CLIMATES

Climates

ANDRÉ MAUROIS

Translated from the French
by Adriana Hunter

With an Introduction by Sarah Bakewell

OTHER PRESS
New York

Copyright © The Maurois Estate,
Anne-Mary Charrier, 2006, Marseille, France
Originally published in France as *Climats*
by Éditions Grasset & Fasquelle, 1928
Translation Copyright © 2012 Adriana Hunter

Cet ouvrage a bénéficié du soutien des Programmes d'aide à la publication
de l'Institut Français.
The work, published as part of a program of aid for publication,
received support from the Institut Français.

Production Editor: Yvonne E. Cárdenas
Text Designer: Jennifer Daddio/Bookmark Design & Media, Inc.
This book was set in 13 pt Fournier by
Alpha Design & Composition of Pittsfield, NH.

10   9   8   7   6   5   4   3   2   1

Library of Congress Cataloging-in-Publication Data

Maurois, André, 1885–1967.
[Climats. English]
Climates / by André Maurois ; translated by Adriana Hunter.
p. cm.
ISBN 978-1-59051-538-9 (trade pbk.) — ISBN 978-1-59051-539-6 (ebook)
I. Hunter, Adriana.   II. Title.
PQ2625.A95C4513 2012
848'.91209—dc23

2012008856

To Simone

We always hope to find the eternal somewhere other than here; we always orient our minds toward other things than the present situation and the present aspect; or we wait to die as if every moment were not dying and coming back to life. With each moment we are offered a new life. Today, now, immediately, it is our only foothold.

—ALAIN

INTRODUCTION

by Sarah Bakewell

Is there any human topic more interesting than love?

The French don't think so. Ever since Pierre Abelard's twelfth-century *Historia Calamitatum*, they have been writing lucid, passionate first-person accounts of their loves. Sometimes they write autobiographically; sometimes they turn reality into fiction. Their books may be vast, like the swathes of Proust's *In Search of Lost Time* that deal with jealousy and desire. Or they may be slim tales or treatises, distilling love to its essence and running it through endless filters of analysis, imagination, reflection, and interrogation. It is not only

French writers who do this, of course, but they are more than usually observant and often merciless with themselves. They reveal every power game, every change of emotional weather. Every painful or embarrassing moment is needled out for us on the page. Among the miniature masterpieces in this genre are Benjamin Constant's *Adolphe*, André Gide's *Strait Is the Gate*, Stendhal's *On Love*, Roland Barthes's *A Lover's Discourse*—and André Maurois's 1928 novel, *Climates*.

Like the other works, *Climates* stays close to its author's own experience, while making it feel universal. His setting is local: bourgeois France just after the First World War. His people are precisely located too, behaving in ways typical of their sex, class, and upbringing. Yet they dramatize the deepest structures of love's psychology, as well as other strange phenomena: jealousy, self-delusion, fantasy, and the desire both to lose control and to impose it on someone else.

At first sight, *Climates* is a simple fable. It tells of Philippe Marcenat, heir to a provincial paper-mill business, who falls in love with the woman of his dreams, Odile Malet. He loses her, but is later loved in turn by Isabelle de Cheverny, a woman *not* of his dreams at all, although he tries (*Vertigo*-ishly) to make her so. We follow first Philippe and then Isabelle as they reflect on their love. There is a happy ending of sorts, though not for Philippe. Maurois has summarized his first vision of the story, in its bare-bones form, as:

Part 1. I love, and am not loved.
Part 2. I am loved, and do not love.

Put that way, it sounds like a perfectly balanced diptych. In fact, it is neither balanced nor anywhere near as simple. Each of these four "love" and "non-love" elements conceals some complication, something moving at cross-purposes to it. Beneath what seems to be love, there lurks tyranny or submission, or a mixture of both. Beneath what seems to be non-love, there is . . . it's hard to say what, but something indefinable that looks very much like love.

Climates is about reading, writing, and talking, and also about silence. It is a novel in which a wife cannot find the words to tell her husband where she has been all day, a husband can think of nothing interesting to say to his wife, and everybody fails to say out loud what he or she can write in notebooks and letters. All this silence points backward into Philippe's childhood. His father and mother never talked about anything at all, he complains, and certainly never about emotion.

Maurois's family was similar. In his memoirs, he calls his father "bashful" and his mother "reserved." Between them, they filled the house with "melancholy reticences and unexpressed doubts." Some of the silence surrounded a particular subject: the family's Jewishness. This was not exactly hidden, but it was not brought to the fore either. Maurois, who was born Émile Herzog on July 26, 1885, found out that he was Jewish at the age of about six, when a friend at the local Protestant church told him so. His parents confirmed it, but they also spoke highly of Protestantism. When he became famous, after World War I, Maurois changed his name, probably more because it sounded German than because it sounded Jewish. He chose "André" from a cousin killed in combat, and "Maurois" from a village near Cambrai, because he liked the name's "sad sonority." It was a veiled name, and a melancholy one, but it accompanied him through a generally very cheerful literary career.

The Herzog family had fled their native Alsace during the Franco-Prussian War (1870–1871) and settled in the town of Elbeuf in Normandy, where they ran a successful textile mill. The bourgeois and provincial atmosphere of Elbeuf horrified Maurois sometimes, but he felt at home there and liked to return to breathe in "the moist, vapid odor of steam and the heavy odor of greasy wool," and to admire the bright colors of the river, which ran blue, green, and yellow from the mill's dye works. The whole town reverberated to the clang of the looms, which pounded like a heartbeat.

He had a good education at the lycée in Rouen, falling under the influence of a charismatic teacher, Émile-Auguste Chartier, known as "Alain." Alain inspired other pupils too, including Simone Weil and Raymond Aron, urging them to think for themselves and to question received ideas. He awakened in Maurois a love of literature, but also, perhaps surprisingly, urged him to take up the mill business after leaving school. Maurois did so, but in his Elbeuf office he kept a secret cupboard filled with Balzac novels and notebooks, and copied out pages of Stendhal to improve his writing style. He became a Kipling enthusiast, and learned excellent English.

He traveled to Paris at least one day a week, and frequented brothels there. One can almost see him starting to turn into one of those coarse provincial industrialists who keeps a mistress in the city and a stifling respectable household at home. But he was diverted away from this path by falling madly in love.

It happened on vacation in Geneva. An actress friend with whom he was traveling introduced him to a sixteen-year-old schoolgirl of Russo-Polish origin, Jane-Wanda de Szymkiewicz, nicknamed Janine. Janine's father was dead and her relationship with her mother was troubled; she was emotionally vulnerable, beautiful, and charming. Photographs show a fashionably dressed, very young woman with a forthright gaze, delicate lips, and a languid droop to the lower eyelids, which gives her an air both soft and sad.

Maurois and Janine went walking in the town, and she told him that she had dreams of walking on a seabed, surrounded by fish. They looked at flower stalls and cheap jewelry, just the kind of trinkets he normally despised. She loved them, so they became instantly magical to him too. "I have been waiting for you for twenty years," he cried.

He meant this literally. Janine matched a template that had originated in a novel he had read in adolescence called *Les Petits soldats russes—The Little Russian Soldiers*. (The same novel appears in *Climates* and plays the same role.) It told of a schoolgirl who is elected a queen by the boys in her class; they become her willing slaves and compete to make ever greater sacrifices for her. It influenced Maurois's erotic fantasies permanently. He too longed for "a love that would be at once suffering, discipline, and devotion," as he wrote in his memoirs. With her Slavic features and her cool, rather fey manner, Janine de Szymkiewicz made a perfect Russian Queen.

She was wiser than he, for she responded to his "twenty years" announcement by warning, "Don't put me too high." But he did just that—or rather, he treated her with the same mix of submission and domination that he later ascribed to Philippe. Maurois arranged for Janine to transfer from Switzerland to a finishing school in England, where he visited her frequently. In 1912 they married, despite his family's disapproval, mostly silent of course. Janine's mother was rumored to have a lover, which was scandalous, and they suspected rightly that

Janine would have difficulties fitting into Elbeuf society.

Still, the marriage started well. They took a house near the mill; Maurois worked, and Janine poured her creativity into flower arranging and gardening. She bought vases of Venetian glass and Lalique crystal; Maurois balked at the expense but marveled at her ability to spend hours "studying the curve of a stem or a green cloud of asparagus ferns." She called him Minou, he called her Ginou. Amid the throbbing of looms and the bubbling of blue-yellow waters, they built their private Eden.

But life in Elbeuf *was* difficult. Janine made few friends. "I don't know whether I can live here," she told Maurois. "It seems so sad, so sad . . ." The image with which their love had begun, walking on the bottom of the sea, summed up the marriage's combination of enchantment and oppressiveness. Janine gave birth to the first of their three children in May 1914, but the war began and Maurois went away, leaving her more isolated than ever.

With his excellent English, Maurois was posted as liaison officer to the British Army. That experience inspired his first novel, *Les Silences du Colonel*

Bramble. After the war he returned to the mill, but was also lionized in Paris, and spent more and more time writing. The children's nurse complained, "Instead of scribbling in the evenings, Monsieur would do better to go out with Madame, and instead of scribbling during the day Monsieur would do better to look after his business." Janine scribbled too, filling notebooks with records of her migraines, stomachaches, cramps, and aching legs. She wrote notes, in English, of times when she felt "moody" or "awfully bad," and wrote, chillingly, "Something is broken."

Sometime in the early 1920s, Maurois began having affairs. Janine had them too, or at least flirtations, especially on their seaside vacations in Deauville. Maurois enjoyed great success with *Ariel*, a biography of Percy Bysshe Shelley—more a novelization of his life, really. (It became memorable for later English-language readers for being reprinted in 1935 as Number 1 in Penguin's first series of paperbacks.) It recounts Shelley's disastrous marriage to Harriet Westbrook, who drowned herself in the Serpentine River after the poet abandoned her. Maurois put a lot of his own personality into

Shelley, and wrote of Harriet as a "child-wife" made bitter by unhappiness. He could be savage: "Even when she had the air of being interested in ideas, her indifference was proved by the blankness of her gaze. Worst of all, she was coquettish, frivolous, versed in the tricks and wiles of woman."

Both he and Janine were suffering from each other, and Janine obsessed over the portrait of herself in *Ariel*. It is heartbreaking to learn, from Maurois's own memoir, that she read it repeatedly—the manuscript once and the printed book twice—and copied out passages. "You talk about women better than you've ever talked to me about them," she said. Yet she could see that Maurois was aware of his own weaknesses too. "Since he understands so well," he imagined her thinking, "why doesn't he change?" Their relationship had begun under the sign of *Les Petits soldats russes*, and its disintegration was similarly reflected in literature, through *Ariel*. Side by side, they looked into the book as into a double mirror, seeing each other's faces as well as their own.

In the early 1920s, and like her counterpart in *Climates*, Janine got the idea that she was destined to die soon. She was right. Becoming pregnant again in late 1922, she developed septicemia, was operated on unsuccessfully, and died on February 26, 1923. Maurois was bereaved, and free.

It was not long before he married again, to the woman who would be his lifelong companion, Simone de Caillavet. The granddaughter of Anatole France's mistress Léontine Arman de Caillavet, Simone was highly educated, patient, and well-balanced, and she devoted herself to Maurois's work. She typed his manuscripts and learned shorthand so as to be able to help him further by taking dictation. If it is disturbing to think of Janine's constant reading of *Ariel*, it is at least as much so to imagine Simone working on the drafts and typescripts of *Climates*, in which she is cast, very little changed, as Isabelle de Cheverny.

What are we to make of Maurois and his love life? By his own account, he married one unsuitable young woman because of a romantic idea that had nothing to do with her true personality, and made her life miserable as well as his own. Afterward he married another woman who, he hints, loved him more than he loved her. Yet, as Janine saw, he was aware of his dark side, and channeled his literary talents into exploring it in fiction and biography. He was a writer to the core, and this is one vital difference between him and Philippe in the novel. It changed everything, at least for him. Perhaps it changed everything for the women in his life too, so deeply interwoven was his work with his relationships.

There was another difference. Love makes Philippe Marcenat dull, not to the reader, but to his long-suffering beloved. He realizes only belatedly how tedious Odile must find the long evenings in which he does little but gaze adoringly at her. Working long hours at the factory, consumed by jealousy, Philippe forgets how to have an entertaining conversation. Maurois, by contrast, was energetic and vibrant. A friend, Edouard Morot-Sir, wrote of "the gentle expression of his eyes, his smile, the finesse and warmth of his voice" and remembered Maurois's endless fund of stories. He was a man of infinite curiosity about human nature—a mark of a person who surely can never be boring.

Climates began life in the mid-1920s, after the death of Janine, as a short story called "La Nuit ·

marocaine." Set in Morocco, it was about an eminent personage who falls ill and is told he will die. He summons his friends and confesses to them the true story of his life, which revolves around his love for three women, each of whom he has hurt in some way. Unfortunately, he then proceeds not to die. He lives on, but must adjust to the changed image that others now have of him.

Starting from this point, Maurois first realized that the middle woman, an actress named Jenny Sorbier, was less interesting than the other two, so he dumped her. This gave him more space to explore the relationships with the others, and the book became the two-parter we have today. He also disposed of the Moroccan setting and the framing story. The novel was easy to write, largely because, as Maurois wrote, "I was able to nourish my imaginary characters on real emotions." He adjusted many details: his own family owned a wool mill, so Philippe's owns a paper mill. He met Janine in Switzerland; Philippe meets Odile in Italy. And he moved the action from Elbeuf to Paris, because that created more scope for flirtations and jealousies.

In turning short story to novel, he also introduced an elaborate literary device. In the first half,

Philippe recounts his love for Odile in the form of a letter to his second wife, Isabelle—a bizarre and cruel thing to do, one might think, but something that Isabelle seems to welcome because it enables her to understand him better. In the second half, she responds by writing the story of *her* love for Philippe. Perhaps because Maurois needs to continue conveying Philippe's emotions directly as well, he has Philippe write a diary, which Isabelle reads and quotes at length in her letter back to him. Part Two strains credulity at times, but the device is worth the trouble, for it highlights the novel's themes of reading, writing, reflecting, reenacting, and transcribing.

For love is interwoven with these activities throughout the book. As in real life, Philippe's love for Odile is born from literature in the form of *The Little Russian Soldiers*. Odile's decline is measured out in her habit of reading poems about death. With Isabelle, Philippe reads constantly: Balzac, Tolstoy, Proust, Stendhal, Merimée. At first Isabelle finds Proust and the others dull, but she wills herself to adapt to Philippe's preferences, though not before remarking, "Nothing could have been easier than understanding Philippe's taste in books: he was one of those readers who look only for themselves in what they read." Philippe has already admitted this at the end of the first part: trying to get over Odile, he writes, "books flung me straight back into my dark meditations; all I looked for in them was my pain and, almost in spite of myself, I chose those that would remind me of my own sad story."

This is Philippe all over: he looks for himself in every book he reads, just as he looks for his "queen" in every woman he is involved with. Isabelle has a less self-centered approach, and reads mainly to understand the man she loves. At novel's end, she even reads his old copy of *The Little Russian Soldiers*. These are two extreme models of reading: looking in books to see oneself mirrored again and again, or reading to enter another person's experience, and thus to enlarge oneself.

Which way are *we*, the readers, to approach *Climates*? Its characters seem to invite us to relate their sorrows or triumphs to our own. I recognized aspects of myself and my life in each character, yet there were moments of remoteness too. For one thing, Isabelle's self-abnegating idea of love can be unnerving for a female reader. It is one of the elements that keeps *Climates* from becoming too comfortable, or too blandly universal. It speaks to everyone, yet it is also a historical document about France in the 1920s. It comes from a time when Frenchwomen did not yet have the vote (they got it in 1944), and when it would not have entered Philippe Marcenat's head that *he*, not Isabelle, might make real, concrete, everyday sacrifices for a domestic monarch.

Maurois's sense of the psychology of love, in all its fits and agonies, manages to be dated yet eternally insightful. His analysis of jealousy rivals Proust's, and he shows how Philippe helplessly destroys the genuine but fragile love Odile feels for him. And *Climates* is as good as Stendhal on the first phase of enchantment, in which the lover undergoes what Stendhal calls "crystallization"—the ability to perceive somebody ordinary as a magical, dazzling, twinkling disco ball of fascination. (The crystal image comes from the salt mines of Salzburg, where it was the custom to hang a branch at the mine's entrance, then retrieve it a few months later, when— says Stendhal—"its smallest twigs, those no larger than a titmouse's foot, are spangled with an infinity of diamonds, dancing and dazzling.") Philippe is blinded by Odile. Never seeing her as she really is, he fetishizes her clothes, her flowers, the trinkets she carries everywhere on her honeymoon ("a small clock, a lace cushion, and a volume of Shakespeare bound in gray suede"), and her taste in furnishings. She even decorates their home rather like a salt cave, all white flowers and sleek white carpeting. He adopts Odile's tastes as his own, to the extent of later trying to make Isabelle imitate them.

Clothes, houses, flowers, and furniture are all important in *Climates*. When Isabelle wants to move into her family home, or at least take some furniture from it, Philippe refuses, because he cannot stand their red damask drapes and gargoyle-infested, pseudomedieval chairs. "Don't you think that what's important in life is people not furnishings?" asks Isabelle, but he brushes her aside. Yes, yes, that's the conventional wisdom, he says, but a house's atmosphere affects one more deeply than people acknowledge. "I just know I wouldn't be happy in that house."

Isabelle gives in, as she tends to, but it is his *own* natural environment that Philippe is rejecting. Those tasteful oceans of white carpeting were never the real Philippe, and he admits, "My true tastes and my cautious Marcenat mind were things I was now far more likely to find in Isabelle." Her parents have molded her as his did; when Isabelle and Philippe first meet, they compare notes on "that sort of rural bourgeois heritage that so many French families share." He can be himself with Isabelle, in a way he could not with Odile—and certainly not with her noisy, bohemian family, in whose company he used to become unrecognizable to himself. "I seemed solemn, boring, and even though I loathed my own silences, I withdrew into them." It was "not my sort of climate," he felt.

This is why the novel is called *Climates*: in its examination of love, it also becomes an examination of the atmospheres we need to be fully ourselves. Philippe's complaint about Odile's family goes to the heart of the book. One cannot just transfer one's personality intact from one environment to the next. Relationships have different qualities of air, different barometric pressures. With Odile, Philippe is first expanded and enchanted, then he contracts and distorts into a jealous monster. With Isabelle, despite himself, he *is* himself.

Moreover, Isabelle has a huge advantage in having a certain control over her own climate. She is able to *choose* her servitude, even to affirm it, rather than be helplessly in the grip of her emotions as Philippe had been with Odile. Looking back to his treatment of Odile, Philippe reflects that he showed "no unkindness, but no generosity of spirit either," but this is never mirrored in Isabelle's half of the story. She is all generosity. She even puts forward a strange argument: that we should not attach importance to our loved one's failings, or to what a person actually does, for what matters is that that person alone enables us to live in a particular "atmosphere," or, as she also puts it, in a "climate." That is all we need; it is a devotion that is called forth from our deepest being, but it is not a blind devotion.

"I wanted to love you without trickery, to fight with an open heart," writes Isabelle to Philippe. "It should be possible to admit to loving someone and yet also succeed in being loved." Should it? Is it? It should, and sometimes it is. But oh, how complicated human beings are. And, in the end, something compelled Maurois to take Philippe away from Isabelle after all, thus parting company both with

Isabelle's optimism and with the story of his own second, successful marriage.

For it *was* a successful marriage. Maurois lived with Simone for the rest of his life, and she seems to have tolerated his occasional affairs.

His other marriage, to the written word, succeeded too. He became a sought-after lecturer and speaker, and was elected to the Académie in 1938. His output was prodigious: he wrote biographies of Byron, Disraeli, Balzac, Dumas père and fils, Hugo, and Proust, among others, as well as novels, memoirs, and collections of essays, including works on politics that aired his genial, mild brand of conservatism.

During the Occupation, he and Simone fled to the United States, then returned to set up a country estate, Essendiéras, in Périgord. Simone ran it as an artists', writers', and filmmakers' haven; people would stay for months and work in peace. When money ran short, she and Maurois converted part of the property into a lucrative apple orchard. The Herzog mill in Elbeuf eventually went out of business, the victim of international competition and cheap 1960s artificial fabrics. Maurois does not seem to have mourned it much. He and Simone had one great sorrow, losing their daughter, Françoise, to liver disease; otherwise, he lived a generally pleasurable, productive life until his death in 1967.

His last lecture, prepared in that year but never delivered, was called *Illusions*. In it, he included a kind of manifesto of his art and life. Most of human existence is neither extreme nor tragic, he says, yet:

> *[W]e know that in his daily life man is ever, to a greater or a lesser degree, hagridden. Even when all goes well, all does not go perfectly well. Life remains, on the face of it, absurd. What is the meaning of this strange carnival? Why are we here on this fleck of mud, revolving in darkness? . . . We want peace, concord and the affection of other peoples, and lo and behold here we are at war, massacring and being massacred. Or again we are in love with a woman who at times seems to love us in return and, at others, for no reason known to us, grows cold and distant. We do not understand the universe; we do not understand those who hate us; we do not understand those who love us; often we do not even understand our parents, our children. We do not understand ourselves.*

The only possibility of introducing meaning into such a world lies in art, he concludes, and especially in literature. It is the author's task to create stories that are orderly enough to be coherent, but not so neat that they fail to reflect the true mystery and complexity of human life.

Climates is such a story. It is orderly, yet unsettling. It breathes an air that is profoundly civilized, yet there is something violent and shattering about it too. "Even when it's mutual, love is terrible," says Philippe. It is terrible simply to be human—and there can be no subject more interesting to write about, or more beautiful, than that.

FURTHER READING

André Maurois. Bibliothèque Nationale, 1977. An exhibition catalog.

Dominique Bona, *Il n'y a qu'un amour*. Bernard Grasset, 2003. An account of the lives of Jane-Wanda de Szymkiewicz and Simone de Caillavet.

Jack Kolbert, *The Worlds of André Maurois*. Associated University Press, 1985.

André Maurois, *Memoirs 1885–1967*. Translated by Denver Lindley. Harper and Row, 1970.

André Maurois, *Ariel: A Life of Shelley*. Translated by Ella d'Arcy. Kessinger, 2003.

André Maurois, *Illusions*. Introduction by Edouard Morot-Sir. Columbia University Press, 1968.

Stendhal, *On Love*. Hesperus, 2000.

CLIMATES

PART ONE

Odile

Philippe Marcenat
to Isabelle de Cheverny

. I .

You must have been surprised when I left so suddenly. I apologize for that but do not regret it. I cannot tell whether you too can hear the hurricane of internal music stirring inside me over the last few days like Tristan da Cunha's towering flames. Oh! I would so like to succumb to the tempest that, only the day before yesterday, in the forest, urged me to touch your white dress. But I am afraid of love, Isabelle, and of myself. I do not know what Renée or anyone else may have told you about my life. You and I have sometimes talked of it; I have not told you the truth. That is the charm of new acquaintances: the hope that, in their eyes and by denying the truth, we can transform a past that we wish had been happier. Our friendship has gone beyond the point of overly flattering confidences. Men surrender their souls, as women do their bodies, in successive and carefully defended stages. One after the other, I have thrown my most secret troops into battle. My true memories, corralled in their enclave, will soon give themselves up and come out into the open.

I am a long way from you now, in the very room in which I slept as a child. On the wall are the shelves laden with books that my mother has been keeping for over twenty years "for her eldest grandson." Will I have sons? That wide red spine stained with ink is my old Greek dictionary; those gold bindings, my prizes. I wish I could tell you everything, Isabelle, from the sensitive little boy to the cynical adolescent, and on to the unhappy, wounded man. I wish I could tell you everything in complete innocence, exactitude, and humility. Perhaps, if I manage to finish writing this, I will not have the courage to show it to you. Never mind. It is still worthwhile, if only for my own sake, to assess what my life has been.

Do you remember one evening on the way back from Saint-Germain when I described Gandumas to you? It is a bleakly beautiful place. A torrential river cuts between our factories, built in the depths of a wild gorge. Our house, a small nineteenth-century château like many others in Limousin, looks out over heather-clad heaths. As a young boy I was already proud that I was a Marcenat and our family reigned over the canton. My father took the tiny paper business that had been a mere laboratory for my maternal grandfather and built it into a huge factory. He bought up local smallholdings and transformed Gandumas, which had been all but neglected before his time, into the very model of an estate. Throughout my childhood I watched buildings being constructed and saw the hangar housing paper pulp stretch out along the river.

My mother's family was from Limousin. My great-grandfather, a notary, had bought the Château de Gandumas when it was sold off as national property. My father, an engineer from Lorraine, had been in the region only since he married. He summoned one of his brothers, my uncle Pierre, who settled in the neighboring village of Chardeuil. On Sundays, if it was not raining, the two families met by the ponds in Saint-Yrieix. We traveled in carriages, and I would sit facing my parents, on a small, hard pull-down seat. The horse's monotonous trot sent me to sleep; I used to like watching its shadow on the walls in villages or on the banks by the side of the road: it contorted and moved forward, overtaking us, and then, as we went around corners, it reappeared behind us. Every now and then the smell of droppings (a smell which, like the sound of bells, will always be associated with Sundays in my mind) would hang over us like a cloud, and great fat flies would land on me. I hated the hills more than anything; the horse slowed to a walk and the carriage climbed unbearably slowly while the old coachman, Thomasson, clicked his tongue and cracked his whip.

At the inn, we met up with my uncle Pierre, his wife, and my cousin Renée, who was their only child. My mother would give us bread and butter, and my father would say, "Go and play." Renée and I used to walk under the trees or by the ponds, collecting pinecones and chestnuts. On the way home, Renée climbed into the carriage with us, and the coachman folded down the sides of my seat to give her somewhere to sit. My parents did not speak during the journey.

Any form of conversation was made difficult by my father's extraordinary sense of propriety; it seemed to pain him if the least feeling were expressed in public. At mealtimes, if my mother mentioned our education, the factory, our uncles, or our aunt Cora who lived in Paris, my father would gesture anxiously, pointing out to her the servant clearing the plates. She would fall silent. I noticed very early on that if my father and my uncle had some small criticism to direct at each other, they always ensured it was their wives who conveyed this with tremendous tact. I also grasped very early that my father abhorred sincerity. In our house, it was taken for granted that all conventional feelings held true, that parents always loved their children, children their parents, and husbands their wives. The Marcenats liked to see the world as a decent, earthly paradise, and I feel that, in their case, this had more to do with candor than hypocrisy.

. II .

The sunlit lawn at Gandumas. And, on the plain below, the village of Chardeuil veiled in a shimmering heat haze. A little boy stands waist-deep in a hole he has dug, beside a heap of sand, scouring the vast expanses around him for an invisible enemy. This game was inspired by my favorite book, Driant's *Fortress War*. I was a soldier, Private Mitour, stationed in that hole for skirmishes to defend Fort de Liouville, under the command of a colonel for whom I would gladly have given my life. I must apologize for writing about these puerile ideas, but in them I see the first expression of a need for passionate devotion that has been a dominant feature of my character, although it was later applied to quite different subjects.

If I analyze the tiny but still identifiable trace of the child I was then, I can see that, even at that early stage, there was a hint of sensuality in this sacrifice.

Besides, my game quickly developed into something else. In another book, one I was given on New Year's Day that was called *Little Russian Soldiers*, I read about a gang of schoolboys who decide to form an army and choose a fellow pupil as their queen. The queen was called Ania Sokoloff. "She was a remarkably beautiful, slender, elegant, and able girl." I liked the oath the soldiers swore to their queen, the work they undertook to please her, and the smile that was their reward. I did not know why this story suited me so well, but it did, I loved it, and it must have been from that book that I formed the image of the woman I have so often described to you. I can see myself walking beside her on the lawns at Gandumas; she is talking to me in a serious voice, her sentences sad and beautiful. I do not know at what point I started calling her the Amazon, but I know the notion of audacity and risk was always mingled with the pleasure she afforded me. I also loved reading with my mother about Lancelot of the Lake and

Don Quixote. I could not believe that Dulcinea was ugly, and I tore the engraving of her from my book so that I could imagine her as I chose to.

Although my cousin Renée was two years younger than me, she studied alongside me for several years. Then, when I was thirteen, my father sent me to the Lycée Gay-Lussac in Limoges. I lived at a cousin's house and went home only on Sundays. I really enjoyed school life. I had inherited my father's love of learning and reading, and was a good pupil. The characteristic Marcenat pride and shyness were becoming apparent in me, as inevitably as their shining eyes and rather high-set eyebrows. The only counterpoint to my pride was the image of the queen to whom I remained faithful. At night, before going to sleep, I told myself stories with my Amazon as the heroine. She now had a name, Helen, because I liked Homer's Helen (a Mr. Bailly, one of my teachers, was responsible for that).

Why do some images remain as clear to us as when we first saw them, while others that might seem more important grow hazy and fade so quickly? Right now, on a perfectly focused internal screen, I am projecting Mr. Bailly coming into the classroom with his slow, steady step, on a day when we are to do French composition. He hangs his distinctive coat on a peg and says, "I have found a wonderful subject for you: Stesichorus's palinode . . ." Yes, I can still see Mr. Bailly very clearly. He has a thick mustache, a shock of hair, and a face heavily lined by what were no doubt painful passions. He takes from his briefcase a sheet of paper and dictates: "The poet Stesichorus, having cursed Helen in his verse for the ills she brought to the Greeks, is struck blind by Venus and, now realizing his mistake, composes a palinode expressing his regret for blaspheming against beauty."

Oh! I would so love to reread my eight pages from that morning. Never again have I found such a perfect reconciling of deeper life and the written word, never, except perhaps in a few letters to Odile and, scarcely a week ago, in a letter intended for you that I never sent. The theme of sacrifice to beauty awakened such profound resonances in me that, despite my tender years, I felt terrified and worked with almost painful ardor for two hours, as if I could sense that I too would have many, many reasons to write Stesichorus's palinode during the course of my difficult earthly life.

But I would be giving you a very false idea of a fifteen-year-old schoolboy's nature if I did not admit that my exultation remained internal and perfectly hidden. My conversations with my classmates about women and love were cynical. A few of my friends described their experiences in brutal technical detail. I, on the other hand, had incarnated my Helen in a young woman from Limoges, a friend of the cousins with whom I lodged. Her name was Denise Aubry; she was pretty and was said to be fickle. If I heard anyone say she had lovers, I thought of Don Quixote and Lancelot, and wished I could hurl lances at these slanderers.

On the days when Madame Aubry came for dinner I was beside myself with a blend of happiness and fear. Everything I said in her presence sounded absurd to me. I loathed her husband, an inoffensive and well-meaning porcelain maker. I always hoped to meet her in the street on the way home from school. I had noticed that, around noon, she often went to buy flowers or cakes on the rue Porte-Tourny, opposite the cathedral. I made sure I was on the sidewalk between the florist and the patisserie at that sort of time. On several occasions she allowed me to escort her, with my schoolbag under my arm, all the way back to her door.

When summer came, I found it easier to see her at the tennis court. One particularly warm evening a number of young couples decided to dine there. Madame Aubry, who knew very well that I loved her, asked me to stay too. It was a lively, cheerful supper. Night fell. I was lying on the grass at Denise's feet; my hand drifted to her ankle and I gently encircled it, with no protest from her. There were syringas behind us, and I can still smell their strong fragrance. You could see the stars through their branches. It was a moment of perfect happiness.

When it was quite dark, I crawled closer to Denise and made out a fellow beside her, a twenty-seven-year-old lawyer famous in Limoges for his wit, and I could not help hearing their whispered conversation. He asked her to meet him in Paris, at an address that he gave her. She murmured, "Do be quiet," but I knew she was laughing. I did not relinquish her ankle, which she left to me happily, indifferent, but I felt hurt and immediately conceived a savage contempt for women.

On the table in front of me now, I have the little schoolboy notebook in which I kept a reading record. In it I find: "June 26, D.," an initial ringed with a small circle. Beneath it I copied out a sentence from

Barrès: "We need not make much of women, but should be moved when we look at them and should admire ourselves for having such pleasant feelings for such meager things."

Throughout that summer I wooed young girls. I discovered that you could catch them by the waist in dark alleys, kiss them and toy with their bodies. The Denise Aubry episode seemed to have cured me of my romantic flights of fancy. I established a technique for licentious seductions, and it had a guaranteed success rate that filled me with pride and despair.

. III .

The following year, my father, who had been a regional councillor for some time, was appointed senator for Haute-Vienne. Our way of life changed, and I finished my philosophy studies at a lycée in Paris. Gandumas was now merely our summer residence. It was agreed that I would study law and undertake my military service before choosing a career.

During the summer vacation, I saw Madame Aubry when she came to Gandumas with my cousins from Limoges; I was under the impression it was she who asked to come with them. I offered to show her the grounds and took great pleasure in directing her toward a pavilion that I called my observatory. Back in the days when I loved her, it was here that I had spent entire Sundays aimlessly daydreaming. She was impressed by the deep wooded gorge in whose depths we could make out rocks surrounded by foaming waters, and the fine smoke from the factories. When she stood up and leaned forward to have a better view of the work-men in the distance, I put my hand on her shoulder. She smiled. I tried to kiss her, but she deflected me gently, not sternly. I told her I would be returning to Paris in October. I would have a small apart-ment to myself on the Left Bank and would like to see her there. "I don't know," she murmured. "It's difficult."

In my diary for the winter of 1906–1907, I can see a good many days marked with the letter D. Denise Aubry disappointed me. I was wrong. She was a nice enough woman but, though I cannot say why, I had hoped she would prove to be a study-ing companion as well as a mistress. She came to Paris to see me and to try on gowns and hats. This inspired strong feelings of contempt in me: I lived inside books and could not understand how any-one could do otherwise. She asked me to lend her

Gide, Barrès, and Claudel about whom I talked so much; what she then said about them wounded me. She had a pretty body, and I longed for her desperately the moment she went home to Limoges. But after two hours spent with her, I wished I could die, evaporate, or have a proper conversation with a male friend.

My two greatest companions were André Halff, an intelligent but rather touchy young Jew I had met at law school, and Bertrand de Jussac, a classmate from Limoges who had enrolled at the Saint-Cyr military academy and came to spend Sundays with us in Paris. When I was with Halff or Bertrand I felt I was diving into a seam of perfect sincerity. On the surface was the Philippe my parents knew, a simple creature sharing some Marcenat conventions along with some feeble elements of resistance, then came Denise Aubry's Philippe, prone to bouts of sensuality and tenderness and reacting to this with brutality, then Bertrand's Philippe, courageous and sentimental, and last the one Halff knew, precise and uncompromising. I was also well aware that, somewhere underneath, there was yet another Philippe, one who was more real than all the others, and he alone could have made me happy if I had coincided with him, but I made no effort even to get to know him.

Have I told you about the room I rented in a small house on the rue de Varenne, furnished in the austere style I favored at the time? A mask of Pascal and one of Beethoven hung on the bare walls. Strange witnesses to my exploits. The divan that served as my bed was covered with a large gray cloth. On the mantelpiece there was one book by Spinoza, one by Montaigne, and a few scientific volumes. Was that out of a desire to surprise or a genuine love of ideas? A mixture of the two, I would say. I was studious and inhuman.

Denise often told me my room frightened her but that she liked it all the same. She had had many lovers before me; she had always dominated them. She grew fond of me—I mention that in all humility. Life teaches us all that, where love is concerned, modesty is easy. Even the most underprivileged can sometimes appeal and the most alluring fail. I can tell you that Denise felt more for me than I did for her, but I will be just as sincere in describing the far more significant episodes in my life when the situation was completely reversed. In the period we are looking at, that is, between the ages of twenty and twenty-three, I was loved but I loved little myself. If the truth be known, I had no idea what love was. The thought that it could cause pain struck me as intolerably romantic. Poor Denise, I can picture her lying full length on that divan, leaning over me and anxiously asking questions of my face that remained so utterly closed to her.

"Love," I would say, "what is love?"

"Don't you know what it is? You shall . . . You'll be caught too."

That word *caught* struck me, I found it crude. I did not care for Denise's vocabulary and resented her for not talking like Juliet or Clelia Conti. I responded to her person with the sort of exasperation some might show for a badly cut gown. I drew back, then came closer, trying to find an impossible balance. I learned later that over this period she earned a reputation in Limoges for her intelligence, and that my efforts had helped her win the heart of one of the most difficult men in the province. It seems women's minds are made up of the successive sediments laid down by the men who have loved them, just as men's tastes retain jumbled, superimposed images of the women who have come into their lives, and the appalling suffering inflicted on us by one woman often becomes the reason we inspire love in another . . . and the cause of her unhappiness.

M was Mary Graham, a little English girl whose eyes were shrouded in mystery and whom I met at my aunt Cora's house. I must tell you about this aunt because she has an intermittent but not insignificant role in the rest of my story. She is one of my mother's sisters. She married a banker, Baron Choin, and, although I have never known why, always cherished ambitions of playing host to as many ministers, ambassadors, and generals as possible. She established her first nucleus of acquaintances by being mistress to a fairly well-known politician, and earned her victory by exploiting this success methodically and with admirable perseverance. She was to be found on the avenue Marceau from six o'clock every evening, and every Tuesday she gave a dinner for twenty-four. Aunt Cora's dinners were one of the few subjects about which my Limousin family joked. My father claimed, and I think he was right, that the series never suffered an interruption. In summer, the dinners moved to the villa in Trouville. My mother said that when she knew my uncle was about to die (he was suffering from stomach cancer), she went to Paris to help her sister and arrived on a Tuesday evening to find Cora setting the table.

"What about Adrien?" she asked.

"He's very well," Cora replied, "as well as his condition will allow, only he won't be able to dine at the table."

At seven o'clock the following morning, a servant called my mother: "Madame the Baroness regrets to inform Madame Marcenat that Monsieur the Baron died suddenly in the night."

When I first came to Paris, I had no wish to see my aunt, having been brought up by my father to abhor the social scene. When I met her I did not dislike her. She was a very good woman who liked to help others and, through her connections with men who held a variety of positions, had acquired a haphazard but genuine knowledge of the workings of a company. For the inquisitive, provincial young man that I was, she was a mine of information. She could see I enjoyed listening to her and took to me as a friend. I was invited to avenue Marceau every Tuesday evening. Perhaps there was added coquettishness in her inviting me because she knew that my mother and father were hostile to her salons, and she was not against triumphing over them by commandeering me.

Aunt Cora's gatherings inevitably included a number of young ladies as necessary bait. I undertook to win several of them over. I wooed them without loving them, as a point of honor and to prove to myself that victory was possible. I remember that whenever one of them left my bedroom with a tender smile, I would calmly sit down in an armchair, pick up a book, and effortlessly drive away her image.

Do not judge me too severely. I think that, like me, many young men who do not quickly find a truly remarkable mistress or wife almost inevitably resort to this aloof egotism. They are hoping to find a way of living. Women instinctively know that these enterprises are pointless and enter into them only condescendingly. Desire creates illusions for a while and then invincible boredom rears up within these two almost hostile characters. Was I still thinking of Helen of Sparta? That was a feeling I glimpsed deep below the surface, an underwater cathedral beneath the dark depths of my cold strategies.

Occasionally when I went to concerts on Sunday evenings, I would catch sight of a ravishing profile in the distance, and with a strange jolt I would remember the blond Slavic queen of my childhood and the chestnut trees of Gandumas. All through the concert I would offer the powerful emotions stirred by the music to this stranger's face, and I had the fleeting feeling that if I could only get to know this woman, I would finally find in her the perfect, almost divine creature for whom I wished to live. Then the fallen queen would be lost in the crowd and I would go back to a mistress I did not love on the rue de Varenne.

I now struggle to grasp how I could have harbored two such contradictory personalities. They lived on different planes and never met. The tender lover who hankered for devotion had realized that his beloved did not exist in real life. Refusing to confuse an adored but ill-defined image with the unworthy, vulgar individuals who had walk-on parts in his life, he took refuge in books and saved his love for Madame de Mortsauf and Madame de Rênal. The cynic dined with Aunt Cora and, if he liked the woman seated beside him, entertained her with bright and daring conversation.

After my military service, my father invited me to run our factory with him. He had now moved his offices to Paris, where most of his customers, major newspapers and publishing houses, were based. I was very interested in his business and helped develop it while still pursuing my studies and my reading. I went to Gandumas once a month in winter; in summer my parents lived there and I spent a few weeks with them. I enjoyed rediscovering my solitary childhood walks through Limousin. When I was not at the factory, I worked either in my bedroom (still the same one) or in my little observatory overlooking the Loue ravine. Every hour I would get to my feet, walk to the end of the long avenue of chestnut trees, and walk back at the same brisk pace and return to my reading.

I was glad to be rid of the young women who strung a flimsy but unavoidable web of meetings, complaints, and gossip over my life in Paris. The Mary Graham I mentioned earlier was the wife of a man I knew well. I did not like shaking her husband's hand. Most of my friends would actually have taken ironic pride in doing so. But my family's traditions on such subjects were strict. My father's marriage of convenience had, as is so often the case, become a marriage of love. He was happy in his own silent and serious way. He never had affairs, at least not after he was married, and yet I sensed a romantic side to him and was obscurely aware that if, like him, I were lucky enough to find a woman something like my Amazon, I too could be happy and faithful.

. IV .

In the winter of 1909 I was struck down by bronchitis twice in succession and, toward the month of March, our doctor recommended I spend a few weeks in the south. I thought it would be more interesting to visit Italy, a country I did not know. I saw the northern lakes and Venice, and settled in Florence for the final week of my vacation. The first evening, I noticed a young lady at the next table in the hotel; she had an ethereal, angelic beauty, and I could not take my eyes off her. She was accompanied by her mother, who seemed still young, and a somewhat older man. As I left the dining room, I asked the headwaiter who my neighbors were. He told me they were French, they were Madame and Mademoiselle Malet. Their companion, an Italian general, was not staying in our hotel. At lunchtime the following day their table was empty.

I had letters of recommendation for several inhabitants of Florence including one for Professor Angelo Guardi, the art critic whose publisher was a customer of mine. I had the letter delivered to him and the very same day received an invitation to take tea with him. There, in the gardens of a villa in Fiesole, I discovered some twenty people among whom were my two neighbors. Beneath a wide straw hat and wearing an unbleached linen dress with a blue sailor collar, the young lady looked as lovely as she had the day before. All at once I felt shy and moved away from the group she was in, to go and talk to Guardi. Below us there was a pergola covered in roses.

"I made my garden myself," Guardi said. "Ten years ago all the land you can see was a meadow. Over there . . ."

As I looked to where he was pointing, my eyes met those of Mademoiselle Malet, and I was surprised and delighted to find that hers looked directly into mine. An infinitely brief glance, but that was the minute grain of pollen loaded with unknown forces from which my greatest love blossomed. This look told me without a word that she gave me permission to behave naturally, and as soon as I could I went over to her.

"What a wonderful garden!" I said.

"Yes," she agreed, "and what I love best about Florence is that wherever you are, you can see the mountains and trees. I loathe cities that are simply cities."

"Guardi told me the view from behind the house is quite delightful."

"Let's go and see," she said gaily.

We found a thick screen of cypress trees and, through the middle of it, a stone staircase leading up to a rocky recess that housed a statue. Farther on to the left there was a terrace with views of the city.

Mademoiselle Malet leaned on the balustrade close to me for a long time, silently gazing at the pink domes and wide, gently sloping roofs of Florence, and, in the distance, the blue mountains.

"Oh! I do love this," she said, enraptured.

With a very young, very graceful movement, she tipped her head back as if to inhale the scenery.

From that first conversation, Odile Malet treated me with trusting familiarity. She told me that her father was an architect, that she admired him a great deal, and that he had stayed in Paris. It pained her to see the general as her mother's escort. After ten minutes we had moved on to truly intimate confidences. I told her about my Amazon and how impossible it was for me to have any appetite for life if I were not sustained by potent and deep-seated feelings. (My cynical tendencies had been instantly swept aside by her presence.) She described how one day, when she was thirteen, her best friend, whom she called Misa, had inquired, "If I asked you to, would you throw yourself off the balcony?" and she had nearly jumped from the fourth floor. That story enchanted me.

"Have you visited the churches and museums much?" I asked.

"Yes," she replied. "But what I like best of all is strolling through the streets . . . Except I do so hate walking with Maman and her general, so I rise very early in the mornings . . . Would you like to come with me tomorrow morning? I shall be in the hotel lobby at nine o'clock."

"I think I would . . . Do I need to ask your mother for permission to walk with you?"

"No," she said, "leave that to me."

The following morning I waited for her at the foot of the stairs and we went out together. The wide flagstones along the embankment gleamed in the sunlight; a bell was ringing somewhere; carriages trotted past. Life suddenly seemed so straightforward; happiness would be always having this blond head beside me, taking this arm when crossing a street and, for a moment, feeling beneath her dress the warmth of her young body. She took me to the Via Tornabuoni; she loved shoe shops, florists, and bookshops. On the Ponte Vecchio, she stood for some time looking at necklaces of large pink and black stones.

"Aren't they fun?" she said. "Don't you think?"

She had some of the tastes I had once condemned in the poor Denise Aubry.

What did we talk about? I do not really remember. In my diary, I see: *Walk with O. San Lorenzo. She described the large light above her bed at the convent, coming through a shutter lit from the outside by a streetlamp. As she fell asleep she would watch it grow larger and believed she was in heaven. She told* *me about the Bibliothèque rose;* she hates Camille and Madeleine; she herself cannot bear the role of the "good little girl." Her favorite reading matter is fairy tales and poetry. She sometimes dreams of wandering under the sea with skeleton fish swimming around her, sometimes of a weasel dragging her underground. She likes danger; she rides horses and jumps difficult obstacles on horseback . . . She does the prettiest thing with her eyes when trying to understand something; she furrows her brow slightly and looks forward as if having trouble seeing, then says "yes" to herself; now she understands.*

I am well aware as I copy those words out for you that I am powerless to describe the happy memories she conjures for me. Why did I feel such a sense of perfection? Were the things Odile said remarkable? I think not, but she had what all the Marcenats lacked: a lust for life. We love people because they secrete a mysterious essence, the one missing from our own formula to make us a stable chemical compound. I may not have known women more beautiful than Odile, but I knew plenty who were more brilliant, more perfectly intelligent, yet not one of

---

* Literally "Pink Library," this collection of books, which began publishing in 1856, was deemed suitable for girls.

them managed to bring the physical world within my grasp as she did. Having been distanced from it by too much reading, too much solitary meditation, I now discovered trees and flowers and the smell of the earth, all sorts of things picked by Odile every morning and laid in bunches at my feet.

When I had been alone in the city, I had spent my days in museums, or I stayed in my room reading about Venice and Rome. It was as if the outside world reached me only through masterpieces. Odile immediately introduced me to the world of colors and sounds. She took me to the flower market under the lofty arches of the Mercato Nuovo. She mingled with local women buying sprigs of lily of the valley or branches of lilac. She liked the old country priest haggling over laburnum shoots coiled around tall reeds. On the hills below San Miniato, she showed me narrow roads framed by stiflingly hot walls above which burgeoning wisterias trailed their clusters of flowers.

Did I bore her when I explained with my characteristic Marcenat earnestness the rivalries between the Guelphs and the Ghibellines, Dante's life, or Italy's economic situation? I do not think so. Who is it who said that, between man and woman, it is often a naïve, almost stupid, utterance from the woman that makes the invincible man want to kiss that childish mouth, whereas for the woman it is often when the man is at his most serious and most uncompromisingly logical that she in turn loves him best? Perhaps this was true of Odile and me. In any event, I know that when she murmured pleadingly "Do let's stop" as we passed some shop selling fake jewelry, I never criticized her but simply thought "how I love her," and I heard ever more powerfully the theme of the guardian knight and of devotion unto death that had gone hand in hand with my notion of love ever since childhood.

Every part of me picked up on this theme again now. Just as in an orchestra where one isolated flute outlines a short phrase and seems to waken by turns the violins and cellos, then the brass section, until a great rhythmic wave sweeps through the concert hall, so a picked flower, the smell of wisteria, black and white churches, Botticelli and Michelangelo all successively joined the formidable chorus that expressed my happiness in loving Odile and protecting her perfect fragile beauty from an invisible enemy.

On my first evening, I might have wished for the inaccessible privilege of a two-hour walk with the young lady I had glimpsed. But a few days later, it felt like intolerable slavery having to return to the hotel for dinner. Not knowing much about me, Madame Malet was anxious and tried to slow the progress of our intimacy, but you know what the first stirrings of love are like in two young people; the forces they awaken feel irresistible. We genuinely felt waves of empathy forming wherever we went. Odile's beauty alone would have been enough for that. But she told me that as a couple we were even more successful among this Italian population than she had been on her own. The Florentine coachmen were grateful to us for being in love. Museum attendants smiled at us. Boatmen on the Arno looked up to watch indulgently as we leaned on a parapet, standing close together to feel the warmth of each other's body.

I had wired my father to tell him I believed I could make a full recovery if I stayed another week or two. He consented. I now wanted Odile to myself all day. I hired a carriage and we took long drives together through the Tuscan countryside. On the way to Siena, we felt we were traveling through the background of a Carpaccio painting. The carriage launched up hillsides the shape of children's sand

castles, and at the top we found improbable crenel-
lated villages. We were enchanted by Siena's vast
shadows. As I lunched with Odile in a cool back-
street hotel, I already knew I would spend my whole
life looking across at her. On the way back, in the
darkness, her hand came to rest on mine. The day of
that outing, I find in my diary: *Undeniable affection
toward us from coachmen, chambermaids, and farm-
hands. Doubtless they can tell we love each other. The
professionalism demonstrated by the staff in this little
hotel . . . What I find exquisite is that with her I feel
mere contempt for everything that is not her, and she
for everything that is not me. She does something quite
delectable with her face to express abandon and delight.
There is a touch of melancholy in it, as if she wanted to
capture the moment and keep it in her mind's eye.*

Oh! I still so love the Odile of those weeks in
Florence! She was so beautiful that I sometimes
doubted she was real. I would turn to her and say,
"I shall try to last five minutes without looking at
you." I never managed to resist longer than thirty
seconds. There was extraordinary poetry in everything she said. Although she was very cheerful,
there was occasionally something darker like the
note of a cello in her words, a melancholy discord

that promptly filled the air with a strange and tragic threat. What was the phrase she would quote then? "Fatally condemned." Wait, yes: "Under the influence of Mars, fatally condemned, oh girl with the golden hair, beware." In what puerile novel, what melodrama had she read or heard those words? I forget. The first time she gave me her lips, at dusk in a warm furtive olive grove, she looked at me with the sweetest air of sadness: "My darling, do you remember Juliet's words? . . . 'I am too fond, and therefore thou mayst think my behavior light.'"

It is a pleasure remembering our love in those days; it was a beautiful emotion, equally strong in Odile as it was in me. But with Odile, emotions were almost always restrained by pride. She explained later that first the convent and then life with her mother whom she did not love had constrained her to "closing herself" like this. When this hidden fire appeared, it was as brief violent flames that warmed my heart all the more keenly because I knew they were involuntary. There is a comparison to be drawn with women's clothing: some fashions entirely hide women's bodies from men's eyes, thereby contriving to give more impact when a dress subtly skims the figure; similarly, a modest hold on emotions veiling the usual signs of passion brings out all the value and grace of imperceptible nuances in the choice of words. The day my father finally recalled me to Paris with a fairly disgruntled telegram, I had to announce the fact to Odile at the Guardis' house because she had arrived there before me. Other guests, who were quite indifferent to my leaving, went back to a rather unlikely conversation about Germany and Morocco.

"That was interesting, what Guardi was saying," I said to Odile on our way out.

"I heard only one thing, that you were leaving," she replied, almost in despair.

. V .

I left Florence an engaged man. I needed to discuss my plans with my parents, and I contemplated this not without anxiety. For the Marcenats, marriage had always been seen to concern the clan as a whole. My uncles would intervene and glean information about the Malets. What would they find? I myself knew nothing of Odile's family and had never even laid eyes on her father. I have already said that peculiar Marcenat traditions meant serious news was never transmitted to the concerned parties, but through an intermediary, and tempered by endless precautions. I asked my aunt Cora, my favorite confidante, to tell my father of my engagement. She was always happy to prove the efficiency of her information-gathering service, which was indeed remarkable, although it had the drawback of comprising agents too highly placed in society, for if one wanted details on the life of a corporal, Aunt Cora could only consult the minister of war, or on some local doctor in Limoges, only a surgeon in a Paris hospital. When I gave her Monsieur Malet's name, she replied, as I expected, with, "I don't know him, but if he is anyone, I'll find out right away from old Berteaux, you know, the architect at the institute who comes to a couple of Tuesdays in the winter because poor Adrien used to go hunting with him."

I saw her again a couple of days later and found her pessimistic but animated with it.

"Oh, my poor dear!" she said. "You're lucky you consulted me; this is no marriage for you . . . I saw old Berteaux. He knows Malet very well; they were in lodgings together for the Prix de Rome scholarships. He says he is a pleasant man who had some talent but has not had any success because he never does any work. He is the sort of architect capable of designing a project but who fails to oversee the work and loses all his clients . . . I was aware of that when I had Trouville built . . . Your Malet married a woman I once knew, when she was Madame Boehmer, it came back to me when Berteaux reminded me . . . Hortense Boehmer, I think . . . He is her third husband . . . Now it seems, as you told me, that the daughter is ravishing, and it's only natural that you should be taken with her, but, please believe my experience, my little Philippe, don't marry her, and don't mention this to your father or your mother . . . It's not the same with me—I have seen so many people in my life—but your poor mother . . . I cannot picture her with Hortense Boehmer, Oh! Good Lord, no!"

I told my aunt that Odile was quite different from her family, and besides I had made my decision and it would be better if Odile found approval with my family immediately. After resisting a little, Aunt Cora consented to speak with my parents, partly because she was kind, partly also because she was like an old ambassador with an impassioned taste for negotiating who views a period of international difficulties ahead with both fear, because he likes peace, and secret glee, because it will allow him to exercise his true talent.

My father proved calm and indulgent. He asked me to think things over. As for my mother, she initially greeted the idea that I was to be married with joy, but a few days later she met an old friend who knew the Malets and told her they moved in circles with very liberal customs. Madame Malet had a bad reputation; she was still said to take lovers. Nothing precise was known about Odile, but there was no doubt she had been badly brought up, went out alone with young men, and was far too pretty besides.

"Do they have a fortune?" asked my uncle Pierre, who was inevitably privy to the conversation.

"I don't know," said my mother. "They say this Monsieur Malet is an intelligent man but rather odd . . . They're not people like us."

"Not people like us" was a real Marcenat saying and a terrible condemnation. For a few weeks I thought it would be very difficult for me to have my marriage accepted. Odile and her mother came home to Paris a fortnight after I did. The Malets lived on the rue Lafayette, in a third-floor apartment. A door hidden in paneling led to Monsieur Malet's offices, and Odile took me to see him. I was used to the rigorous order that my father demanded of his employees, both at Gandumas and on the rue de Valois. When I saw those three ill-lit rooms, the partly torn green boxes, and the septuagenarian draftsman, I realized that my aunt's informer had been right to describe Monsieur Malet as an architect with no work. Odile's father was talkative, easygoing; he received me with a cordiality that was rather too perky, talked to me about Florence and Odile in affectionate terms full of emotion, then showed me the drawings for some villas he "hoped" to build in Biarritz.

"What I should really like to build is a large modern hotel, in Basque style. I submitted a project for Hendaye, but I didn't secure the commission."

As I listened to him, I pictured the impression he would make on my family with trepidation and discomfort.

Madame Malet invited me to dinner the following day. When I arrived at eight o'clock, I found Odile alone with her brothers. Monsieur Malet was in his office reading; Madame Malet had not yet come home. The two boys, Jean and Marcel, looked like Odile and yet I instantly knew we would never be close friends. They tried to be amicable, brotherly, but several times during the course of the evening I caught them exchanging glances and smirks that clearly meant, "He's not much fun . . ." Madame Malet came home at half past eight and made no apology. When Monsieur Malet heard her, he appeared like a good little boy, book in hand, and just as we were sitting down, the chambermaid showed in a young American, a friend of the children's who had not been invited but was greeted with great cries of joy. In all this disorder, Odile still looked like an indulgent goddess. She sat beside me, smiling at her brothers' quips and calming them down when she felt I was overwhelmed. She seemed as perfect as she had in Florence, but it pained me, although I could not properly define my pain, to see her surrounded by this family. Beneath the booming triumphal march of my love, I could hear a muted Marcenat motif.

My parents paid a visit to the Malets and, surrounded by the generous effusiveness of Odile's parents, maintained an air of polite rebuke. Luckily, my father was very susceptible to women's beauty although he never talked of it (and in that I knew I was similar to this stranger): he was won over by Odile from the first.

"I don't think you're right," he said as we left, "but I can understand you."

"She's certainly pretty," my mother said. "She's unusual; she says such funny things; she'll have to change."

In Odile's view there was another meeting more important than our families': the meeting between her best friend, Marie-Thérèse (whom she called Misa), and myself. I remember feeling intimidated; I could tell that Misa's opinion meant a great deal to Odile. In the event I rather liked her. Although she did not have Odile's beauty, she was very graceful and had regular features. Next to Odile she looked a little hardy, but side by side, their faces formed a pleasing contrast. I soon grew accustomed to seeing them as a single image and thinking of Misa as Odile's sister. And yet there was an innate refinement in Odile that made her very different from Misa, although by birth they were from the same social circles. During our engagement I took them to a concert every Sunday, and I noticed how much more attentively Odile listened than Misa. Eyes closed, Odile would let the music flow through her, she seemed happy and forgot about the world. Misa's eyes were inquisitive as she looked around, recognized people, opened the program, read it, and irritated me with her agitation. But she was a pleasant friend, always cheerful, always satisfied, and I was grateful to her for telling Odile, who then told me, that she thought I was charming.

We spent our honeymoon in England and Scotland. I cannot recall a happier time than those two months alone together. We stopped in small hotels decked in flowers, beside rivers and lakes, and spent our days lying in flat, varnished boats fitted with cushions in pale floral fabrics. Odile gave me the lovely scenery as a gift, meadows invaded by the blue of hyacinths, tulips rearing up from tall grass, supple close-cropped lawns, and weeping willows trailing their leaves in the water like women with unkempt hair. I came to know a different Odile, even more beautiful than the one in Florence. Watching her live was enchantment itself. The moment she stepped into a hotel room, she transformed it into a work of art. She had a naïve, touching attachment to certain childhood mementos she took everywhere with her: a small clock, a lace cushion, and a volume of Shakespeare bound in gray suede. When, much later, our marriage broke down, it was still with her lace cushion under her arm and her Shakespeare in her hand that Odile left. She skimmed over the top of life, more of a spirit than a woman. I wish I could paint her as she walked on the banks of the Thames or the Cam, her footsteps so light they might have been a dance.

On our return, Paris seemed absurd. My parents and Odile's assumed that our one desire would be to see them. Aunt Cora wanted to organize dinners in our honor. Odile's friends complained they had been deprived of her company for two months and begged me to let them have her back some of the time, but all we wanted, Odile and I, was to carry on living alone. The first evening, when we took possession of our little home with its smell of paint and its carpets not yet laid, Odile, on a jubilant girlish impulse, went to the front door and cut the wire for the doorbell. It was her way of dismissing the world.

We went all around our apartment and she asked me whether she could have a small study next to her bedroom: "It will be my little corner . . . You could only come in if I invited you; you know I have a fierce need for independence, Dickie. (She had been calling me Dickie since hearing a young lady in England hailing a young man by this name.) You don't know me yet, you'll see, I'm terrible."

She had brought champagne, cakes, and a bouquet of asters. With a low table, a couple of armchairs, and a crystal vase, she improvised a charming homely scene. We had the most cheerful, tender evening meal. We were alone and we loved each other. I do not regret those times, although they were fleeting. Their last chords still resonate within me, and if I listen very carefully and silence the noise of the present, I can make out their pure but already doomed sound.

. VI .

Nevertheless, it was on the very morning after this supper that I have to register the first knock to send a fine crack through the transparent crystal of my love. An insignificant episode but one that prefigured everything to come. It was at the upholsterer's, where we were ordering our furnishings. Odile had chosen curtains that I thought expensive. We discussed this briefly, very amicably, then she demurred. The salesman was a good-looking fellow who had energetically taken my wife's part and had irritated me. As we were leaving, I caught sight in a looking glass of a glance of understanding and regret exchanged between this salesman and Odile. I cannot describe how I felt. Since my engagement I had sub-consciously developed an absurd conviction that my wife's mind was now linked to my own and that, by constant transfusion, my thoughts would always be hers. The concept of independence in a living being by my side was, I think, incomprehensible to me. Still more so the concept that this being might conspire against me with a stranger. Nothing could have been more fleeting or more innocent than that glance. I could make no comment, I was not even sure of what I had seen, and yet I feel it is to that moment that I can trace the revelation of jealousy.

Before my marriage, not once had I thought of jealousy, other than as a theatrical emotion and one worthy of utmost contempt. I saw Othello as a tragic jealous figure, and Molière's George Dandin as a comic one. Imagining that I might some-day play one of these characters, or perhaps both at once, would have seemed quite ridiculous. I had al-ways been the one to abandon my mistresses when I tired of them. If they were unfaithful to me, I never knew it. I remember when a friend told me he was suffering from jealousy, I replied, "I can't under-stand you . . . I simply wouldn't be able to carry on loving a woman who didn't love me . . ."

Why did Odile make me anxious the moment I saw her surrounded by male friends? She was so gentle and even tempered but, I could not say how, she created an aura of mystery around her. I had not noticed it during our engagement or our honeymoon because our solitude and the total intermixing of our two lives at the time left no room for any mystery, but in Paris I immediately perceived a distant, as yet undefined danger. We were very close, very tender, but—as I want to be honest with you here—I have to confess that as early as the second month of our married life I knew that the real Odile was not the one I had loved. I did not love the one I was discovering any the less, but it was with a quite different sort of love. In Florence I believed I had met the Amazon; I myself had created a perfect mythical Odile. I was wrong. Odile was no goddess made of ivory and moonlight; she was a woman. Like me, like you, like the entire unhappy human race, she was divided and multiple. And she too doubtless now realized I was very different from the besotted man who had walked beside her in Florence.

As soon as I was back in France, I had to take a serious part in running the factory in Gandumas and the office in Paris. My father, who had considerable parliamentary commitments, had been overrun with work in my absence. When I met with them, our best clients were quick to complain of being neglected. The business quarter was a long way from the home we had rented on the rue de la Faisanderie. I soon realized it would be impossible for me to return home for lunch. If you add to this the fact that I had to spend one day a week at Gandumas and that this hasty journey was too tiring to allow me to take Odile with me, you will understand how our lives were immediately separated against our will.

On my way home in the evenings, I felt happy knowing I would soon see my wife's beautiful face. I liked the furnishings with which she had surrounded herself. I was not accustomed to living among lovely things, but it seemed I had an innate need for them, and Odile's taste delighted me. In my parents' house in Gandumas, too many pieces of furniture accumulated over three or four generations cluttered salons whose walls were hung with fabrics in blue-green tones, featuring crudely drawn peacocks wandering between stylized trees. Odile had had our walls painted in soft single colors; she liked bedrooms to be almost bare, with great deserted plains of pale carpeting. When I went into her boudoir, I felt such an acute sense of beauty that I found it obscurely disturbing. My wife would be lying on a chaise longue, almost always in a white dress, and beside her (on the low table of our first supper) stood a narrow-necked Venetian vase bearing a single flower and sometimes some scant foliage. Odile loved flowers more than anything, and I in turn was learning to love choosing flowers for her. I learned to follow the changing seasons in florists' windows; I was happy to see chrysanthemums or tulips appear once more, because their strident or delicate colors gave me an opportunity to solicit from my wife's lips the happy Odile smile. When she saw me come home from work with a crisp-edged white paper package in my hands, she would jump up happily: "Oh! Thank you, Dickie . . ." She admired them, enchanted, before becoming serious and saying, "I'm going to arrange my flowers." She would then spend an hour finding the correct vase, stem length, and lighting to ensure a single iris or rose curved as gracefully as possible.

After this, though, the evening would often become peculiarly sad, like on sunny days when the shadows of huge clouds take the world by surprise as they envelop everything. We had little to say to one another. I tried often enough to talk to Odile about my business, but she had no interest in it. She had exhausted the novelty of listening to me describing my youth; my ideas did not change much because I had no time to read, and she was uncomfortably aware of this. I tried to bring my two closest friends into our life. Odile instantly disliked André Halff, whom she found sarcastic, almost hostile, and indeed he was so with her.

"You don't like Odile," I once said to him.

"I think she's very beautiful," he said.

"Yes, but not very intelligent?"

"True . . . There's no need for a woman to be intelligent."

"Anyway, you're wrong; Odile is very intelligent, but it's not your sort of intelligence. She's intuitive, concrete."

"You could be right," he said.

It was different with Bertrand. He tried to have a deep, confidential friendship with Odile and found her rebellious, defensive. Bertrand and I could happily spend an entire evening sitting together, smoking, and putting the world to rights. Odile preferred to spend the end of the day at theaters, cabarets, or amusement parks. One evening she made me spend three whole hours roaming around between shops, fairground rides, raffles, and shooting galleries. Her two brothers came with us; Odile always had fun with these two spoiled, boisterous, and slightly unpredictable children.

"Come on, Odile," I said toward midnight, "haven't you had enough? Can't you see that it's rather ridiculous. Surely you can't actually enjoy throwing balls at bottles, going around in circles in fake automobiles, and winning a boat made of spun glass on the fortieth attempt?"

She replied with a quote from a philosopher I had told her to read: "What does it matter if a pleasure is false, so long as we believe it is real . . ." And, taking her brother's arm, she ran off toward a shooting gallery; she was a very fine shot and, after hitting ten eggs in as many shots, went home in good spirits.

At the time of our marriage, I believed that, like me, Odile could not bear the social scene. This was not the case. She liked dinners and balls; as soon as she discovered the dazzling animated group that revolved around Aunt Cora, she wanted to go to avenue Marceau every Tuesday. My only desire since our marriage had been to have Odile to myself;

I could rest easy only when I knew that so much beauty was perfectly contained within the narrow confines of our home. This was something I felt so powerfully that I was happier when Odile, who was always fragile and often laid low by exhaustion, had to keep to her bed for a few days. Then I would spend the evening in an armchair beside her. We would have long conversations together that she called "waffling," and I would read to her. I quickly learned what sort of book would capture her attention for a few hours. She had quite good taste, but in order to please her a book had to be both melancholy and passionate. She liked *Dominique*, Turgenev's novels, and a few English poets.

"It's strange," I said. "Someone who doesn't know you well might think you frivolous, and yet deep down you like only rather sad books."

"But I'm very serious, Dickie; perhaps that's why I'm frivolous. I don't want to show everyone what I'm really like."

"Not even me?"

"Well, you, yes . . . Remember Florence . . ."

"Yes, in Florence I came to know you well . . . But you're very different now, darling."

"We mustn't always stay the same."

"You don't even say anything kind to me anymore."

"People don't say kind things to order. Be patient; it will come back . . ."

"Like in Florence?"

"Well, of course, Dickie. I haven't changed."

She held out a hand to me and I took it, then another great "waffling" began about my parents, hers, Misa, a dress she had ordered, life. On these evenings when she was tired and gentle, she really was like the mythical Odile as I had conceived her. Kindly and weak, in my power. I was grateful to her for this languor. The moment she felt stronger and could go out, I was confronted with the mysterious Odile again.

She never told me spontaneously, as many chatty transparent women might, what she had done in my absence. If I inquired about this, she would reply with very few, almost always vague words. What she told me never allowed me to picture at all satisfactorily the succession of events. I remember one of her friends telling me long afterward (with that harshness that women have toward each other), "Odile always embroidered the truth." This was not true, and at the time I felt indignant about the comment, but when I thought about it later I could easily see what it was about Odile that might give this judgment some weight: the nonchalant way she described things . . . her contempt for precision . . . If, surprised by an improbable detail, I questioned her, she would shut down like a schoolboy when an insensitive master asks questions beyond his scope.

One day when, unusually, I was able to come home for lunch, Odile asked the maid for her hat and coat at two o'clock.

"What are you doing this afternoon?" I asked.

"I have an appointment with the dentist."

"Yes, darling, but I heard you on the telephone; your appointment isn't until three. What will you do until then?"

"Nothing. I'd like to go there slowly."

"But, my child, that's absurd; the dentist lives on the avenue de Malakoff. It will take you ten minutes to get there and you have an hour. Where are you going?"

"You do amuse me," she replied and went out.

After dinner that evening, I could not help asking her, "So what did you do between two and three?"

She tried to joke at first, then, because I pressed the point, she got up and went to bed without saying good night. This had never happened before. I went to ask her forgiveness. She kissed me. Before leaving the room, when I could see she was pacified, I asked, "Now, do be kind and tell me what you did between two and three."

She burst out laughing. But later in the night I heard some noise, turned on my light, and went to her room to find her crying softly. Why was she crying? With shame or concern?

She answered my questions: "Be careful about this. I love you very much. But beware: I'm extremely proud . . . I have it in me to leave you, even though I love you, if there are more scenes like this . . . I may be in the wrong, but you will have to accept me as I am."

"Darling," I said, "I shall do my best, but you too must try to change a little. You say you're proud; could you not occasionally overcome your pride?"

She shook her head obstinately. "No, I cannot change. You always say that what you like about me is how natural I am. If I changed I would no longer be natural. It is up to you to be different."

"My darling, I could never be different enough to understand what I do not understand. I was brought up by a father who always taught me to respect the truth and precision above all else . . . It's the very way my mind works . . . No, I could never say with any sincerity that I understand what you did today between two and three o'clock."

"Oh, I've had enough!" she said bluntly. And, turning to one side, she pretended to sleep.

The following morning I was expecting to find her displeased, but, quite the reverse, she greeted me gaily and seemed to have forgotten everything. It was a Sunday. She asked me to go to a concert with her. They were playing Wagner's "Good Friday Spell," a piece we both liked very much. As we emerged, she asked me to take her somewhere for tea. There was nothing more touching than Odile when she was happy, glad to be alive; she gave such a powerful impression of being made for happiness, that it seemed criminal not to give it to her. Looking at her that Sunday, so animated and dazzling, I could scarcely believe our quarrel the previous evening had been real. But the more I came to know my wife, the better I understood that she had a capacity for forgetting that likened her to a child. Nothing differed more from my own nature, my own mind, which noticed, accumulated, and recorded. That day, life for Odile was a cup of tea, hot buttered toast, and cream. She smiled at me and I thought, "What truly divides people could be the fact that some live mostly in the past while others only in the present moment."

I was still suffering slightly but was incapable of resenting her for long. In my head I upbraided and lectured myself, swore I would no longer ask pointless questions, would have faith. We went home on foot, across the Tuileries Gardens and the Champs-Elysées; Odile inhaled the cool autumn air with delight. It seemed to me, as it had in Florence in the spring, that the russet-colored trees, the shifting gray and golden light, the happy bustle of Paris, the children's boats whose sails leaned over the large pond, and the flexible spray of the fountain in their midsts—everything was singing the Knight's theme in unison. I kept repeating a sentence from Rondet's *Christian Manual* to myself, one I liked very much and that I had grown accustomed to applying to my relationship with Odile: "Here I am before you like a slave and I am ready to do anything, for I want nothing for myself, but for you." When I succeeded in conquering my pride like this and humiliating myself, not before Odile but to be more precise before my love for Odile, I felt pleased with myself.

The person Odile saw most often was Misa. They telephoned each other every morning, sometimes talking for more than an hour, and went out together in the afternoon. I was in favor of this friendship, which kept Odile occupied without danger while I was at work. I even enjoyed seeing Misa at our apartment on Sundays and, more than once, it was I who suggested this friend accompany us when Odile and I made little two- or three-day trips. I want to try to explain the feelings that guided me in this, because they will help you understand Misa's unusual role in my life. First, if, as in the early weeks of our marriage, I still wanted to be alone with Odile, it was now more out of a vague fear of what new friends might bring than for positive pleasure. I loved her no less, but I knew that exchanges between us would always be limited and that she would accept truly serious, in-depth conversations only with listless goodwill. On the other hand, it is fair to say that I was developing a taste for the slightly mad, slightly sad, often frivolous, and always gracious chattering, the "waffling" that was Odile's real form of conversation when she was quite natural. But Odile was never more herself than with Misa. When they talked together, they both displayed a puerile side, one I found very entertaining and touching too, in that it showed me what Odile might have been like as a child. I was delighted one evening while we were staying in Dieppe when they argued like children, and Odile ended up throwing a pillow at Misa's face, crying, "Beastly girl!"

I also harbored more unsettling feelings, the sort that must appear every time circumstances rather than love cause a young woman to be involved in a man's daily life. Thanks to our journeys and thanks to Odile's own familiarity that permitted my own, I found I was almost as intimate with Misa as with a mistress. One day when we were discussing women's physical strength, she challenged me. We wrestled for a moment; I tipped her over, then stood up, slightly ashamed.

"Really, you're such children!" said Odile.

Misa stayed on the floor a long time, staring at me.

In fact she was the only human being Odile and I received at home with equal pleasure. Halff and Bertrand hardly came anymore and I did not miss them much. I very soon felt the same way about them as Odile did. And when I listened to her talking to them, I experienced a strange duality. Seeing her through their eyes, I felt she treated serious subjects with inappropriate levity. But at the same time I managed to prefer her flights of fancy to my friends' theories. I was ashamed of my wife in front of them but proud of her in front of myself. When they left, I would think to myself that, in spite of everything, Odile was superior to them in her more direct contact with life and nature.

Odile did not like my family and I did not care much for hers. My mother had wanted to give her advice on her choice of furniture, our way of life, and a young wife's duties. Advice was Odile's least favorite thing in the world. When she talked about the Marcenats, she adopted a tone I found rather shocking. I was bored at Gandumas and felt that there all life's pleasures were sacrificed to a family conformism whose sacred origins were utterly unproved, and yet I was quite proud of the austerity of our traditions. Life in Paris, where the name Marcenat meant nothing, should have cured me of my insistence on granting them such importance, but like a small religious community transported to a barbarous continent and whose religious faith remains undisturbed by the sight of millions of people worshipping different gods, so we Marcenats, transported into a pagan world, remembered Limousin and recalled our greatness.

My own father, who admired Odile, could not help but be irritated by her. He did not show it; he was too good and too reserved for that. But, being familiar with and having inherited his propriety, I knew how much Odile's tone of voice must have pained him. When my wife had cause to doubt something or to be angry, she would express her views forcefully and then forget about them. This was not how we Marcenats had been taught that human beings communicate with each other. When Odile said, "Your mother came here while I was away and took the liberty of making certain comments to the manservant; I shall call her to tell her I won't tolerate that . . . ," I begged her to wait.

"Listen, Odile, deep down you're right, but don't try to tell her yourself, you'll only make her angry. Let me do it or, if you prefer—and it would actually be better—ask Aunt Cora to tell my mother that you told her that . . ."

Odile laughed in my face. "You have no idea," she said, "how comical your family is . . . Except, it's also terrible . . . Yes really, Dickie, it's terrible, because I actually love you less when I see the caricatures of you that all these people effectively are . . . I do understand that you're not like that by nature, but you've been affected by them."

The first summer we spent together at Gandumas was quite difficult. At home, my family had lunch at exactly noon, and it had never occurred to me to keep my father waiting. But Odile would take a book down to the meadow or go for a walk along the river and forget the time. I watched my father pacing backward and forward in the library, and ran across the park looking for my wife, only to come back out of breath having failed to find her. Then she would appear, all calm and smiling, and happy to be warmed by the sun. At the beginning of the meal we would sit in silence to show our disapproval, which (given that it came from a group of Marcenats) could only be indirect and unspoken, and she would watch us with a smile in which I could read amusement and defiance.

In the Malet household, with whom we dined once a week, the situation was completely reversed; I was the one who felt scrutinized and judged. Here meals were not solemn ceremonies. Odile's brothers would get up to fetch bread; Monsieur Malet might mention some saying he had read, could not quote it exactly, and he too would go out to consult a book. Conversation was extremely free, and I did not like to hear Monsieur Malet discussing improper subjects in front of his daughter. I knew how ridiculous it was to attach so much importance to such small details, but it was not a judgment, it was an uncomfortable impression. I was not happy in the Malet house; it was not my sort of climate. I did not like myself, I seemed solemn, boring, and, even though I loathed my own silences, I withdrew into them.

But in the Malet household and at Gandumas alike, my discomfort was only skin-deep because I had the still potent pleasure of watching Odile live. When I was seated opposite her at a dinner, I could not help watching her. She had a dazzling, luminous whiteness and reminded me of a beautiful diamond twinkling in the moonlight. At the time she almost always dressed in white and surrounded herself with white flowers at home. It suited her well. What a fantastic combination of candor and mystery she was! It felt like living alongside a child, but sometimes, when she spoke to another man, I caught glimpses of unfamiliar sentiments in her expression and something like the distant murmurings of a passionate and savage race.

. VIII .

I have tried to help you grasp the entrance, the first exposition—half hidden beneath louder instruments—of the themes around which the unfinished symphony of my life has been built. You have seen the Knight and the Cynic, and perhaps you have also noticed, in the ridiculously intricate ornamentation, that I have scrupulously chosen not to omit the first distant call of Jealousy. Be indulgent now and try not to judge but to understand. It is painful and difficult for me to tell you what happened next, and yet I want to be accurate. And this desire is all the greater because I believe I am cured, and I will try to describe my madness with the objectivity of a doctor who has had a fit of delirium and forces himself to write about it.

There are illnesses that begin slowly with slight, increasingly frequent dizzy spells; others explode in the space of an evening with a bout violent fever. For me jealousy was a sudden and terrible scourge. If I try now, in a calmer state, to trace its causes, they strike me as very varied. First there was my great love and the natural desire to keep for myself the tiniest portions of the precious materials that were Odile's time, her words, her smiles, and her expressions. But that desire was not the most important element, for when I could have Odile to myself (if, for example, we were alone at home in the evening, or if I went away with her for a couple of days), she complained that I was much more interested in my books and thoughts than in her. It was only when she could have been taken by others that I wished I had her to myself. This sentiment was mostly due to pride, a subterranean pride masked by the modesty and reserve characteristic of my father's family. I wanted to rule over Odile's mind in the same way that, in the Loue valley, I ruled over the waters, the forests, the long machines sliding across the white paper pulp, the peasants' houses and the workmen's cottages. I wanted to know what was going on inside her pretty little head, beneath that curly hair, just as I knew, from the clear printed statements that came every day from Limousin, how many kilos of Whatman were left and what the factory's daily output had been over the last week.

Judging by the pain it reawakens when I press on this precise spot, I can see that here was the root of the problem, in my acute intellectual curiosity. I never conceded that I did not understand. Yet understanding Odile was impossible, and I believe that no man (if he loved her) could have lived with her without suffering. I even think that, had she been different, I might never have known what it is to be jealous (because man is not born jealous, he comes only with a certain receptiveness that predisposes him to contract this illness), but Odile, by her very nature and without meaning to, constantly aroused my curiosity. Things that happened, the events of one day, were for me and for all my relations precise facts and needed only to be described scrupulously for each sentence, each element of the account to slot in perfectly with all the others, leaving no room for doubt. But when they were filtered through Odile's mind they became a hazy, muddled landscape.

I would not like to give the impression that she deliberately dissimulated. It was far more complex. What happened was that, to her, words and sentences had little value; just as she had the beauty of a character in a dream, she spent her life in a dream. I have said that she lived mostly in the present moment. She invented the past and the future as and when she needed them, and then forgot what she had invented. If she had wanted to mislead, she would have made a concerted effort to coordinate what she said, to give it at least an air of truthfulness; I never saw her go to that trouble. She could contradict herself within a single sentence. On my return from a trip to the factory in Limousin, I asked her, "What did you do on Sunday?"

"Sunday? I don't remember . . . Oh, yes, I was very tired. I stayed in bed the whole day."

Five minutes later we were talking about music and she suddenly cried, "Oh! I forgot to tell you: at the concert last Sunday I heard Ravel's *Waltz* you told me about. I really liked—"

"But, Odile, do you realize what you're saying? It's lunacy . . . Surely you must know whether you were at a concert or in bed on Sunday . . . and you don't think I could possibly believe both."

"I'm not asking you to believe that. When I'm tired I talk complete nonsense . . . I don't even listen to what I'm saying myself."

"All right, but now, try to think of a precise memory: what did you do last Sunday? Did you stay in bed or did you go to the concert?"

She looked perplexed for a moment, then said, "Well, I don't remember now. You get me all confused when you behave like the Inquisition."

I emerged from this sort of conversation very unhappy: anxious, agitated, and unable to sleep. I spent hours trying to reconstruct how she had actually spent her day, from the tiniest scraps she had let slip. I then reviewed all the worrying male friends whom I knew had filled Odile's life as an unmarried woman. As for Odile, she had the same capacity for forgetting these scenes as everything else. I could leave her sulky and uncommunicative in the morning and find her jubilant that evening. I would arrive home prepared to say, "Listen, darling, this can't go on. We'll have to think about a separation. It's not what I want, but you really will have to make an effort, you need to behave differently," only to be greeted by a girl in a new dress who kissed me and said, "Guess what! Misa called and she has three tickets for the theater, and we're going to see *A Doll's House*." And, out of weakness and love, I would accept this unrealistic but consoling fiction.

I was far too proud to let my suffering show. My parents in particular had, at all costs, to be unaware of it. In that first year only two people seemed to have guessed what was going on. The first was my cousin Renée, and this surprised me all the more because we saw her so little. She led an independent existence, a fact that had irritated our family for some time, at least as much as my marriage. While my uncle Pierre was staying in Vittel where he went to take the waters every year, she had met a Paris doctor and his wife and grew fond of this couple. Renée had always been a fairly rebellious girl and, since her adolescence, had been very hostile to Marcenat ways. She got into the habit of making longer and longer visits to her new friends in Paris. This Doctor Prud'homme, who was wealthy, did not practice medicine but did research into cancer, and his wife worked with him. Renée had inherited from her father (whom she got along with all the worse for being so like him) a taste for a task well done. She was quickly adopted by the circle of scholars and doctors into which her friends introduced her. At twenty-one, she asked her father to give her her dowry and to consent to her living in Paris. For a few months she was on bad terms with our family. But the Marcenats clung too keenly to the notion of an indestructible love uniting parents and children to tolerate the reality of indifference for very long. Once my uncle Pierre had accepted the firm conviction of his daughter's decision, he capitulated to restore peace. From time to time he would still have fits of anger, though they were increasingly brief. Then he begged his daughter to marry and she refused, threatening never to set foot at Chardeuil again. Horrified, my aunt and uncle promised there would be no more talk of marriage.

Renée had witnessed my engagement and had sent Odile a wonderful basket of white lilies the very same day. I remember being surprised by this. Her parents had given us a handsome gift; why these flowers? A few months later we dined with her at Uncle Pierre's house, and I then inivted her to come to us. She was very friendly toward Odile and I was extremely interested by the tales of her travels. Since I had stopped seeing most of my former friends, I hardly ever heard such robust, informed conversation. When she left, I saw her to the door. "Your wife's so pretty!" she said with sincere admiration. Then she looked at me sadly and added, "Are you happy?" and from her tone of voice I understood she thought I was not.

The other woman who I felt lifted the veil for a moment was Misa. After a few months, her behavior became rather odd. It seemed to me that she now sought far more to be my friend than to remain Odile's. One evening when Odile was unwell in bed (she had had two consecutive miscarriages and it was unfortunately looking unlikely that she would ever have children), Misa, who had come to see her, sat beside me on the sofa at the foot of the bed. We were very close together and the high wooden footboard concealed us almost entirely from Odile's eyes so that, as she lay there, she could see only our heads. All at once, Misa moved closer, pressed herself to me, and took my hand. I was so surprised that I do not understand to this day how Odile failed to read this in my face. I moved away, but only reluctantly, and later, when I walked Misa home, with an abrupt involontary movement I kissed her lightly. She allowed me to.

"This is too bad. Poor Odile . . . ," I said.

"Oh! Odile!" she said with a shrug.

I found this unpleasant and became rather cold toward Misa. It worried me too because I wondered whether her "Oh! Odile!" might mean, "Odile doesn't deserve to be fussed over."

. IX .

Two months later Misa was engaged. Odile told me she did not understand Misa's choice. My wife thought this Julien Godet horribly mediocre. He was a young engineer fresh from the Central School of Engineering and in Monsieur Malet's words "had no position." Misa seemed more to *want* to love him than actually to love him. He, on the other hand, was very much in love. For some time my father had been looking for a director to run an additional paperworks he had set up at La Guichardie near Gandumas, and when he heard us discussing Misa's marriage he had the idea of taking on our friend's husband. This only half pleased me.

I no longer felt I could trust Misa, but Odile, who so liked helping people and making them happy, thanked my father and immediately passed on the offer.

"Be careful," I told her. "You're sending Misa off to live in Limousin and depriving yourself of her company in Paris."

"Yes, I know that, but I'm doing it for her, not for me. Anyway, I'll see her during those awful stays in Gandumas, which will be a precious bonus for me, and if she ever wants to come to Paris she can always stay with her parents or with us . . . And this boy really does have to do something, and if we don't take him on, he'll trail her off to somewhere like Grenoble or Castelnaudary."

Misa and her husband accepted the position at once, and Odile herself traveled to Gandumas, in midwinter, to look for a house for them and to recommend them to the locals. This was a trait of Odile's, one I have not mentioned enough, devoting herself so generously to her friends.

I think that Misa's leaving was a blow to our marriage, because it had the instant result of bouncing Odile back into a group of people I seriously disliked. Before we were married, Odile had frequently gone out alone with young men; they had taken her to the theater and she had traveled with her brothers and their friends. She had, very loyally, informed me of this when we became engaged and told me she could not relinquish this freedom. At the time, I wanted her more than anything in the world. I told her in good faith that this struck me as quite natural and I would never be an obstacle to her friendships.

It is so unfair and absurd holding people to account on their promises! When I gave that promise I had made no attempt to imagine what I might feel if I saw another man welcomed with the same gaze, the same smile I so loved. You may be surprised to hear that I was also aggrieved by the rather mediocre nature of most of Odile's friends. I should have found this reassuring, when in fact it wounded me. If someone loves a woman as much as I loved my wife, everything connected with her image ends up being invested with imaginary qualities and virtues by that love. In the same way that the place where he met this woman seems more wonderful than it actually is, and the restaurant where he dined with her is suddenly better than any other, rivals themselves, even though despised, have their share of this aura. If the mysterious composer orchestrating our existence were to play the theme for the Rival in isolation, I think it would sound almost the same as the Knight's theme, but ironic and distorted. We want to see our enemy as an adversary worthy of us, which is why, of all the disappointments a woman can afford us, disappointment over a rival is the worst. I would have been jealous but not surprised if I had seen the most remarkable men of our time with Odile; instead I saw her surrounded by young men who, if I judged them impartially, may have been no more mediocre than any others, but who were certainly not worthy of her, and she had anyway not chosen them.

"Odile, why do you flirt so?" I asked. "I can see that an unattractive woman might want to test her powers. But you . . . it's a game you're bound to win every time. It's cruel, darling, it's disloyal . . . But worst of all, your choices are so strange . . . That Jean Bernier, for example, you see him the whole time . . . What on earth can you find interesting about him? He's ugly, vulgar . . . "

"I find him amusing."

"How can you find him amusing? You're refined, you have taste. He makes the sort of jokes I haven't heard since military service and I wouldn't dare tell them in front of you . . ."

"You're probably right. He's ugly and he might be vulgar—although I don't think so—but I like seeing him."

"But you're not in love with him, are you?"

"Oh! For goodness' sake, no! You must be mad! I wouldn't even want him to touch me, he reminds me of a slug . . ."

"My darling, you may not love him, but he loves you; I can see that. You're making two men unhappy, him and me. Why would you do that?"

"You think everyone's in love with me . . . I'm not that pretty . . ."

She said this with such a charming flirtatious smile that I smiled too. And kissed her.

"So, my darling, will you see him a little less?"

Her face hardened, inscrutable. "I never said that."

"You didn't say it, but I'm asking it of you . . . What difference would it make to you? It would make *me* happy. And you yourself have said you're indifferent to him . . ."

She seemed taken aback, lost in thought, then she said with an embarrassed smile, "I don't know, Dickie, I don't think I can do things differently . . . I'm having fun."

Poor Odile! She seemed so puerile and so sincere as she said that. I then showed her, with my implacable but pointless logic, that it would be easy to "do things differently."

"Your downfall," I told her, "is that you accept yourself as you are, as if we were given our characters ready-made. But we can shape our characters, we can alter them . . ."

"Well, alter yours, then."

"I'm completely prepared to try. But you could help me by trying too."

"No, I've already told you plenty of times that I can't. And anyway I don't want to try."

When I think of those now long gone days, I wonder whether she had some deep-seated instinct dictating this attitude. If she had changed in the way I was asking her to, would I have carried on loving her so much? Would I have tolerated the constant presence of that futile little creature, if scenes like that had not made it impossible for either of us to be bored? Besides, it was not true that she had never tried. Odile was not unkind. When she could see I was unhappy, she believed she would go to any lengths to make things better for me, but her pride and weakness were stronger than her goodness, and her life stayed the same.

I had come to recognize what I called her "air of triumph," a heightened cheerfulness, a semitone above the usual, brighter eyes, a more beautiful expression, and her customary languor overcome. When she liked a man, I knew before she did. It was appalling . . . Sometimes this made me think of the phrase she quoted in Florence: "I am too fond, and therefore thou mayst think my behavior light."

What saddens me most when I reflect on that unfortunate period, as I still often do, is the thought that, despite her flirtatiousness, Odile was faithful to me and that, with a little more aptitude, I might have been able to keep her love. But it was not easy knowing how to react with Odile. She found tenderness boring and it produced snappy, hostile reactions in her, whereas threats would have made her determined to take drastic action.

One of her most unwavering characteristics was her love of danger. She liked nothing better than being taken out in a yacht in stormy winds, driving a racing car around a tricky circuit, or jumping unnecessarily high obstacles on horseback. A whole band of bracing young men circled around her. But none of them was preferred over the others, and whenever I had an opportunity to hear their conversations, I felt the tone of Odile's niceties was of the companionable, sporting kind. In fact I am now in possession (I will explain why) of a number of letters these boys wrote to Odile; they all prove that she tolerated a certain amorous banter but had not succumbed to any of them.

"Strange Odile," one of them wrote, "so wild and yet so chaste; too chaste for my liking." And another, a sentimental, religious young Englishman, said, "As it is clear, my dear Odile, that I can never have you in this world, I hope to be close to you in the next." But I am now telling you things I knew only much later and, at the time itself, I could not believe that this free way of life was innocent.

In order to be quite fair to her, I should also add a detail I have been forgetting. Early on in our marriage she had tried to involve me with her friends, old and new; she would happily have shared all her friends with me. We met the Englishman I mentioned during our first summer vacation, in Biarritz. He entertained Odile by teaching her the banjo, which was a new instrument at the time, and by singing her Negro songs. Then, when we left, he insisted on giving her a banjo as a gift, which I found extremely irritating.

Two weeks later she said, "Dickie, I've had a letter from little Douglas, a letter in English. Would you read it for me and help me reply?"

I cannot say what sort of demon took hold of me: I told her with ill-contained fury that I sincerely hoped she would not reply, that Douglas was a little cretin and I found him boring . . . None of this was true. Douglas was well brought up, charming and, before my marriage, I would have liked him very much. But I was getting into the habit of never listening to what my wife was saying without wondering what she was hiding. Every time I spotted something unexplained in what she said, I constructed an ingenious theory to clarify why she wanted it to be unexplained. There was a painful pleasure, a voluptuous torment in believing that she was lying. My memory is usually fairly poor, but where Odile's words were concerned it became astonishing. I remembered her least utterances, made comparisons between them, weighed them. I would find myself saying, "What? You had a fitting for that jacket? But that makes it the fourth fitting. You already went on Tuesday, Thursday, and

Saturday last week." She looked at me, smiled at me with no trace of embarrassment, and replied, "You have a devilish memory . . ." I felt both ashamed of being found out and proud to think I had foiled her tactic. Mind you, my discoveries were pointless, I never acted on them, I had no desire to act, and Odile's mysterious calm gave me no grounds to make a scene. I was both unhappy and passionately interested.

What stopped me from harshly laying down the law and, for example, forbidding Odile from seeing some of her friends, was my acknowledgment of the ridiculous mistakes that my desperate deductions drove me to. In one instance I remember her complaining of headaches and tiredness for several weeks, and she said she wanted to spend a few days in the country. I could not leave Paris at the time, and for a long while I refused to let her go. Please note, I completely failed to notice how selfish it was of me to deny that she was ill.

Eventually it struck me that it would be still more ingenious to agree, to allow her to go to Chantilly, which was what she wanted, and to surprise her there the following evening. If I did not find her alone (and I was quite sure I would not), at least I would know something concrete at last and, more important, I would be able to act on this, to confound her, to leave her (because I believed that was what I wanted, but I was wrong). She left. On the second day I hired a car (I was predicting a scene and did not want my own chauffeur to witness it) and left for Chantilly after dinner. About halfway there, I gave the man the order to turn back to Paris. Then, after a couple of miles, with my curiosity too acutely aroused, I made him turn toward Chantilly once more. At the hotel I asked for Odile's room number. They did not want to give it to me. That was quite clear. I showed them my papers, proved I was her husband, and eventually a bellboy took me up. I found her alone, surrounded by books and the countless letters she had written. But surely she had had time to set up this little scene?

"You don't give up, do you!" she said with a note of pity. "What did you think? What were you afraid of? . . . That I'd be with a man? What would you have me do with a man? . . . What you don't understand is that I want to be alone just to be alone. And, if you want me to be absolutely frank, what I really don't want is to see you for a few days. I'm so exhausted by your fears and suspicions that I have to watch what I say and be careful not to contradict myself, like a defendant in a court of law. I've had the most lovely day here. I've been reading, dreaming, sleeping, I went for a walk in the forest. Tomorrow I'm going to the château to see some miniatures . . . It's all so simple, if you only knew."

But I was already thinking, "Now, spurred on by this success, she'll know that next time she can invite her lover to join her without any danger."

Oh, this lover of Odile's, I tried so hard to work out what he was like! I put him together from everything I found inexplicable in my wife's thoughts and words. I had developed incredible subtlety in my analyses of what Odile said. I made a note of all the finer ideas she expressed, in homage to this stranger. A peculiar relationship had grown between Odile and myself. I now admitted my every thought to her, even those that cast her in the harshest light. She listened to me with an almost indulgent attentiveness, irritated but also flattered to be the object of so much curiosity and interest.

Her health was still poor and she now went to bed very early. I spent almost every evening at her bedside. Strange and rather pleasant evenings.

I explained the flaws in her character to her, she smiled as she listened to me, then reached out her hand and, taking mine, said, "Poor Dickie, what torment over an unhappy little girl who's unkind, stupid, proud, flirtatious . . . because I'm all those, aren't I?"

"You're not at all stupid," I told her. "You're not very intelligent . . . but you have incredible intuition and a great deal of taste."

"Ah!" said Odile. "I have taste . . . So I am left with *something*. Listen, Dickie, I'm going to read you an English verse that I found. I adore it."

Her natural tastes were very refined and she rarely liked anything mediocre, but even in the choice of verses she read to me I was disturbed and surprised to identify a taste for love, a profound knowledge of passion, and sometimes a longing for death. I particularly remember one stanza that she often recited:

From too much love of living,
From hope and fear set free,
We thank, with brief thanksgiving
Whatever gods may be
That no life lives for ever;
That dead men rise up never;

That even the weariest river
Winds somewhere safe to sea.

"'The weariest river,' I like that," she often said. "That's me, Dickie, the weariest river . . . and I'm heading off gently toward the sea."

"You're mad," I said. "You're life itself."

"Oh, I may look like that," Odile retorted with a comically sad pout, "but I'm a very weary river."

When I left her after an evening like this, I would say, "Deep down, with all your faults, Odile, I do love you."

"And so do I, Dickie." She would say.

. X .

My father had been asking me for some time to make a trip to Sweden in connection with the paper factory. We bought wood pulp there through brokers. There was no doubt we could have it at a better price by dealing directly with the supplier, and he was not in good enough health to make the trip himself. I refused to go if Odile did not come with me, and she was in no hurry to do so. I thought this unwillingness suspect; she enjoyed travel. In case she did not want to cross Germany and Denmark by train, I suggested going by boat from Le Havre or Boulogne, which should have been a pleasure for her.

"No," she said, "you go alone. I'm not tempted by Sweden. It's too cold."

"Not at all, Odile, it's a charming country . . . landscapes just made for you, you can get away from things, there are lakes edged with fir trees, old castles . . ."

"Do you think? No, I don't feel like leaving Paris at the moment . . . But your father's keen for you to do this, so you go. It'll do you good to see some other women besides me. Swedish women are ravishing, tall, fair-skinned blondes. Just your type . . . Be unfaithful to me . . ."

In the end it became impossible for me not to make the trip. I humbly admitted to Odile that I was horrified at the thought of leaving her alone in Paris.

"You *are* funny," she said. "I won't go out, I promise. I've lots of books to read and I'll take all my meals with my mother."

I left in a state of anxiety, and the first three days were hellish. During the long journey from Paris to Hamburg, I pictured Odile in her boudoir receiving a man whose face I could not see but who played all the music she loved on the piano. I imagined her smiling and animated, her face lit up by the happy expression that had once been reserved for me and that I wished I could catch, shut away, and guard jealously for myself alone. Which of her regular friends had kept her in Paris? Was it that half-wit Bernier or that American friend of her brothers', Lansdale? In Malmö the varnished new train and unusual colors eventually drew me out of my grim imaginings. In Stockholm I received a letter from Odile. Odile's letters were odd; she wrote like a little girl. It said: *I'm being very good. I'm not doing anything. It's raining. I'm reading. I've read* War and Peace *again. I had lunch with my mother. Your mother came to see me.* And it went on like that with short sentences that implied nothing and—I could not say why but perhaps precisely because they were so vacuous and naïvely simple—had a reassuring effect on me.

The next few days only increased this feeling of relaxation. It was strange, I loved Odile more than in Paris. I pictured her looking serious, lying rather languidly and reading beside a vase in which she had most likely put a beautiful carnation or a rose. Because I was very lucid in spite of my mania, I wondered, "Why on earth isn't this hurting? I should be unhappy. I have no idea what she's doing. She's free and can say whatever she wants in a letter." I realized that while absence, as I already knew, crystallizes love, it also temporarily lulls jealousy to sleep because, by removing all the minor facts and observations on which jealousy has learned to build its monstrous and dangerous edifices, absence compels it to be calm, to rest.

The business I was handling required me to travel through the Swedish countryside. I stayed with squires who owned swathes of woodland; I was offered local liqueurs, caviar, and smoked salmon; the women had a cold, crystalline radiance; I could spend entire days without thinking about Odile or what she was doing.

I particularly remember one evening when I dined out in the country not far from Stockholm, and after dinner my hostess suggested we take a walk through the grounds. We were wrapped up in furs. The air was icy. Tall blond-haired valets opened up a wrought-iron gate, and we ended up beside a frozen lake that gleamed gently in the night sun. The woman beside me was ravishing and very gay; a few minutes earlier she had played piano preludes for me with a light-fingered grace that brought tears to my eyes. For a moment I felt extraordinarily happy. "The world is such a beautiful place," I thought, "and it's so easy to be happy."

Returning to Paris reawakened my phantom fears. Odile's accounts of her long days of solitude were so empty that they invited the most painful hypotheses to fill their vast, deserted expanses.

"What have you been doing all this time?"

"Nothing really. I got some rest, I daydreamed, I read."

"What did you read?"

"I told you in my letter: *War and Peace*."

"Come on, you can't have spent two weeks reading one novel!"

"No, I did things: I tidied my clothes, I sorted out my books, I replied to old letters, I visited some couturiers."

"But who have you seen?"

"No one. I told you in my letter: your mother, my mother, my brothers, Misa . . . And I've listened to a lot of music."

She became more animated and told me about the Spanish music by Albéniz and Granados that she had just discovered.

"And another thing, Dickie, I must take you to *The Sorcerer's Apprentice* . . . It's so intelligent."

"Is it based on the ballad by Goethe?" I asked.

"Yes," Odile replied brightly.

I looked at her. How did she know the ballad? I knew Odile had never read anything by Goethe. Who did she go to the concert with? She could read the anxiety in my face.

"It said so in the program," she said.

The Tuesday after I returned from Sweden, we dined with Aunt Cora. She invited us once every two weeks and was the only member of my family for whom Odile felt any liking. Aunt Cora, who saw Odile as a gracious ornament for her table and was good to her, criticized me, saying I had grown silent since my marriage. "You're gloomy," she said, "and you spend too much time fussing about your wife; couples only work at a dinner once they've reached the indifferent stage. Odile is delightful, but you'll only be ready in a couple of years, maybe three. At least this time you've just come back from Sweden, I hope you're going to be dazzling."

In fact, success at this dinner was not granted to me at all but to a young man I knew well because he was friend of André Halff's. It was at Halff's house that I had previously met him, and Halff spoke of him with a unique combination of admiration, fear, and irony. Admiral Garnier, the naval chief of staff, had introduced this man to the avenue Marceau gatherings. His name was François de Crozant, he was a naval lieutenant and had just returned from the Far East. That evening he described Japanese landscapes and talked of Conrad and Gaugin in powerful, vibrant, poetic language that I could not help but admire, although I did not much like him. Listening to him, I gradually remembered things André had told me about him. He had had several postings in the East and had a small house near Toulon full of things brought back from his travels. I knew he composed music and had written an un-usual opera on a subject from Chinese history. I also knew, though only obscurely, that he was admired in sporting circles for breaking several automobile speed records and had been one of the first naval of-ficers to go up in a seaplane.

A man in love is an extremely sensitive reagent for the feelings of the woman he loves. I could not see Odile, who was seated at the other end of the table, on the same side as me, but I knew the expression on her face at that moment and with what unnecessarily acute interest she would be listening to François's tales. I remember that dinner very well. My feelings were those of a father who loves his only daughter above all else, who realizes that, as a result of unfortunate but inevitable circumstances, he has taken her somewhere contaminated by a terrible epidemic and hopes ardently and desperately that he can save her before she is infected. If I could ensure that Odile did not end up in the same group as François after dinner, if no one told her the details that I had already heard about his life (details so likely to attract her attention), perhaps I could take her home at midnight still quite unsullied by the most terrifying of germs.

It so happens that I was lucky in this, and not thanks to some adept maneuver on my part but because straight after dinner François was scooped up by Hélène de Thianges, who took him off to the Chinese salon that Aunt Cora always kept for couples eager to be left alone. Meanwhile I myself had a peculiar conversation, about François himself, no less, with a pretty woman called Yvonne Prévost, whose husband was also a naval man, a captain who worked alongside the admiral at the ministry.

"Do you find Crozant interesting?" she asked. "I knew him well in Toulon. I lived there for many years before I was married because my father was naval commander there. I remember men found Crozant artificial, some even said disloyal, but women chased after him . . . I was too young myself, but I heard what people said."

"Well, yes, I am interested."

"Oh! I don't remember very clearly. I think he was a tremendous flirt. He would behave as if he cared passionately for a woman, would court her ardently, showering her with letters and flowers, then all of a sudden he would abandon her and start showing an interest in another while the first had no way of knowing what had caused this change . . . He subjected himself to an extraordinarily disciplined routine. In order to stay in shape he went to bed at ten o'clock every evening, and they used to say that, when the appointed hour came, he would have shown the prettiest woman in the world the door . . . In matters of love he was hard and cruel, behaving as if the whole thing was a meaningless game to himself and to everyone else.

You can imagine how much pain he caused with a personality like that."

"Yes, I see what you mean. But why would anyone love him?"

"Oh, well, that, you know . . . All right, I had a friend who loved him, and she told me, 'It was appalling but I couldn't cure myself of him for a long time. He was so complicated, endearing, and demanding, brutal and terse one minute, but sometimes gentle and beseeching too . . . It took me several months to realize he could only bring me unhappiness.'"

"And did your friend manage to escape?"

"Yes, very successfully. She can laugh when she talks about him now."

"And do you think he's trying to cast his spell on Hélène de Thianges at the moment?"

"Oh, for sure! But this time he has more than met his match. Besides, a woman like her, who is young and has some social standing, would do well to save herself. François ruins the lives of women he comes across, because he can't help talking about his lovers to all and sundry. In Toulon, every time he made a new conquest, the whole town would know about it the following day."

"But this François of yours is a loathsome character."

"Oh, no!" she said. "He's very charming . . . That's just the way he is."

We are almost always the craftsman of our own unhappiness. I was wise when I promised myself I would not talk of François to Odile. Why then was it impossible for me not to mention this conversation when we were in the car taking us home? I think it was because arousing Odile's interest, seeing her listen intently to what I was saying was a pleasure whose appeal I had difficulty resisting, perhaps also because I was under the illusion—absurd though it may seem—that this harsh criticism of François would distance Odile from him forever.

"And you say he's a composer?" Odile asked when I stopped talking.

I had unwisely called up the demon. It was no longer in my power to drive him away. I had to spend the rest of the evening relating everything I knew about him and his unusual way of life.

"He must be a strange man to know. Shall we invite him to dinner sometime?" Odile asked with apparent indifference.

"Gladly, if we see him again, but he has to go back to Toulon. Did you like him?"

"No. I really don't like the way he looks at women, as if he can see through them."

Two weeks later we met him again at Aunt Cora's house. I asked him whether he had left the navy.

"No," he said in his abrupt, almost insolent way. "I'm doing a six-month posting with the Hydrographical Service."

This time he had a long conversation with Odile; I can still picture them sitting on the same upholstered sofa, leaning toward each other and talking animatedly.

On the way home, Odile was very quiet.

"Well then," I said, "what do you think of my sailor?"

"He's interesting," said Odile, and she said nothing more all the way home.

. XII .

On several consecutive Tuesdays, François and Odile took refuge together in Aunt Cora's Chinese salon as soon as dinner was over. Naturally, this was very painful for me, but I was keen to do my best not to show it. I could not help talking about François with the other women; I hoped to hear them say they found him boring, so that I could then pass this on to Odile. But almost all of them admired him. Even the sensible Hélène de Thianges, who was so wise that Odile called her Minerva, told me, "He's very attractive, I can assure you."

"But how? I try in vain to be interested in what he's saying; it strikes me it's always the same old things. He talks about Indochina, nations conquering other nations, Gaugin's 'intense' life . . . I thought it quite remarkable the first time I heard it. Then I realized it was a star turn; watching it once is enough."

"Yes, perhaps. You're partly right. But he tells such incredible stories! Women are like big children, Marcenat. They still have a sense of wonder. And, anyway, the scope of their real lives is so limited that they're always longing to escape it. If you only knew how boring it is looking after a household, meals, guests, and children every day! Married men and bachelors in Paris are all part of the same social and domestic machinery, and they have nothing new, nothing fresh to offer us, whereas a naval man like Crozant is like a breath of fresh air, and that's why we find him attractive."

"But really, don't you think Crozant's whole stance smacks of unbearable false romanticism? You mentioned his stories . . . I can't stand all those adventures . . . that he's clearly invented."

"Which ones?"

"Oh, you know perfectly well: the one about the Englishwoman in Honolulu who threw herself in the water after he'd left; the one about the Russian woman who sends him her photograph framed by a coil of hair. I think it's all such bad taste . . ."

"I hadn't heard those stories . . . who told them to you? Odile?"

"No, no, everyone did, why would you think it was Odile? . . . Tell me honestly, don't you think that's unpleasant, shocking, even?"

"If you like, yes . . . All the same, he has unforgettable eyes. And not everything you're saying is accurate. You're seeing him through the prism of myth. You should talk to him in person, you'll see he's very straightforward."

We often saw Admiral Garnier at avenue Marceau. One evening I maneuvered so that I was alone with him and asked him about Crozant.

"Ah!" he said. "A true sailor . . . One of our great leaders of the future."

I resolved to stifle the feelings of disgust that François de Crozant aroused in me, to see more of him and to try to judge him impartially. It was very difficult. When I had met him with Halff, he had been rather disdainful toward me, and I had had the same uncomfortable impression the first time we met again. For a few days now he seemed to have been making an effort to overcome the boredom that my surly, hostile silence inspired in him. But I thought, perhaps correctly, that he was now interested in me because of Odile, and this did nothing to endear him to me. Far from it.

I invited him to dine with us. I wanted to find him interesting, but did not succeed. He was intelligent but, deep down, fairly shy, and he overcame his shyness by affecting a brusque assertiveness that I found exasperating. I thought him far less remarkable than my former friends, André and Bertrand, and could not understand why Odile, who had swept them aside so contemptuously, showed such sustained interest in what François de Crozant had to say. The moment he was there, she was quite transformed and even prettier than usual. One time François and I had a conversation about love in front of her. I had said, I think, that the only thing that makes love a truly beautiful sentiment is faithfulness, in spite of everything and until death. Odile gave François a quick glance that I thought peculiar.

"I really don't understand the importance of faithfulness," he said with the staccato diction that always gave his ideas an abstract, metallic feel. "You have to live in the present. What matters is getting all the intensity out of every moment. There are only three ways of achieving this: with power, with danger, or with desire. But why would you use faithfulness to keep up a pretence of desire when it has evaporated?"

"Because true intensity is to be found only in something lasting and testing. Don't you remember the passage in *Confessions* where Rousseau says that barely touching the gown of a chaste woman affords more acute pleasure than possessing a woman of easy virtue?"

"Rousseau was not a well man," said François.

"I loathe Rousseau," said Odile.

Feeling them united against me, I set about defending Rousseau, about whom I was actually indifferent, with clumsy vehemence, and the three of us realized that we would now never be able to have a conversation together without it becoming confidential and dangerous beneath its veneer of transparency.

Several times when François was talking about his work I became so fascinated that I forgot my hostile feelings for a few minutes. After dinner one evening, as he walked across the salon with his rolling seaman's stride, he asked, "Do you know how I spent my evening yesterday, Marcenat? With

Admiral Mahan's book, studying Nelson's battles," and, in spite of myself, I felt the little thrill of pleasure that seeing André Halff or Bertrand used to give me.

"Really?" I replied. "But were you doing it for your own pleasure or do you think it could be useful for you? Naval procedures must have changed so much. All those stories of boarding enemy ships, favorable winds, and the position to adopt to give a broadside, is that of any value still?"

"Don't go believing that," said François. "The qualities that result in victory, on land and at sea, are the same today as they were in Hannibal's day, or Caesar's. Take the Battle of the Nile, why were the English successful? . . . First, Nelson's tenacity when, having searched all over the Mediterranean for the French fleet and failing to find them, he didn't abandon his hunt; then the promptness of his decision when he finally found his enemy at anchor and the wind in his favor. Well, do you think those fundamental qualities—tenacity and audacity—are no longer valid because the Dreadnought has replaced the Victory? Not at all, and besides the basic principles of any strategy are immutable. Here, look . . ."

He took a piece of paper from a table and a pencil from his pocket.

"The two fleets . . . this arrow is the wind direction . . . This cross-hatching here, the shallows . . ."

I leaned over him. Odile had sat down at the same table, her hands together with her chin resting on them. She was admiring François and, from time to time, watched me from beneath her long eyelashes.

"Would she be listening like this," I thought, "if *I* were describing a battle to her?"

Another fact that struck me during the few visits that François de Crozant made to our house was that Odile often dazzled as she related anecdotes and expressed ideas that I had told her about while we were engaged. She had never mentioned them to me again; I thought she had forgotten everything. Yet now here was all my poor knowledge resuscitated to amaze another man with the masculine clarity of a woman's mind. As I listened to her, I remembered that this had been the case with Denise Aubry too, and that when we take great care to instruct an individual, we are almost always working for another man's benefit.

The strange thing is that the beginnings of a true relationship between them probably coincided with what was a brief period of relative security for me. François and Odile, who had openly compromised themselves in front of me and all our friends for several weeks, suddenly became extremely cautious, rarely appearing together and never in the same group in a salon. She did not talk about him, and if, out of curiosity, another woman pronounced his name in her presence, she replied with such perfect carelessness that I myself was taken in by it for a few weeks. Unfortunately, as Odile herself said, I was demonically intuitive wherever she was concerned, and it was not long before logical reasoning explained their behavior to me. "It's precisely because they are seeing each other freely behind my back," I thought, "and don't have much left to say to each other in the evening, that they now avoid each other and make a show of hardly speaking to each other."

I now habitually analyzed what Odile said with frightening clairvoyance, and I found François hiding in her every sentence. Thanks to Doctor Pozzi, François was now a friend of Anatole France, and he went to the Villa Saïd every Sunday morning. I knew this. Now, in the last few weeks, Odile had taken to telling the most interesting and private stories about France. One evening when we dined with the Thianges, Odile, who was usually so quiet and modest, astonished our friends by commenting with some verve on France's political ideas.

"You were dazzling, my darling!" I told her afterward. "You've never talked to me about all that. How did you know about it?"

"Me?" she asked, both pleased and worried. "Was I dazzling? I didn't notice."

"It's not a crime, Odile, don't be defensive. Everyone thought you were very intelligent . . . Who taught you all that?"

"I don't really know. It was the other day, taking tea somewhere, someone who knew Anatole France."

"But who?"

"Oh, I can't remember . . . I can't see that it matters."

Poor Odile! She did make such blunders. She wanted to keep to her usual tone of voice, not to say anything that might give her away, but still her new love was just beneath the surface of her every utterance. It reminded me of flooded meadows that still look intact at a glance, the grass seems to stand tall and vigorous, but every step you take reveals the treacherous layer of water already seeping into the soil. Though attentive to direct indicators such as naming François de Crozant, she did not see the indirect indicators that flashed over and above her own words and paraded his name for all to see like great illuminated signs. For me who knew Odile's tastes, ideas, and beliefs so well, it was at once easy, interesting, and painful to watch them swiftly altering. Without being very pious, she had always been a believer; she went to mass every Sunday. She now said, "Oh, I'm like the Greeks in the fourth century B.C. I'm a pagan," words I could attribute to François as surely as if he had signed them. She would say, "What *is* life? Forty paltry years spent on a lump of mud. And you expect us to waste a single minute being bored for no gain?" And I thought, "François's philosophy, and a rather vulgar philosophy to boot." Sometimes I needed a moment's thought to spot the link between some newfound interest of hers that struck me as out of the ordinary and the true object of her thoughts. For example, she who never read a newspaper spotted the headline, "Forest Fires in the South," and snatched the page from my hand.

"Are you interested in forest fires, Odile?"

"No," she said, rejecting the newspaper and handing it back to me. "I just wanted to see where it was."

I then remembered the little house surrounded by pine forests that François owned near Beauvallon.

Like a child playing hunt-the-thimble who puts the trinket he wants to hide in the middle of the room, on the carpet, right under everyone's nose, making them all smile indulgently, Odile was almost touching with her endless naïve precautions. When she relayed a fact she had learned from one of her friends or one of our relations, she always named her informer. When this was François, though, she would say: "Someone . . . Someone told me . . . I've heard that . . ." She sometimes displayed an incredible knowledge of naval facts. She knew we were to have a new faster cruiser or a new type of submarine or that the English fleet would be coming to Toulon. People were amazed.

"That's not in the papers . . ." they said.

Terrified and realizing that she had said too much, Odile beat a retreat. "Isn't it? I don't know . . . Maybe it's not true."

But it was always true.

Her entire vocabulary had become François's, and Odile now spouted this man's repertoire—the repertoire that had caused me to tell Hélène de Thianges that his conversation was just a star turn. She talked about the "intensity of life," the joy of conquest, and even Indochina. But filtered through Odile's veiled mind, François's hard-edged themes lost their sharp contours. I could follow them quite clearly through her but could see they were distorted, like a river crossing a wide lake and losing the rigid framework of its banks, reduced to an indistinct shadow eaten into by encroaching waves.

. XIII .

So many corroborating facts proved to me beyond doubt that, even if Odile was not François's mistress, she at least saw him in secret, and yet I could not make up my mind to have it out with her. What was the point? I would reveal all the tiny nuances and verbal coincidences my implacable memory had registered, and she would laugh out loud, look at me tenderly, and say, "You do make me laugh!" What could I reply? Could I threaten her? Did I want to break off with her? And besides, despite appearances, could I have been mistaken? When I was honest with myself, I knew I was not mistaken, but life then felt unbearable and for few days I would cling to some unrealistic hypothesis.

I was very unhappy. Odile's behavior and her secret thoughts had become a constant obsession for me. In my office on the rue de Valois, I now hardly got any work done, I spent days on end with my head in my hands, dreaming and thinking; at night, I could get to sleep only toward three or four o'clock in the morning, after pointlessly mulling over problems whose solution I could see only too clearly.

Summer came. François's posting finished and he went back to Toulon. Odile seemed very calm and not at all sad, which I found quite reassuring. I did not know whether he wrote to her. In any event, I never saw any letters, and I was less aware of his disturbing shadow looming over Odile's sentences.

I could not take a vacation until August because my father was going to take the waters in Vichy in July, but as Odile was unwell for almost the whole winter, it was agreed that she would spend the month of July at the Villa Choin in Trouville. A couple of weeks before she was due to leave, she said, "If it makes no difference to you, I'd rather not stay with Aunt Cora but go to a quieter beach. I can't bear the Normandy coast; there are too many people, especially in that house . . ."

"What do you mean, Odile? Don't tell me you're the one who doesn't want to see people now, when you're always criticizing me for not wanting to see anyone!"

"It depends on one's state of mind. Right now, I need peace and quiet, time to myself . . . Don't you think I could find a little place in Brittany? I don't know Brittany at all and they say it's beautiful."

"Yes, my darling, it's very beautiful, but it's a long way away. I wouldn't be able to come and see you on Sundays as I could in Trouville. Anyway, you'll have the villa in Trouville to yourself, Aunt Cora won't be there until August first . . . Why the change?"

But she was obviously keen to go to Brittany and kept gently bringing the subject up until I gave in. I could not understand. I had been expecting her to ask to be closer to Toulon; it would have been easy because the summer was awful that year, and everyone was complaining about how wet it was in Normandy. Although I was sad to see her go, I derived some pleasure from knowing she was heading in this reassuring direction. I went with her to the

station, feeling rather sad. She was particularly loving that day. On the station platform she kissed me.

"Don't get bored, Dickie, have some fun . . . If
you like, you could go out with Misa, she'd like
that."

"But Misa's at Gandumas."

"No, she's coming to Paris to stay with her parents all of next week."

"I don't feel like going out when you're not
here . . . I stay at home, on my own, moping."

"You mustn't," she said, stroking my cheek in a
motherly way. "I don't deserve that sort of attention. I'm not interesting . . . you take life too seriously, Dickie . . . It's just a game."

"It's not a very cheerful game."

"No," she said, and this time she too had a
note of sadness in her voice. "It's not a cheerful
game. Mostly, it's difficult. We do things we don't
mean to do . . . I think it's time I boarded the
train . . . Goodbye, Dickie . . . Are you going to be
all right?"

She kissed me again, turned on the step and gave
one of those luminous smiles that chained me to
her, and immediately disappeared into the compartment. She hated goodbyes from the window, and

sentimentality in general. Misa later told me she was hard. That was not entirely accurate. She could actually be generous and kind, but she was driven by very strong desires and, precisely because she was afraid that feelings of pity might cause her to resist her own wishes, she refused to give in to them. It was in these circumstances that her face took on the blank, impermeable-looking expression that was the only thing that could make her look ugly.

. XIV .

The following day was a Tuesday and I dined with Aunt Cora. She carried on entertaining up until August but there were fewer people in summer. I ended up next to Admiral Garnier. He talked about the weather, about a thunderstorm that had flooded Paris toward the end of the afternoon, then said, "By the way, I've just found a position for your friend François de Crozant . . . He wanted to study the Brittany coast. I found him a temporary job in Brest."

"In Brest?"

I watched the glasses and flowers spin around me; I thought I would pass out. But the social instinct has become so strong in us that I believe we could even succeed in dying while feigning indifference.

"Oh, I didn't know that," I told the admiral. "Was this recently?"

"A few days ago."

I carried on a long conversation with him about the port of Brest, its value as a naval base, its old houses and its Vauban architecture. My thoughts were racing on two extraordinarily distinct planes. On the surface, they shaped the bland, polite sentences with which I maintained the image of myself in the admiral's mind as a calm creature enjoying this lovely cool evening and the last fleeting clouds. On a deeper level, in a silent veiled voice, I kept saying to myself, "So that's why Odile wanted to go to Brittany." I pictured her walking through the streets of Brest with him, leaning on his arm and wearing that animated expression I knew so well and loved so much. Perhaps she would stay with him one evening. Morgat, the beach she had chosen, was not far from Brest. Perhaps it would be the other way around, François would come to meet her by the sea. He must have a launch. They would walk along the rocks together. I knew how lovely Odile could make the scenery seem on a walk like that.

Something surprising then struck me: although it hurt, I felt a hard, intellectual sort of pleasure now that I knew at last. For all the terrible problems I had wrestled with whenever Odile's decisions were concerned, the conclusion that had come to me with astonishing clarity when she first mentioned going to Brittany was, "François's already there." And he was. My heart was devastated, my mind almost satisfied.

Back at home, I spent nearly the entire night wondering what I would do about it. Take the train to Brittany? I would most likely end up on some small beach to find Odile radiant and rested; I would look foolish and not even feel reassured, because I would immediately think François had been and left again, which would in fact be likely. The awful thing about what I was feeling was that nothing could cure it, because, whatever the facts, they could be interpreted unfavorably. For the first time, I asked myself, "Must I leave Odile, then? Given that her character and mine mean I can never rest easy, given that she does not want, and never will want, to be more considerate toward me, wouldn't it be better for us to live apart? We have no children; divorce would be easy." I then remembered very clearly the state of humdrum happiness and confidence I had known before meeting her. In those days, although my life had little grandeur or power, it was at least natural and pleasant. But, even as I formulated this plan, I knew I had no wish to realize it and that the thought of living without Odile was not even conceivable.

I turned over and tried to get to sleep by counting sheep and picturing a landscape. Nothing works when the mind is obsessed. At some points I was furious with myself. "Why love *her* rather than anyone else?" I asked myself. "Because she's beautiful? Yes, but other women have lovely faces and are far more intelligent. Odile has serious flaws. She doesn't tell the truth; that's the thing I hate most in the whole world. So? Can't I free myself, shake off this hold?" And I kept telling myself, "You don't love her, you don't love her, you don't love her." But I knew perfectly well it was a lie and that I loved her more than ever although I did not understand why.

Toward morning I tried to persuade myself that this coincidence proved nothing and that Odile might not even know François was so near her. But I knew this was not the case. I fell asleep at dawn and dreamt I was walking along a street in Paris near the Palais

Bourbon. The street was lit by an old-style streetlamp, and I could see a man hurrying away ahead of me. I recognized François from behind. I took a revolver from my pocket and fired at him. He fell. I felt relieved and ashamed, and woke up.

Two days later I received a letter from Odile: *The weather's lovely. The rocks are lovely. I've met an elderly lady at the hotel who knows you. Her name is Madame Jouhan; she has a house near Gandumas. I bathe in the sea every day. The water is lukewarm. I have been on excursions locally. I really like Brittany. I went for a trip in a boat. I do hope you're not unhappy. Are you having fun? Did you dine with Aunt Cora last Tuesday? Have you seen Misa?* It finished with: *With fond love to you, my darling.* The writing was slightly larger than her natural hand. It was obvious she had wanted to fill four pages so as not to hurt me but had also had a lot of trouble filling them. She was in a hurry, I thought, he was waiting for her. "But I really must write to my husband," she told him. And, when I imagined my wife's face as she spoke these words, I could not help thinking it beautiful and longing for nothing more than her return.

. XV .

The week after Odile left, Misa telephoned me.

"I know you're on your own," she said. "Odile's abandoned you. I'm on my own too. I've come to stay with my parents because I needed to do some shopping and have a little dose of Paris, but they're away and I have the apartment to myself. Come and see me."

I thought that talking with Misa might help me forget some of the terrible, pointless thoughts in whose midst I was floundering, and I arranged to meet her that same evening. She opened the door to me herself; the staff were out. She looked very pretty; she was wearing a pink silk negligee copied from a pattern lent to her by Odile. I noticed she had changed her hairstyle, and it now looked like Odile's. The weather had changed since the storm and, toward evening, it was very cold. Misa had lit a wood fire in the hearth, and she sat on a pile of cushions by the fire. I sat close to her and we started talking about our families, the terrible summer, Gandumas, her husband, and Odile.

"Have you heard from her?" Misa asked. "She hasn't written to me, which isn't very kind."

I told her I had had two letters.

"Has she met any people? Has she been to Brest?"

"No," I said. "Brest is quite far from where she is."

But it seemed a strange question. Misa was wearing a bracelet of blue and green glass beads. I said I liked it and took her wrist to look at it more closely. She leaned toward me. I put my arm around her waist; she did not resist. I could tell she was naked beneath that pink dress. She looked at me anxiously, questioningly. I leaned toward her, found her lips and, as I had on that day when we wrestled, felt the firm twin pressure of her breasts against my chest. She let herself drop backward and there, before that fire, on those cushions, she was my mistress. I felt no inkling of love, but I desired her and thought, "If I don't take her, I'll look like a coward."

We ended up sitting watching the dying embers of the last log. I held her hand and she looked at me with a happy, triumphant expression. I felt sad; I wished I could die.

"What are you thinking?" asked Misa.

"I'm thinking of poor Odile."

She became hostile; two hard lines formed across her forehead.

"Listen," she said, "I love you, and I want you to stop talking nonsense now."

"Why nonsense?"

She hesitated, looking at me for a long time.

"Do you *really* not understand," she asked, "or do you just pretend not to understand?"

I could anticipate everything she was about to say and knew I should stop her, but I wanted to know.

"It's true," I said. "I don't understand."

"Oh," she said. "I thought you knew but loved Odile too much to leave her or talk to her about it . . . I've often thought I ought to tell you everything . . . only I was Odile's friend. It was hard for me . . . Well, never mind! I now love you a thousand times more than I love her."

So she told me that Odile was François's mistress, that it had been going on for six months, and that Odile had even asked her, Misa, to pass on their letters so that the Toulon postmark did not attract my attention.

"Can you see how difficult that was for me . . . especially because I loved you . . . Haven't you noticed that I've been in love with you for three years? . . . Men don't understand anything. Well, at least everything's all right now. I'll make you so happy, you'll see. You deserve it and I so admire you . . . You're an admirable person."

And she showered me with compliments for several minutes. It afforded me no pleasure whatsoever. I kept thinking, "This is all so wrong. I'm not a good person at all! I can't cope without Odile . . . Why am I here? Why do I have my arm round this woman's waist?" We were still sitting side by side like happy lovers, and I hated it.

"Misa, how can you betray Odile's trust? What you're doing is appalling."

She looked at me in astonishment.

"Oh, this is too much," she said, "I can't believe *you're* defending her."

"Yes, I am. I don't like what you're doing, even if you are doing it for my sake. Odile's your friend . . ."

"She was. I don't like her anymore."

"Since when?"

"Since I've loved you."

"I sincerely hope you *don't* love me . . . *I* love Odile just as she is," I said, looking at Misa defiantly, but she was shaking. "And when I try to work out why I love Odile, I wouldn't know how to describe it . . . I think it's because I'm never bored with her, because for me she is life itself and happiness."

"You are odd," she said bitterly.

"Perhaps."

She seemed to go into a dream for a moment, then let her head drop down onto my shoulder and, in a voice filled with deep-seated passion that should have touched me if I had not been so impassioned and blinded myself, she said, "Well, I do love you and I could make you happy in spite of yourself . . . I would be faithful to you, devoted . . . Julien's at Gandumas; he leaves me well alone.

If you like, you could even come to see me there because he spends two days a week at la Guichardie . . . You'll see, you've lost the habit of being happy, I'll get you back into it."

"I can only thank you," I said coldly, "but I'm very happy."

This scene carried on far into the night. We adopted positions and made gestures associated with love, but I could feel a savage, incomprehensible resentment rising within me. And yet we parted tenderly with a kiss.

I swore to myself that I would never go to see her again, and yet I often went to her house while Odile was away. Misa was unbelievably daring and gave herself to me in her parents' salon when a chambermaid might come in at any minute. I would stay with her until two or three in the morning, almost always without a word.

"What are you thinking?" she kept asking, trying to smile kindly.

I would be thinking, "She's so deceitful to Odile," and would reply, "About you."

Now, when I look back on it all calmly, I can see that Misa was not a bad woman, but I treated her harshly at the time.

. XVI .

Odile eventually came home one eve-
ning, and I went to pick her up at the station. I had
promised myself I would tell her nothing. I was well
aware what such a conversation would be like. I
would be reproachful; she would deny everything.
I would relay what Misa had said; she would say
Misa was lying. I meanwhile would know that Misa
had told the truth. It was all pointless. As I walked
along the station platform, surrounded by strang-
ers and a smell of coal and oil, I kept telling myself,
"Given that I'm only happy when I'm with her and
given that I will never break up with her, I might
as well enjoy the pleasure of seeing her again and

avoid annoying her." Then the next minute I would be thinking, "What a coward! It would take only a week's effort to force her to change her ways or to get used to coping without her."

A member of the staff came and hung up a sign: FAST TRAIN FROM BREST. I came to a stop.

"Come on," I thought, "this is too ridiculous. What if you had gone to stay in a different hotel in Florence in May 1909? You would have spent your whole life not even knowing Odile Malet existed. But you'd be alive, you'd be happy. Why not start, right now at this exact moment, assuming she doesn't exist?"

It was then that I spotted in the distance the headlamps of a locomotive and the curve of a train undulating toward us. It all felt unreal. I could not even picture Odile's face anymore. I took a few steps forward. Heads leaned out of windows. Men were jumping from the train before it stopped. Then a walking crowd formed. Porters pushed trolleys. All at once I spotted Odile's outline some way away, and a moment later she was beside me flanked by a porter carrying her gray bag. She looked well and I could tell she was in good spirits.

As we climbed into the car she said, "Dickie, we're going to stop to buy some champagne and some caviar, and we'll have a little supper like the day we came home from our honeymoon."

This might strike you as the height of hypocrisy, but you had to know Odile to judge her. She had most likely truly savored the few days she had spent with François; she was now prepared to enjoy the present moment and make it as wonderful for me as she could. She noticed I was glum and not smiling.

"What *is* the matter, Dickie?" she asked desperately.

My resolutions to be silent were never very solid, and I let the thoughts I was trying to hide burst out in front of her.

"The matter is that people say François is in Brest."

"Who told you that?"

"Admiral Garnier."

"That François is in Brest? And then what? What difference does that make to you?"

"The difference it makes to me is that he was very close to Morgat and it would have been easy for him to come to see you."

"Very easy, so easy that, if you must know, he did come to see me. Does that upset you?"

"You didn't tell me that in your letters."

"Are you sure? But I honestly thought . . . Anyway, if I didn't tell you in a letter it's because I couldn't see that it was in the least bit important, and it wasn't."

"That's not what I think. I've also heard that he was engaged in a secret correspondence with you."

This time it looked as if I had hit home: Odile was almost beside herself. It was the first time I had seen her look like that.

"And who told you that?"

"Misa."

"Misa! She's a wretch! She lied to you. Did she show you any letters?"

"No, but why should she invent something like that?"

"Well, I don't know . . . Out of jealousy."

"That's a cock-and-bull story if ever I heard one, Odile."

We reached the house. Odile mustered a pure and charming smile for the staff. She went to her bedroom, took off her hat, looked at herself in the glass to tidy her hair and, spotting me behind her, looked directly at my reflection and smiled at me too.

"What am I to do with you, Dickie!" she said. "I can't leave you alone for a week without the black moths descending . . . You're thankless, sir. I thought about you the whole time and I'm going to prove it to you. Pass me my bag."

She opened it and took out a small parcel that she handed to me. It contained two books, *Reveries of a Solitary Walker* and *The Charterhouse*, both in vintage editions.

"But, Odile . . . Thank you . . . these are in-credible . . . How did you find them?"

"I sifted through the bookshops in Brest, sir. I wanted to bring something back for you."

"So you went to Brest, then?"

"Of course. It was very close to where I was, there was a ferry service, and I've been wanting to see Brest for ten years now . . . Well, aren't you going to kiss me for my little present? And there I was thinking it would be such a success . . . I went to a lot of trouble, you know . . . They're very rare, Dickie. All my little savings went on those."

So I kissed her. I had such complex feelings for her that I had trouble understanding them myself.

I loathed her and adored her. I thought her innocent and guilty. The violent scene I had prepared for turned into a friendly, trusting conversation. We talked all evening about Misa's betrayal as if the revelations made to me (which were no doubt true) had not been about Odile and myself but a couple of friends whose happiness we wanted to protect.

"I do hope," Odile said, "that you won't see her again."

I promised I would not.

I have never known what happened between Odile and Misa the following day. Did they talk it out over the telephone? Did Odile go to see Misa? I knew she was candid and brutal. That was all part of the almost insolent courage that both shocked and charmed my silent inherited reserve. I myself stopped seeing Misa. I did not hear her mentioned again, and my memories of that brief affair were like those left by a dream.

. XVII .

Suspicions planted in the mind are trig-
gered like a series of mines and destroy love gradually with their successive explosions. On the
evening that Odile came home, her kindness and
adroitness, along with the pleasure I felt seeing
her again, managed to delay the catastrophe. But
from that moment, we both knew we were living
in a minefield and it would all go up one day. Even
when I loved her best, I could now talk to Odile
only in terms laced, however delicately, with bitterness. Like the shadow of clouds in the distance, my
most banal sentences bore the shadow of unspoken
resentments. The cheerful optimistic philosophy I

had espoused in the first months of our marriage was replaced by a melancholy pessimism. The natural world, which I had so loved since Odile had revealed it to me, now sang only sad tunes in a minor key. Even Odile's own beauty was no longer perfect, and I could sometimes see traces of deceitfulness in her face. It was fleeting; five minutes later I would see only her smooth forehead and candid eyes, and would love her again.

In early August we left for Gandumas. The isolation, the distance, and the complete absence of letters or telephone calls received reassured me and gave me a few weeks' respite. The trees, sunny meadows, and dark hillsides covered in firs had a strong influence on Odile. Nature afforded her almost sensual pleasures, and she inadvertently transmitted these to whoever was with her, even if that was me. Shared solitude, if it does not last long enough to produce satiation or boredom, favors a steady rise in affection and trust that brings those concerned much closer together. "Deep down," Odile thought, "he's kind . . . ," and I for my part felt very close to her.

I remember one evening in particular. We were alone on the terrace, which looked out over a vast horizon of hills and woods. I can still see so clearly the heather on the slopes opposite. The sun was setting; it was very quiet, very warm. Human affairs seemed trifling. I suddenly started saying the humblest, most tender things to Odile, but (and this is peculiar) they were the words of a man already resigned to losing her.

"We could have had such a wonderful life, Odile . . . I've loved you so much . . . Do you remember Florence and the days when I couldn't last a single minute without looking at you? . . . I'm still right on the brink of being like that, darling . . ."

"It makes me happy to hear you say that . . . I've loved you very tenderly too. My God! I had such faith in you . . . I used to tell my mother, 'I've found the man who'll settle me down once and for all.' Then I was disappointed . . ."

"It was all my fault . . . Why didn't you explain all this to me?"

"You know why, Dickie . . . Because it was impossible. Because you put me on a pedestal. You see, Dickie, your big mistake is you ask too much of women. You expect too much of them. They can't . . . But it still makes me happy to think you'll miss me when I'm no longer here . . ."

She spoke these words in a painfully prophetic way, which had a profound effect on me.

"But you'll always be here."

"You know perfectly well I won't," she said.

At that point my parents joined us.

During that stay, I often took Odile to my observatory, and we would spend a long time watching the tiny torrent deep down in the wooded funnel of the gorge. She liked it there and talked about her childhood, Florence, our daydreams along the Thames; I would put my arm around her with no resistance from her. She seemed happy. "Why not accept that we're constantly beginning new lives?" I thought, "and that, in each of these lives, the past is just a dream? Am I now the same man who put his arms round Denise Aubry in this same spot? Perhaps, since we've been here, Odile has quite forgotten François?" But while I tried everything I could to put my happiness back together, I knew this happiness was unrealistic and that the dreamy beatitude on Odile's face as she leaned on the parapet was due to the fact that she thought François loved her.

———

There was one other person at Gandumas who understood with extraordinary lucidity what was going on in my marriage, and that was my mother. I have said that she never much liked Odile, but she was a good woman, could see I was in love, and had never wanted to reveal her feelings toward my wife. On the morning of the day before we left, I came across her in the vegetable garden, and she asked me if I would like to go for a walk with her. I checked my watch; Odile would not be ready for a long time, so I said, "Yes. What I'd really like is to go right down into the valley. I haven't done that since I was about twelve or thirteen."

She was touched by this memory and became more confidential than usual. She spoke first about my father's health; he had arteriosclerosis, and the doctor was worried. Then, keeping her eyes on the stones along the path, she said, "What's happened between you two and Misa?"

"Why do you ask?"

"Because you haven't seen them a single time since you've been here . . . Last week I asked them to lunch and Misa declined. She's never done that before . . . I can see something's happened."

"Yes, something has, Mother, but I can't tell you about it . . . Misa behaved badly toward Odile."

My mother walked on in silence for a while, then said quietly and almost reluctantly, "Are you quite sure it's not Odile who behaved badly toward Misa? Listen, I certainly don't want to intervene between you and your wife, but I do have to tell you at least once that everyone blames you, even your father. You're too weak with her. You know how I loathe gossip; I want to believe that everything people say is nonsense but, if it is nonsense, you should insist that she lives in such a way that people don't say it."

While I listened to her I flicked seed heads off stalks of grass with my walking stick. I knew she was right and had held this back a long time; I also thought that Misa had probably spoken to her and might have told her everything. My mother had grown very close to Misa since Misa had come to live at Gandumas and had a great deal of respect for her. Yes, she most likely knew the truth. But hearing this attack on Odile, this fair and measured attack, my reflex reaction was to play the Knight and to defend my wife rigorously. I professed a trust in her that I did not have, I endowed Odile with virtues that I would not grant her when I talked to her in person.

Love develops strange solidarities and, on that morning, I thought it my duty to form a common front with Odile against the truth. I think I needed to make myself believe she still loved me. I told my mother about all the characteristics that might prove Odile cared for me, the two books she had gone to such lengths to find in Brest, her kindness in her letters, the way she had behaved since we had been at Gandumas. I was so ardent that I believe I undermined my mother's conviction, but—alas!— not my own, which was all too strong.

I did not mention this conversation to Odile.

. XVIII .

As soon as we were back in Paris, François's shadow hovered over our lives again, vague but
ever present. Since the falling-out with Misa, I did
not know how he communicated with Odile. I still
have no idea, but I noticed that Odile had adopted
a new habit of running to the telephone whenever it
rang, as if she feared my intercepting a communication that needed to remain secret. The only books she
read were about the sea, and she fell into a voluptuous
languor looking at the most banal engravings if they
happened to be of waves and boats. One evening a
telegram arrived for her. She opened it, said, "It's
nothing," and tore it into little pieces.

"What do you mean nothing, Odile? What is it?"

"A dress that isn't ready," she said.

I knew, because I had made inquiries with Admiral Garnier, that François was in Brest. I should have been calm, but was not, and with good reason. But there were still times when, under the influence of a moving concert or a beautiful autumn day, we had brief moments of tenderness.

"What if you told me the truth, darling, the whole truth about the past . . . I would try to forget and we could start again, trusting each other, start a new, perfectly transparent life."

She shook her head, not unkindly or resentfully but with a sense of despair. She no longer denied this past, not that she admitted anything to me, but there was a silent, implicit admission.

"No, Dickie, I can't, I know it would be pointless. It's all such a muddle now, such a tangle . . . I'd never find the strength to sort it out . . . And I couldn't explain why I said or did certain things . . . I can't even remember why I did . . . No, I can't do it . . . I won't."

In fact, these tender conversations almost always ended in hostile interrogations. Just one thing she said would strike a chord, and I would embark on a line of reasoning, no longer listening to her as the dangerous question teetered on the tip of my tongue. I would hold it back for a moment, then, suffocating, unleash it. Wherever possible, Odile tried to take the scene lightly but, seeing how serious I was, she eventually flew into a temper.

"Oh! Stop! Stop! Stop!" she said. "An evening with you is like a torture session now. I'd rather leave. If I stay here, I'll lose my mind . . ."

My terror of losing her then restrained me. I apologized to her, with only halfhearted sincerity, and could see that each of these quarrels was helping untie an already fragile knot. What on earth was it that kept her there so long, given we had no children? Strong feelings of pity for me, I think, and even a little love, because emotions can sometimes overlap without canceling each other out, and women in particular can have a peculiar desire to keep everything as it is.

Besides, Odile had religious beliefs—she rarely expressed them but they persisted, though much weakened by François's influence—that meant she abhorred divorce. Perhaps she also felt ties, if not to me then to our life together, thanks to her childish love of material things? She loved this house that she herself had furnished so tastefully. On a small table in her boudoir she kept her favorite books and the little Venetian vase that always held a single flower, just one but a really beautiful one. When she took refuge there alone, she felt sheltered from me and from herself. She would find it difficult tearing herself away from that setting. Leaving me to live with François would mean living in Toulon or Brest for most of the year; this in turn would mean being away from most of her friends. François was no more able to fill her life than I was. What she needed, I now realize, was a sense of movement around her, the strange spectacle of varied characters that all those different men laid on for her.

But she herself did not understand this. She knew it was painful for her being separated from François and believed she would find happiness if she could only be with him. To her, he had all the prestige of those we do not know well, and, their charms not yet exhausted, they seem rich with previously unimagined possibilities. I had once been this mythical seductive character in her eyes, back in Florence and on our trip to England. I had not succeeded in living up to the fictitious person she had attached to me. I was condemned. It was now François's turn.

He too would be put to trial by familiarity. Would he stand up to it?

Had he lived in Paris, I think François's relationship with Odile would have evolved like almost every illness of this type and ended without incident when Odile discovered how wrong she had been about what sort of man François was. But he was far away, and she could not live without him. What feelings did he have? I do not know. It would be impossible for him not to be touched by conquering so lovely a creature. All the same, if he was the man I had heard described, then the idea of marriage would not have been to his liking.

This I do know: he stopped off in Paris sometime around Christmas, on his way back to Toulon from Brest. He spent two days there, and during this time Odile behaved with a foolish lack of caution. She was alerted to his arrival by telephone in the morning, before I left for the office. I knew instantly that it was him from the astonishing expression on Odile's face when she talked to him. I had never seen her look so submissive and tender, almost beseeching. She certainly could not have known that standing there holding that black receiver and so far from her love, she betrayed her feelings to me by adopting that pure and ravishing smile.

"Yes," she said, "I'm delighted to hear from you . . . Yes . . . Well, yes but . . . Yes, yes but . . ." She looked up at me awkwardly and added, "Listen, call me back in half an hour."

I asked her who she had been talking to and she hung up with apparent indifference but did not reply, as if she had not heard me. I made sure I was free to come home at lunchtime. The chambermaid gave me piece of paper on which Odile had written: *If you come home, don't worry. I've had to go out for lunch. See you this evening, darling.*

"Has Madame been out for long?" I asked.

"Yes," said the chambermaid, "since ten o'clock."

"In the car?"

"Yes, sir."

I had lunch alone. Then I felt so terrible that I decided not to go back to the rue de Valois. I wanted to see Odile the moment she came home and had made up my mind that this time I would ask her to choose between us. The afternoon was pure torture. Toward seven o'clock the telephone rang.

"Hello, is that you Juliette?" Odile's voice asked.

"No," I said, "it's me, Philippe."

"Oh," she said, "are you home already? Listen, I wanted to ask whether you mind if I have dinner here."

"What?" I asked. "Where's 'here'? And why? You've already had lunch out."

"Yes, but listen . . . I'm in Compiègne. I'm calling from Compiègne and whatever I do, I'd be home too late for dinner anyway . . ."

"What are you doing in Compiègne? It's dark already."

"I came for a walk in the woods; it's gorgeous in this clear cold weather. I didn't think you'd be home for lunch."

"Odile, I don't want to discuss this on the telephone, but it's all quite ridiculous. Come home."

She came in at ten o'clock in the evening and replied to my reproachful comments with, "Well, it'll be the same tomorrow. I can't shut myself away in Paris in weather like this."

She had the same expression of merciless resolution that so struck me when she took the train to Brest, and it made me think at the time that, even if I had lain down on the tracks, she would still have left.

The following day it was she who asked me very sadly to agree to a divorce and to let her live with her parents until she was able to marry François.

We were in Odile's boudoir, before dinner. I offered very little resistance. I had known for a long time that it would end like this, and even her behavior during François's time in Paris had persuaded me that I would be better off not seeing her anymore. And yet the first thought that crossed my mind was a petty one: no Marcenat had ever been divorced and I would feel terribly humiliated when I told my family about this drama in the morning. Then I was so ashamed for thinking this that I made it a point of honor to see only what was in Odile's best interests. The conversation soon reached high moral ground and, as was often the case when we were sincere, became affectionate. We were told dinner was ready and went downstairs. Sitting facing each other, we hardly spoke a word now because of the servants. I looked at the plates, the glasses, all those things that bore the mark of Odile's taste. Then I looked at her and thought that it might be the last time I had that face in front of me, that face that had represented so much happiness. She was looking at me too, meeting my eyes, pale and pensive. Perhaps, like me, she wanted to secure in her memory these features she would not see again. The manservant, indifferent and tactful, moved silently between the table and the sideboard. The thought that he knew nothing established a mute complicity between Odile and myself. After dinner, I joined her in her boudoir, and we talked at length, seriously, about what our life would become. She gave me some words of advice.

"You must remarry," she said. "You'll be a perfect husband for someone else, I'm sure of it . . . But I wasn't right for you . . . Just don't marry Misa, it would hurt me and she's an unkind woman. I know someone who would suit you very well, your cousin Renée . . ."

"You're mad, darling. I'll never marry again."

"You will, you will . . . You must . . . And then when you think of me, don't be too resentful. I loved you well, Dickie, and I do know how good you are. I can assure you I never paid you many compliments because I'm shy, and I don't like to anyway . . . But I often saw you doing things that no other man would ever have done in your shoes. I used to think, 'Dickie really is a tremendously good man.' And I even want to tell you something that might please you: in lots of ways, I like you better than François, it's just . . ."

"It's just?" asked.

"It's just . . . I can't get by without him. When I've spent a few hours with him, I feel strong, I feel I'm living more fully, better. It may not be true; I might have been happier with you. But there it is, it didn't work out. It's not your fault, Philippe, it's no one's fault."

When we parted company late in the evening, she spontaneously offered her lips for a kiss.

"Oh dear," she said, "how miserable we are!"

A few days later I received a letter from her, a sad and well-meaning letter. She told me she had loved me for a long time and had never had a lover before François.

That was the story of my marriage. I don't know whether, in relating it to you, I have managed to do justice to my poor Odile as I would have liked to. I wish I could make you feel her charm, her mysterious melancholy, her profound childishness. People around us, our friends and my family, naturally judged her harshly after she left. I who knew her well, as well as that silent little girl could be known, think no woman was ever less reprehensible.

. XIX .

After Odile left, my life was very unhappy. The house felt so gloomy that I found it difficult being there. Sometimes, in the evening, I went into Odile's bedroom and sat in an armchair by her bed as I used to when she was there and thought about our life. I was troubled by vague feelings of remorse, and yet I had nothing specific to hold against myself. I had married Odile because I loved her, when my family would have wanted a more dazzling marriage for me. I was faithful to her until the evening with Misa, and my brief betrayal was caused by hers. I may well have been jealous, but she did nothing to reassure a loving husband who was clearly concerned. All this was true, I knew it was, but I felt responsible. I started to glimpse what was for me a quite new understanding of the relationship there needed to be between men and women. I saw women as unstable creatures always striving to find a strong directing force to pin down their wandering thoughts and longings; perhaps this need made it man's duty to be that infallible compass, that fixed point. Love, however strong, is not enough to set your beloved free if you do not also fill that person's life with a wealth of constantly changing interests and pleasures. What can Odile have seen in me? I came home every evening from my office where I had seen the same men and dealt with the same questions; I sat in an armchair, looked at my wife, and was happy that she was beautiful. How could she have found happiness in this static contemplation? Women are naturally drawn to men whose lives move on, who take them along in that movement, who give them something to do, who ask a lot of them . . . I looked at Odile's bed. What would I not have given to have seen her body lying there, her head of blond hair? And how little I had given in the days when it would have been easy to keep all that. Instead of trying to understand her tastes, I condemned them; I wanted to impose my own onto her. The almost terrifying silence around me now in that empty house was punishment for an attitude that held no unkindness, but no generosity of spirit either.

I should have moved, left Paris, but I could not make up my mind to; I took painful pleasure in clinging to the least thing that reminded me of Odile. At least in that house, when I lay half awake in the morning, I felt I could hear her clear soft voice calling, "Good morning, Dickie!" through the door. That January was a springlike month, the naked trees stood out against perfectly blue skies. If Odile had been there, she would have put on what she called "a little jacket," wound her gray fox around her neck, and gone out first thing in the morning. "Alone?" I would have asked in the evening. "Oh!" she would have replied, "I don't remember . . ." Confronted with this absurd mystery, I would have felt a pang of anxiety that I now missed.

I spent my nights trying to establish when this trouble had begun. On our return from England we were perfectly happy. Perhaps all it needed was for one sentence in some early conversation to have been said in a different tone, gently but firmly. Our fates are determined by a single gesture, a word: in the beginning it would have taken only the smallest effort to stop it, but then a vast mechanism was set in motion. I now felt that the most heroic acts could not have rekindled in Odile the love she had once had for me.

Before she left we had come to an understanding about the divorce proceedings. We had agreed that I would write her an insulting letter, thereby allowing her to cite the letter against me. After a few days I was summoned to the law courts for the conciliation process. It was appalling seeing Odile in such circumstances. There were some twenty couples waiting, the men separated from the women by a wire mesh to prevent difficult scenes. People threw insults at each other, some women were in tears. The man next to me, a chauffeur, said, "I find it comforting that there are so many of us." Odile nodded at me very gently, very affectionately, and I knew I still loved her.

At last it was our turn. The judge was a kindly man with a gray beard. He told Odile not to be distressed. He talked to us about the memories we shared, about the bonds of marriage, then he encouraged us to try one last time to be reconciled. I said, "Unfotunately, that's no longer possible." Odile stared straight ahead. She seemed to find this painful. "Perhaps she has some regrets . . ." I thought. "Perhaps she doesn't love him as much as I think she does . . . Perhaps she's already disappointed?" Then, because we were both silent, I heard the judge say, "Then, would you kindly sign this statement." Odile and I left together, side by side.

"Would you like to walk a little?" I asked.

"Yes," she said. "It's such a lovely day. What a gorgeous winter."

I reminded her she had left a lot of things that belonged to her at home and asked whether I should arrange to have them taken to her parents' house.

"If you like, but, you know, keep anything you want . . . I don't need anything. Anyway, I won't live very long, Dickie, you'll soon be rid of my memory."

"Whatever makes you say that, Odile? Are you ill?"

"Oh, no! Not at all! It's a feeling I have . . . Whatever happens, find someone else soon. If I could be sure you're happy, it will help me to be."

"I could never be happy without you."

"Of course you could, quite the opposite. You'll soon see what a relief it is being free of this intolerable woman . . . I'm not joking, you know, it's true: I am intolerable . . . Isn't the Seine pretty at this time of year!"

She stopped by a window display of marine maps; I knew she liked them.

"Would you like me to buy them for you?"

She looked at me very sadly and tenderly.

"You're so kind," she said. "Yes, I'd like that; they can be the last present I have from you."

We went in to buy the two maps. She called a taxi to take them away and took off her glove to give me her hand to kiss.

"Thank you for everything . . . ," she said.

Then she climbed into the car without a backward glance.

. XX .

Plunged into the depths of solitude, I found my family were of little help. Deep down, my mother was happy to see me rid of Odile. She did not say as much, because she could see I was suffering but also because we spoke so little at home; all the same, I could tell, and that made conversation with her difficult for me. My father was very ill. He had had a stroke, which had left his left hand paralyzed and his mouth slightly deformed, spoiling his handsome face. He knew his days were numbered and had grown very quiet, very serious. I did not want to go back to see Aunt Cora, whose dinners stirred too many sad memories. The only person I could see at the time without too much distaste and discomfort was my cousin Renée. I saw her one day at my parents' house; she behaved very tactfully and did not mention my divorce. She was working and studying for a law degree. Rumor had it she did not want to marry. Her conversation, which was most interesting, was the first to tear me away from the constant analyses of my emotional troubles with which I was consumed. She had devoted her life to research and a profession; she seemed calm and contented. Was it possible to renounce love, then? I could not yet conceive of any other purpose for my life than devotion to Odile, but I found Renée's presence very soothing. I asked her to have lunch with me. She accepted, and I went on to see her quite frequently. After a few such meetings, I tamed my emotions and talked about my wife with great sincerity, trying to explain what it was about her I had loved.

"When your divorce is pronounced, will you remarry?" she asked.

"Never," I said. "And you? Have you never thought of marrying?"

"No," she said. "I have a career now; it fills my life. I'm independent. I've never met a man I really liked."

"What about all your doctors?"

"They're friends."

Toward the end of February I wanted to spend a few days in the mountains but was recalled by telegram because my father had had another stroke. I went home and found him dying. My mother tended to him with admirable devotion; during the last night when he had already lost consciousness, I remember watching her standing beside that inert body, wiping that brow and moistening those poor twisted lips, and was almost amazed by the serenity she maintained in her enormous pain. I thought she owed that calm to the sense she must have of his life's perfection. An existence like my parents' struck me as both beautiful and almost impossible to understand. My mother had not pursued any of the pleasures sought by Odile and most other young women I knew. She had renounced all romance and change when she was very young, and she was now reaping the rewards. I made a painful appraisal of my own life. It would have been sweet indeed if, toward the end of this difficult journey, I could picture Odile standing beside me, wiping a brow already drenched in the sweat of my death throes, a white-haired Odile softened by the passing years and who had long since left behind the storms of youth. Would I be alone, then, when I faced death? I hoped it would be as soon as possible.

I no longer received any news, even indirectly, of Odile. She had warned me that she would not write, because she thought my pain would be abated more swiftly by total silence; she had also stopped seeing our mutual friends. I thought she had rented a small villa near François's, but I was not sure of this. For my part, I had decided to leave our house, which was too large for me alone and held too many memories. I found a delightful apartment in an old mansion block on the rue Duroc, and I worked hard to furnish it as Odile would have liked. Who could tell? Perhaps one day she would come there, unhappy, hurt, and asking for shelter. When I was moving house, I found fragments of letters Odile had received from her male friends. I read them. Perhaps I was wrong to, but I could not resist the acute longing to know. I have already told you that these letters were tender but innocent.

I spent the summer at Gandumas, in almost complete solitude. The only calm I could find was by lying in the grass far from the house. It then felt as if all links to society were broken and, for a few moments, I was in contact once more with deeper, more real needs. Was a woman worth such torment? . . . But books flung me straight back into my dark meditations. All I looked for in them was my pain and, almost in spite of myself, I chose those that would remind me of my own sad story.

I returned to Paris in October. A few young women took to coming to visit me on the rue Duroc, drawn—as they always are—by a man's loneliness. I do not want to describe them to you; they merely passed through my life. What I should point out is that it took no effort (but afforded some surprise) for me to revert to the attitude of my youth. I behaved as I had toward my mistresses in the days before my marriage. Pursuing them was a game, and I was amused to see the effect a single sentence or bold move could have. Once the game was won, I would forget the woman and seek to start all over again with another.

Nothing provokes more cynicism than a great love that was not shared, but nothing produces more modesty either; I was utterly surprised to feel loved. The truth is: a passion that fully preoccupies a man draws women to him when he least wants them. Even if he is sentimental and tender by nature, when he is obsessed with another he becomes indifferent and almost brutal. Because he is unhappy, he sometimes allows himself to be tempted by the offer of affection. As soon as he has tasted this affection, he tires of it and does not disguise the fact. Without wishing to and without even realizing it, he plays the most appalling game. He becomes dangerous and conquers because he himself has been vanquished. This was the case with me. I had never been more convinced of my own inability to attract women, I had never felt less desire to attract them, and I had never received so much clear proof of devotion and love.

But my mind was still too disturbed for me to derive any pleasure from these successes. When I look at my diaries for 1913, all I can find in among the meetings and assignations noted on every page are memories of Odile. I have written out a few of them for you at random:

October 20—Her demands. We love difficult creatures so much better. It was such a pleasure, with a hint of anxiety, putting together a bouquet of wild flowers for her, cornflowers, oxeyes, and chrysanthemums, or a symphony in white major, arums, and white tulips . . .

Her humility. "I know exactly how you would like me to be . . . very serious, very pure . . . very much the bourgeois French lady . . . and yet sensual, but only with you . . . You'll have to mourn her passing, Dickie, I'll never be like that."

Her modest pride. "I do have some little qualities, though . . . I've read more than most women . . . I know many beautiful poems by heart . . . I can arrange flowers . . . I dress well . . . and I love you, yes, sir, you may not believe it but I love you very much."

October 25—There must be a love so perfect that a man could share all his loved one's feelings at the exact same moment. There were times (in the days when I did not know him well) when I was almost grateful to François for being so like what Odile might love . . . then jealousy became stronger and François was too imperfect.

October 28—Loving the little bit of you that other women have in them.

October 29—There were times when you wearied of me; I loved that weariness too.

A little farther on, I come across this brief note: *I have lost more than I possessed.* It very clearly expresses what I felt at the time. When Odile was there, beloved though she was, she had flaws that distanced her from me a little; when Odile was gone, she became the goddess once more. I decked her out with virtues she did not have and, having finally modeled her on the eternal concept of Odile, I could be her Knight. A superficial acquaintance and the distortions of desire had had their effect during our engagement, and now forgetting and distance were having the same effect in turn, and, alas, I loved the unfaithful faraway Odile in a way that I never managed to love Odile nearby and tender.

. XXI .

Toward the end of the year, I learned that Odile and François were married. It was a painful time, but the certainty that the harm could not now be remedied actually helped me find the strength to live again.

Since my father's death, I had introduced a lot of changes to the administration of the paper factory. I spent less time on it, which gave me more free time. This meant I was able to renew contact with friends from my youth who had been distanced from me by my marriage, particularly André Halff, now a member of the Council of State. Occasionally I also saw Bertrand, who was a cavalry lieutenant stationed in Saint-Germain and came to spend Sundays in Paris. I tried to return to books and studies I had abandoned several years earlier. I followed courses at the Sorbonne and the Collège de France. In doing this I discovered that I had changed a great deal. I was surprised to find how little importance the problems that once filled my life now had. Can I really have wondered so anxiously whether I was a materialist or an idealist? Any form of metaphysics now felt like a puerile game.

Even more than these male friends, I now also saw a number of young women, as I have told you. I left the office at about five o'clock in the afternoon. I spent more time at social events than in the past and even realized rather mournfully that on these occasions (perhaps in an attempt to rekindle her memory) I tried to find pleasures that Odile had struggled to impose on me in the past. Knowing that I was now alone and fairly free, a lot of women I had met through Aunt Cora sent me invitations. At six o'clock on Saturday evenings I went to Hélène de Thianges, who was at home every Saturday. Maurice de Thianges, Member of Parliament for the Eure region, brought connections of his. Alongside these politicians, there were writers, friends of Hélène's, and eminent businessmen because Hélène was the daughter of an industrialist, Monsieur Pascal-Bouchet, who came up from Normandy some Saturdays with his second daughter, Françoise. There was a great deal of intimacy between the regulars at this salon. I liked to sit beside a young woman and discuss the finer points of feelings with her. My wound still caused me suffering, but I could spend whole days without thinking of Odile or François. Occasionally I would hear someone talking about them; because Odile was now Madame Crozant, there were some who did not know she had once been my wife, and, having met her in Toulon where she was now famous as the city's greatest beauty, they would tell stories about her. Hélène de Thianges tried to stop them or take me to another room, but I was keen to hear.

Most people did not think the marriage was particularly sound. Yvonne Prévost often spent time in Toulon, and I asked her to tell me very frankly what she knew.

"It's terribly difficult to explain," she said. "I haven't seen much of them . . . It strikes me that when they married, they both already knew they were making a mistake. But she *does* love him . . . I apologize for telling you that, Marcenat, but you wanted to know. She certainly loves him a great deal more than he loves her, it's just she's proud; she doesn't want to show it. I had a meal at their house, and there was an awkward atmosphere . . . Do you know what I mean? She kept saying kind little niceties, some of them rather naïve, the sort of things you so liked, and François rebuffed her . . . He can be so brutal. I can assure you I felt for her . . . You could see she was trying to please him, that she longed to talk about subjects he would find interesting . . . of course she didn't talk about them very skillfully and François answered irritably and contemptuously: 'Yes, yes, Odile, all right.' Roger and I felt sorry for her."

I spent the whole winter of 1913–14 in trivial intrigues with women, on business trips undertaken rather unnecessarily, and studies that I never pursued in any depth. I did not want to take anything seriously. I broached ideas and people's lives with caution, always prepared to lose them, so that it would not hurt me if I did. Toward May it was warm enough for Hélène de Thianges to entertain in her garden. She threw cushions on the lawn for the ladies, and the men sat on the grass. On the first

Saturday in June, I found an entertaining group of writers and politicians there, surrounding Father Cénival. Hélène's little dog was lying at his feet, and Hélène asked very earnestly, "Tell me, Father, do animals have a soul? Because if they don't, then I really don't understand. How could it be? My poor dog who's suffered so much . . ."

"Well yes, Madame," said the abbot, "why wouldn't they have one? . . . They have a very small soul."

"That's not very orthodox," someone said, "but it's disturbing."

I myself was sitting some way away with an American woman called Beatrice Howell; we were listening to the conversation.

"Well, *I'm* quite sure animals have a soul . . . When it comes down to it, there's no difference between them and ourselves. I was thinking that earlier. I spent the afternoon at the Zoological Gardens. I adore animals, Marcenat."

"And so do I," I said. "Would you like to go there together one day?"

"I'd be delighted . . . What was I saying? Oh yes! I was watching the sea lions this afternoon. I love them because they gleam like wet rubber. They were swimming around in circles underwater and popping their heads up every two minutes to breathe, and I felt sorry for them. I kept thinking, 'Poor creatures, what a monotonous life!' Then I thought, 'And what about us? What do we do? We go around in circles underwater all week, and at about six o'clock on a Saturday evening we pop our heads out of the water at Hélène de Thianges's salon, then on Tuesday at the Duchess of Rohan's, or Madeleine Lemaire's, and Madame de Marel's on Sunday . . .' It's all the same thing. Don't you think?"

Just then I saw Major Prévost and his wife arrive, and I was struck by their somber expressions. They walked anxiously, as if the gravel in the garden were fragile. Hélène stood up to say hello. I watched her because I liked the gracious, animated way she greeted her guests. I always used to tell her she was like a white butterfly barely coming to rest on people.

The Prévosts started telling her something and I saw her face darken. She looked around in some embarrassment and, spotting me, averted her eyes. They moved a few paces away.

"Do you know the Prévosts?" I asked Beatrice Howell.

"Yes," she said. "I've been a guest of theirs in Toulon. They have a beautiful old house . . . I do so like the seafront in Toulon. Those old French houses set against the sea . . . it's a lovely combination."

Several people had now joined Hélène and the Prévosts. They had formed quite a group and were talking almost loudly; I thought I heard my name.

"What *are* they up to?" I asked Mrs. Howell. "Let's go and see."

I helped her up and brushed off a few blades of grass clinging to her dress. Hélène de Thianges saw us and came over to me.

"Do excuse me," she said to Beatrice, "I'd like a word with Marcenat. Listen," she said to me, "I'm so sorry to be the first to tell you such a dreadful thing, but I don't want to run the risk . . . Well, the Prévosts have just told me that your wife . . . that Odile took her own life this morning, in Toulon, with a revolver."

"Odile?" I said. "My God! Why?"

I pictured Odile's frail body punctured by a bleeding wound, and a single sentence went around and around inside my head: "Under the influence of Mars, fatally condemned . . ."

"No one knows," she said. "Leave without saying goodbye to anyone. When I hear anything, I'll telephone you."

I started walking aimlessly toward the Bois de Boulogne. What had happened? My poor little child, why had she not called me if she was so unhappy? I would have gone to help her with such wild joy, would have taken her back home, would have consoled her. From the very first time I saw François, I knew he would be Odile's downfall. I remembered that dinner and had that same acute impression again, the father who had carelessly taken his child somewhere contaminated. At the time, I felt she had to be saved as soon as possible. I had not saved her . . . Odile dead . . . Women who passed me on the street peered at me anxiously. Perhaps I was talking out loud . . . So much beauty, so much charm . . . I could see myself beside her bed, holding her hand as she recited:

From too much love of living,
From hope and fear set free . . .

"The weariest river, Dickie," she used to say in a comically doleful voice.

And I would reply, "Don't say it like that, dar-ling, you'll make me cry."

Odile dead . . . Ever since I had known her, I had watched her with superstitious concern. Too beautiful . . . One day when we were in Bagatelle, an old gardener had seen Odile and me, and said, "The most beautiful roses are the first to wilt . . ." Odile dead . . . I thought that if I could have seen her once more just for a quarter of an hour and then died with her, I would have agreed at once.

I do not know how I arrived home, how I got to bed. I fell asleep toward dawn and dreamed I was dining with Aunt Cora. André Halff, Hélène de Thianges, Bertrand, and my cousin Renée were all there. I looked everywhere for Odile. At last, after worrying for ages, I found her lying on a sofa. She was pale and seemed very ill, and I thought, "Yes, she's unwell but she's not dead. What a terrible dream I had!"

. XXII .

My first thought was to leave for Toulon the next day, but I was feverish and delirious for a week. Bertrand and André tended to me most devotedly; Hélène came several times to bring me flowers. When I felt a little restored, I asked her anxiously what she had gathered. The accounts she had heard, like those I myself had, were contradictory. The truth seemed to be that François, who was used to being very independent, had quickly tired of the marriage. Odile had disappointed him. Spoiled by me, she proved gently demanding at the point when François already loved her less. He had thought her intelligent; she was not, at least not in the popular sense of the word. I knew this perfectly well myself, but it had been of no consequence to me. He tried to insist she respect a degree of discipline in her thinking and her behavior. Odile and François, both proud creatures, had clashed violently.

Much later, some six months ago, a woman told me some confidential comments François had made about Odile. "She was very beautiful," he had told her, "and I really loved her. But her first husband had trained her badly. She was an extraordinary coquette. She's the only woman who's managed to hurt me, *me* . . . I defended myself . . . I took her to pieces . . . I laid her out on the table, open and bare . . . I saw the workings of all her little lies . . . I showed her I could see them . . . She thought she could get me back with a bit of her charm . . . Then she realized she was beaten . . . Of course I regret what happened, but I feel no remorse. I couldn't do anything about it."

Once I knew of this conversation, I was filled with disgust for François. And yet there were times when I admired him. He was stronger than I had been, and perhaps more intelligent; mostly stronger, because like him I had understood Odile, but the difference between us was that I had not had the courage to tell her. Was François's cynicism any better than my weakness? After thinking about it at length, I too felt no regret for what I had done. Defeating people and driving them to despair is easy. To this day, after that failure, I still believe it is finer to try to love them, even in spite of themselves.

Besides, none of this clearly explained Odile's suicide. One thing is certain: François was not in Toulon the day she killed herself. During the war, Bertrand met a boy who had dined with Odile, along with three other young women and three naval officers, on the eve of her suicide. The conversation had been very gay. Odile had sipped champagne and laughed as she said to the man next to her, "Do you know, I'm going to kill myself at noon tomorrow." She was very calm throughout the evening, and this stranger noticed (because he described this to Bertrand) the luminous white glow of her beauty.

I was unwell for three months. Then I left for Toulon. I spent several days there, covering Odile's grave with white flowers. One evening an old woman came over to me in the cemetery, told me she had been Madame de Crozant's chambermaid, and said she recognized me because she had seen my photograph in one of her mistress's drawers. She then told me that in the early weeks, although Odile seemed very cheerful in public, she descended into despair the moment she was alone. "Sometimes," the woman told me, "when I went into Madame's room, I would find her sitting in a chair with her head in her hands . . . As if looking death in the face."

I talked to her for a long time and was delighted to see that she had adored Odile.

There was nothing I could do in Toulon, so in early July I decided to go and live at Gandumas. There I tried to work and read. I took long walks through the heather and managed to sleep by tiring myself out.

I carried on dreaming of Odile almost every night. Most often I would see myself in a church or a theater, with the place next to me empty. All at once I would think, "Where's Odile?" and start looking for her. I saw pale women with a mess of hair, but not one of them looked like her. Then I woke up.

I could not work. I had even stopped going to the factory. I did not want to see a single human being. I liked my heartbreak. Every morning I went down to the village alone. I could hear the sound of an organ coming from the church, so light and fluid that it blended with the air and seemed to be its murmuring voice. I pictured Odile by my side in the light-colored dress she wore on the day we first walked together beside the black Florentine cypresses. Why had I lost her? I wanted to find the word, the action that had transformed that great love into this sad, sad story. I could not. There were roses she would have loved in every garden.

It was on a Saturday in August, during one of these walks at Chardeuil, that I heard a drumroll followed by the local policeman crying: "Mobilization of land and sea forces."

PART TWO

Isabelle

. I .

Philippe, I have come into your study to work this evening. As I came in I struggled to believe I would not find you here. You still seem so alive to me, Philippe. I can see you in that armchair, book in hand, your legs bent back beneath you. I can see you halfway through a meal, when your gaze had wandered and you had stopped listening to what I was saying. I can see you welcoming one of your friends, and your long fingers endlessly twiddling a pencil or an eraser. I loved your little gestures.

Three months already since that horrible night. You said, "Isabelle, I can't breathe. I think I'm going to die." I can still hear that voice, it was already so different, no longer yours. Will I forget it? The worst thing for me is thinking that even my pain will most likely die. If you only knew how sad I felt when you said so earnestly, "Now I've lost Odile forever. I can't even remember her features."

You loved her very much, Philippe. I have just reread the long exposition you sent me around the time we were married, and I envied her. At least that is something that will be left of her. There will be nothing of me. And yet you loved me too. I have your first letters here in front of me, the ones from 1919. Yes, you loved me then, you loved me almost too much. I remember once saying, "You value me at three hundred when I'm worth forty, Philippe, and that's awful. When you realize your mistake, you'll think I'm worth ten, or nothing." You were like that. You told me Odile used to say, "You expect too much of women. You put them on a pedestal; it's dangerous." She was right, poor little thing.

For the last two weeks I have been resisting an urge that is growing stronger by the day. For my own sake, I would like to make a record of my love as you did of yours. Philippe, do you think I will succeed—however ineptly—in writing our story? I shall have to do it as you did, fairly, being very careful to say everything. I can tell it will be difficult. We are always tempted to sentimentalize ourselves and depict ourselves as we would like to be. Particularly me; it is one of the things you held against me. "Don't be self-pitying," you used to say. But I have your letters, I have this red notebook that you hid so carefully, and the little journal I started and you asked me to give up on. If I were to try . . . I am sitting at your desk. The image of your hand is all part of this ink-stained green leather. I am surrounded by terrifying silence. If I were to try . . .

. II .

The house on the rue Ampère. Potted palms in cachepots surrounded by green cloths. The gothic dining room, the sideboard with its protruding gargoyles in high relief, the chairs—they were so hard—with Quasimodo's head sculpted on the chair back. The red damask living room and its armchairs with too much gilding. The bedroom I grew up in, painted in a white that was once virginal but had grown dirty. The schoolroom, a junk room where I took my meals with my teacher when there were grand dinners. Mademoiselle Chauvière and I often had to wait until ten o'clock. A grumpy, sweating, overstretched valet would bring us a tray of viscous soup and melted ice cream. I felt as if, like me, he understood the unobtrusive, almost humiliating role that the only child played in that household.

Oh, my childhood was so sad! "Do you think so, darling!" Philippe would say. No, I am not wrong about this. I was very unhappy. Was it my parents' fault? I have often held it against them. Now soothed by a stronger pain, when I look back at the past with fresh eyes, I can see they thought they were doing the right thing. But their methods were strict and dangerous, and I feel as if the results condemn them.

I say "my parents" but I should say "my mother" because my father was very busy and scarcely asked more of his daughter than to be invisible and silent. For a long time his distance gave him tremendous prestige in my eyes. I considered him a natural ally against my mother because, two or three times, I heard him reply with amused skepticism when she revealed a bad aspect of my character. "You remind me of my director, Monsieur Delcassé," he said. "He puts himself behind Europe and says he's helping it move forward . . . do you yourself believe we can mold a human being? . . . well, of course we can't, dear friend, we think we're actors in this drama when we're only ever spectators." My mother flashed reproachful looks at him, pointing anxiously at me. She was not unkind, but she sacrificed my happiness and her own to her fear of imaginary dangers. "Your mother's only affliction," Philippe told me later, "is overdeveloped cautiousness." That was exactly it. She saw every human life as a hard battle, and we needed to be toughened up for it. "A spoiled little girl makes an unhappy woman," she would say. "You mustn't get a child used to thinking she's rich; God knows what life has in store for her." And: "It doesn't do a young woman any favors paying her compliments." Which was why she repeatedly told me I was far from beautiful and would have a lot of trouble appealing to anyone. She could see this made me cry, but in her view childhood represented what earthly life was for those who feared hell: even if it meant harsh penitence, my soul and body had to be steered toward a worldly salvation at whose gates marriage would be the final judgment.

This upbringing might, in fact, have been very wise had I had her strong personality, her self-confidence, and great beauty. But being naturally shy, my fear made me withdrawn. By the age of eleven, I avoided human company and sought refuge in reading. I was particularly passionate about history. At fifteen, my favorite heroines were Joan of Arc and Charlotte Corday; at eighteen, Louise de la Vallière. I felt peculiarly happy reading about a Carmelite's suffering or Joan of Arc's final moments. I felt I too could summon infinite physical courage. My father was very contemptuous of fear and had made me stay out in the garden at night when I was very young. He also asked that I not be shown pity or tenderness when I was ill. I learned to view visits to the dentist as stages toward a heroic sanctity.

When my father left the Foreign Office and was appointed French minister in Belgrade, my mother took to closing our house on the rue Ampère for several months every year and sending me to my grandparents in Lozère. There I was unhappier still. I did not like being in the country. I preferred monuments to landscapes, and churches to woodland. Reading through the journal I wrote as a girl is like flying over a desert of boredom in a very slow airplane. I felt I would go on being fifteen, sixteen, seventeen forever. My parents, who honestly believed they were bringing me up well, killed any taste for happiness in me. My first ball, something most women remember as such a dazzling, lively event, stirs only feelings of painful and enduring humiliation. It was in 1913. My mother had had my dress made at home by her chambermaid. The dress was ugly, I knew that, but my mother was scornful of luxury. "Men don't look at dresses," she said. "People don't like women for what they wear." I had little success in society. I was very awkward and had a desperate need for affection. I was seen as stiff, clumsy, and pretentious. I was stiff because I spent my life restraining myself, clumsy because I had always been denied any freedom of movement or thought, and pretentious because I was too shy and too modest to talk graciously about myself or anything amusing, so I took refuge in serious subjects. My slightly pedantic seriousness at balls meant the young men kept their distance. Oh! How I longed for the man who would tear me away from this slavery, from those long months in Lozère when I saw no one, when I knew every morning that nothing would interrupt the day except for an hour's walk with Mademoiselle Chauvière. I pictured him handsome and charming. Every time *Siegfried* was put on at the opera, I begged Mademoiselle Chauvière to secure permission for me to watch it because, in my view, I was a captive Walkyrie who could only be delivered by a hero.

My secret exaltation, which took the form of religion at the time of my first communion, found another outlet during the war. I had a nursing diploma, so I asked to be sent to a hospital in the military zone as early as August 1914. My father was on a posting a long way from France at the time, and my mother was abroad with him. My grandparents, panicked by the declaration of war, allowed me to go. The ambulance I was assigned to in Belmont had been inaugurated by Baroness Choin. The nurse who ran the hospital was called Renée Marcenat. She was quite a pretty woman, very intelligent, and proud. She saw immediately that there was a contained but very real strength in me and, despite my youth, she made me her assistant.

There I discovered I could appeal to men. Renée Marcenat once told Madame Choin in front of me that, "Isabelle is my best nurse; she has only one fault—she's too pretty." This absolutely delighted me.

A second lieutenant in the infantry whom we had treated for a minor injury asked for permission to write to me when he left the hospital. The dangers I knew he would be exposed to drove me to replying with more emotion than I would have liked. He became affectionate and, as one letter led to another, I found I was engaged. I could not believe it. It seemed unreal, but life is mad in times of war and everything happened very quickly. When they were consulted, my parents wrote to say that Jean de Cheverny was from a good family, and they approved of my plans. I myself knew nothing of Jean. He was playful and good-looking. We spent four days alone together in a hotel on the place de l'Étoile. Then my husband rejoined his regiment and I went back to the hospital. That was my entire married life. Jean was hoping to secure more leave during the winter but was killed at Verdun in February 1916. At the time I believed I loved him. When I was sent his papers and a small photograph of myself that was found on him after his death, I cried a great deal and in good faith.

. III .

When the armistice was announced, my father had just been appointed minister in Peking. He invited me to accompany him, but I declined. I was now too accustomed to independence to tolerate family slavery again. My income allowed me to live on my own. My parents agreed to my turning the second floor of their house into a small apartment, and I linked my life closely with Renée Marcenat's. After the war she had joined the Pasteur Institute, where she worked in the laboratory. She was extremely useful to them and had no trouble arranging for me to be taken on alongside her.

I had grown fond of Renée. I admired her. She acted with an authoritativeness that I envied, and yet I sensed she was vulnerable. She wanted to give the impression she had turned her back on marriage, but from the way she talked about one of her cousins, Philippe Marcenat, I thought I deduced that she wanted to marry him.

"He's a very secretive person," she said, "and he seems distant if you don't know him well, but he's actually almost frighteningly sensitive . . . The war did him good by getting him away from his usual life. He's about as suited to running a paper factory as I am to being a great actress . . ."

"But why? Does he do anything else?"

"No, but he reads a great deal, he's very cultured . . . He's a remarkable man, I assure you . . . You'll like him very much."

I was convinced she loved him.

There were now several men of varying ages prowling around me. Behavior had become much freer after the war. I was alone, and, in that world of doctors and young scholars frequented by Renée, I had met some men I found interesting. But I had no trouble resisting them. I could not bring myself to believe them when they said they loved me. I was obsessed by my mother's "unfortunately, you're ugly," despite the refutations it had been given during my time as a nurse. I still had a deep lack of faith in myself. I thought men wanted to marry me for my fortune or saw me as a mistress for a few evenings—convenient but not demanding.

Renée told me that Baroness Choin would like to invite me to dinner. She often went there herself on Tuesdays.

"I'd be bored," I said. "I so hate the social scene."

"No, you'll see, she almost always has interesting people. Besides, next Tuesday my cousin Philippe will be there and if you're bored we can always find a quiet corner for the three of us."

"Oh well, in that case, yes!" I said. "I'd like to meet him."

It was true. Renée had succeeded in making me want to meet Philippe Marcenat. When she told me the story of Philippe's marriage, I remembered once meeting his wife and thinking her very beautiful. People said he was still in love with her, and although Renée clearly did not admire everything Odile had done, she herself said it would be impossible to find a more perfect face. "It's just . . . the thing I can't forgive her is that she behaved badly toward Philippe, while *he* was loyalty personified." I had asked for a lot of details about their relationship. During the war I had even read some passages from Philippe's letters to Renée and liked their melancholy tone.

Madame Choin's imposing staircase and her countless footmen were not to my liking. When I went into the salon I immediately spotted Renée standing by the fireplace beside a very tall man with his hands in his pockets. Philippe Marcenat was not handsome, but I thought he had a kind, reassuring look about him. When we were introduced, it was the first time in my life I did not feel shy in front of a stranger. As we sat down to dinner I was delighted to see I was seated next to him. After dinner an instinctive maneuver brought us together.

"Would you like to find somewhere quiet to talk?" he asked. "Come with me, I know this house well."

He took me to a Chinese drawing room. The thing I still remember about that conversation was talking of our childhoods. Yes, on that first evening Philippe told me about his life in Limousin, and we were amused to find that our younger years and our families were so alike. The house at Gandumas was furnished like the rooms on the rue Ampère. Like mine, Philippe's mother used to say, "Men don't look at dresses."

"Yes," said Philippe, "that sort of rural bourgeois heritage that so many French families share is very strong. In some ways it's quite fine, but I just can't keep it going, I've lost faith . . ."

"Oh, I haven't," I said, laughing. "You see, there are some things I just *can't* do . . . Even though I live alone, I just couldn't buy flowers or candy for myself. It would feel immoral and wouldn't give me any pleasure."

He looked at me in astonishment. "Is that true?" he asked. "You can't buy flowers?"

"I can for a dinner, for entertaining. But for me, just for the pleasure of looking at them, no, I couldn't."

"But do you like them?"

"Yes, I do quite like them . . . still, I manage perfectly well without them."

I thought I saw a sad, ironic expression in his eyes and talked about something else. And it is most likely this second part of the conversation that struck Philippe because I found this in his red notebook:

March 23, 1919—Dinner with Aunt Cora. Spent the whole evening with Renée's pretty friend, Madame de Cheverny, on the sofa in the Chinese drawing room. She is nothing like Odile, and yet . . . Perhaps it is simply because she was wearing a white dress . . . Gentle, shy . . .

I had trouble getting her to talk. Then she became more trusting: "Something happened this morning which, how can I put this? Well, it shocked me. A woman I hardly know, not even a close friend, you know, telephoned to say, 'Don't make any blunders, Isabelle. I'm lunching with you today.' How can anyone lie like that and find herself an accomplice? I thought it very low."

"You should be more indulgent. A lot of women have such difficult lives."

"They have difficult lives because they want it that way. They think that if they don't create an air of mystery around them, they'll be bored . . . It's not true; life is not made up of pointless little intrigues. We don't always have to rub our sensibilities up against others' . . . Wouldn't you say?"

Renée came and sat down beside us and said, "Are we allowed to come and disturb this flirting?" Then, because neither of us said anything, she stood up laughing and left.

Her friend sat there thoughtfully for a moment, then went on: "Anyway, wouldn't you say the only love worth having is where there's complete trust between two people, pure crystal you can look through without seeing a single mark?"

At that point she must have thought she had caused me pain, and she blushed. True, her words had rather hurt me. She then said a few kind words, so awkwardly it was touching. Then Renée came over with Doctor Maurice de Fleury. Talk about the secretions of the endocrine glands. "We have to give them out," he said. "Doctors who don't prescribe them are ruining their reputations." Amusing technical information. Admired Renée's incisive mind. Lovely farewell glance from her friend.

It's true. I too remember the words that hurt Philippe. I too thought about it when I arrived home that evening, and the following morning I wrote a few lines to Philippe Marcenat to say I regretted that the previous evening I had been so tactless in expressing my feelings and inclinations, because, through Renée, I had felt great friendship toward him for some time. I added that, given he was on his own, I would be very happy if he would like to come and visit me from time to time. He replied:

Your letter, Madame, confirmed what your face had already told me. You have the tactful kindness that gives a good mind such charm. From the first moment I saw you, you spoke to me of my sadness and loneliness with a kindness that was so straightforward and so obviously spontaneous that I immediately felt a sense of trust. I do not think you could imagine how precious that will be to me.

I invited Philippe and Renée to lunch in my rooms on the rue Ampère, then Philippe asked the two of us for lunch. I very much liked the little apartment where he entertained us. I particularly remember two wonderful Sisleys (views of the Seine in lavender blue) and an arrangement of pastel-colored flowers on the table. Conversation was easy, both amusing and serious, and it was clear that the three of us enjoyed seeing each other.

Renée in turn invited Philippe and myself to dinner. That evening, he offered to take us to the theater the next day, and we fell into a routine of going out with him two or three times a week. I was amused to notice, during the course of these outings, that Renée was at pains to show that she and Philippe were a twosome and I was the guest. I accepted this stance but knew, although he had never told me so, that Philippe preferred to be alone with me. One evening when Renée was unwell and could not come, I went out with him. During dinner he was first to raise the subject of his marriage (and to talk very lucidly of it). I then realized that everything Renée had told me about Odile, although true, was not accurate. From what Renée said of Odile, I had pictured a very beautiful but very dangerous woman. Listening to Philippe, I saw a fragile little girl who had done her best. I very much liked Philippe that evening. I admired the terribly affectionate memories he still had of a woman who had made him suffer. For the first time it occurred to me that he might be the hero I had been waiting for.

At the end of April he went on a long journey. He was not in very good health, was coughing a great deal, and the doctors recommended a warm climate. I received a card from Rome: *Cara signora, I am writing to you beside my open window; the sky is cloudless and blue; the pillars and triumphal arches in the Forum rise up from sandy, golden mists. Everything is extraordinarily beautiful.* Then a card from Tangier: *First stage of a dreamlike voyage on the smooth sea colored pearl gray and violet. Tangier? It has elements of Constantinople, Asnières, and Toulon. It is dirty and noble, like all of the East.* Then a telegram from Oran: *Come for lunch at my apartment on Thursday, one o'clock. Respectfully—Marcenat.*

When I saw Renée at the laboratory that morning I said, "So, are we having lunch with Philippe on Thursday?"

"What?" she said. "Is he back?"

I showed her the telegram; her face adopted a pained expression I had never seen before. She pulled herself together immediately.

"Oh yes!" she said. "Oh well! You'll be lunching alone because he hasn't invited me."

I felt very awkward. I gathered later from Philippe himself that the main aim of his travels had been to put an end to his intimacy with Renée. Their family had treated them as an engaged couple, and it had exasperated him. In fact, Renée slipped out of his life without a whimper. She remained our friend, sometimes a slightly bitter one. It was from her that I had learned to admire Philippe, but from that point on she welcomed—with a sadness that was sometimes almost cruel—anything that belittled him. "It's only human," Philippe used to say, but I was less indulgent.

. IV .

Through the summer, Philippe and I spent a lot of time together. He attended to his business interests but took a few hours off every day, and he went to Gandumas only once a month. He telephoned me almost every morning and we arranged to go out later: a walk in the afternoon if the weather was fine, or a dinner or a show in the evening. Philippe was a faultless friend for a woman. He seemed to anticipate my wishes and instantly satisfied them. I was given flowers, a book we had discussed, something he had admired during one of our walks. I say *he* had admired, because Philippe's tastes were very different from my own, and he obeyed his. There was a mystery in this that I strove in vain to understand. If a woman walked into a restaurant where we were dining, he would pronounce a judgment on her dress, the particular nuances of her elegance, and the character that these might reveal. I noticed with a sort of terror that his impressions almost always contradicted my own spontaneous reactions. With my usual application, I tried to find rules for "Philippe thinking" or "translating into Philippe." I could not. I did try.

"But that dress there," I would ask, "it's pretty, isn't it?"

"What!" Philippe would reply, disgusted. "The salmon pink one? Oh, for heaven's sake, no!"

I would concede that he was right but I did not understand why.

On the subject of books and theater, it was more or less the same. From our very first conversation I noticed that he seemed shocked because I sincerely viewed Henry Bataille as a major dramatist and Edmond Rostand a great poet. "Well, yes," he said, "*Cyrano* was good fun, I was even quite taken with it when I was young and, all in all, it's well together, but it's not in the same league as the greats." I thought him unfair but did not dare defend my feelings because I was afraid of shocking him. I found the books he gave me to read (by Stendhal, Proust, and Mérimée) boring at first, but I quickly came to like them because I could see why they appealed to him. Nothing could have been easier than understanding Philippe's taste in books: he was one of those readers who look only for themselves in what they read. I often found the margins of his books covered with notes, notes I had trouble deciphering but that helped me follow his thoughts through the author's. I took a passionate interest in anything that revealed his character to me.

What most amazed me was that he should take so much trouble to instruct and entertain me. I probably had many faults but no vanity at all; I thought myself stupid and not very pretty. I constantly wondered what he could possibly see in me. It was obvious he liked seeing me and wanted to please me. Yet this was not because I had been coquettish with him. In the early days, respect for Renée's prior claim had stopped me envisaging so much as close friendship with Philippe, so he really was the one who chose me. Why? I had the pleasant but also disturbing notion that—rather like hanging a garment on a peg—he was hanging a more beautiful and more complex character onto mine. In the passage I have already cited, he said, "She is nothing like Odile, and yet . . . Perhaps it is simply because she was wearing a white dress . . ." I certainly was nothing like Odile, but we can all give mysterious, fleeting impressions, and these are not the ones with the least influence over our lives.

We are wrong to say love is blind. The truth is that love is indifferent to faults and weaknesses it can see perfectly clearly, if it believes it has found in someone an often indefinable quality that means more to it than anything else. At the bottom of his heart Philippe knew, although he may not have admitted it to himself, that I was a shy, gentle, and unremarkable woman, but he needed me there. He wanted me to be prepared to leave everything in order to be with him. I was not his wife or his mistress, yet he seemed to demand utter fidelity. On several occasions, as had become my habit since the war, I went out with other male friends. I told him I had: he looked so unhappy that I decided not to again. He now telephoned every morning at nine o'clock. On the days when I had already left for the Pasteur Institute (either because he had had trouble placing the call or he had arrived a little too late at his office), he would be so agitated in the evening that I eventually gave up the laboratory so he knew he would get hold of me. He gradually annexed my life in this way.

He took to coming to see me on the rue Ampère after lunch. When the weather was fine we would go out together. I knew Paris very well and liked showing him old mansions, churches, and museums. He found my overly precise erudition amusing. "You," he would say, laughing, "you know the dates for all the kings of France, and the telephone numbers of every great writer." But he enjoyed those walks. I now knew what he liked: the splash of a flower on a gray wall, a slice of the Seine glimpsed from a window on the Île Saint-Louis, a garden hidden behind a church. I would often go out alone in the mornings to explore the terrain so that I could be sure to take him somewhere just right for him that afternoon. Occasionally we went to concerts too; our tastes in music were almost the same. I found this striking because my musical tastes were not at all the result of my upbringing but of extremely strong responses I myself had felt.

And so we led a fairly intimate and in some ways almost conjugal life, but Philippe had never told me he loved me, and even frequently said he did not love me and that this was a very good thing for our friendship. One day when we met by chance in the Bois de Boulogne, where we both happened to be out for a morning walk, he said, "I'm so glad to see you that I feel a bit like a young boy. When I was sixteen I used walk through the streets of Limoges hoping to bump into someone like this, a young woman called Denise Aubry."

"Were you in love with her?"

"Yes, and then I tired of her, just as you will tire of me if I don't keep a measure of happiness myself."

"But why?" I asked. "Don't you believe in mutual love?"

"Even when it's mutual, love is terrible. A woman once told me these words and I thought them very accurate: 'A love that's going very well, in other words trundling along, is difficult enough, but a love that's not going well is hell.' It's true."

I did not reply; I had made up my mind that I would let him go whichever way he wanted and do whatever he wanted. A few days later we went to the opera together to watch my beloved *Siegfried*. It was such a pleasure for me to listen to it beside the man who had become my hero. During the "Forest

Murmurs," without thinking what I was doing, I put my hand on Philippe's; he turned and looked at me with a happy, questioning expression. In the car on the way home, he in turn took one of my hands, brought it to his lips, and then held it. When the car stopped by my door, he said, "Good night, darling." I replied brightly and with some emotion, "Good night, my dear friend." The following morning I received a letter he had written during the night and had had delivered to me: *Isabelle, this unique, demanding emotion is not just friendship . . .* He described a few phases of his romantically inspired childhood; he told me about the woman he had called "the Queen," then "the Amazon," and who had always obsessed him:

> *This sort of woman who put me in such a state of exultation always remained the same. She had to be fragile, unhappy, and frivolous too, and yet wise. You see, the authoritativeness of a Renée could not be associated with her. But the very moment I met Odile, I felt she was the one I had always been waiting for. What can I tell you? You have a little of that mysterious essence that gives life all its value in my eyes and without*

which I wanted to die. Love? Friendship? What does the word matter? It's a deep, tender feeling, a great hope, a vast gentleness. My darling, I long for your lips and the nape of your neck where my fingers can stroke the soft prickle of your close-cropped hair.

Philippe

That evening I went out with him. We had arranged to meet at the Gaveau concert hall and listen to some Russian music. When I arrived I smiled and said, "Hello . . . I received your letter." He looked rather distant and said, "Oh yes," and went on to talk of something else. But in the car on the way home I surrendered to him the lips and the neck he had wanted for so long.

The following Sunday we went to the Fontaine-bleau forest. "You're such a Wagnerian," he said, "it would be fun to show you a place near Barbizon that really reminds me of the climb to Valhalla. There are blocks of rock under the fir trees, great piles of them reaching up to the sky. It's chaotic and gigantic but also very ordered, I mean it's all very *Twilight of the Gods*. I know you don't like landscapes, but you should like this one because it's a bit like a theater."

I wore a white dress, only white, so that I could be a Walkyrie myself. Philippe complimented me on it. Despite my efforts, he rarely liked my dresses; he almost always eyed them critically and said nothing. I could tell he liked looking at me that day. I found the forest as lovely as he had described. A winding path rose up between the huge moss-covered rocks. Philippe took my arm several times to help me climb up over the stones, then he put his hands around me to hoist me up. We lay down in the grass with my head leaning on his shoulder. A circle of fir trees around us formed a dark well shaft whose edges framed the sky.

. V .

I wondered whether Philippe intended to make me his wife or his mistress. I even loved this uncertainty. Philippe would be the arbiter of my fate; the solution must come from him alone. I waited trustingly.

Sometimes a more specific indication seemed to hover beneath the surface of his words. Philippe would say, "I must show you Bruges; it's a delightful place . . . we haven't yet made any sort of trip together." I found the thought of traveling with him enchanting, and smiled tenderly, but over the next few days there would be no more talk of departures.

July was blazing hot. All our friends were dispersing, heading off for vacations. I did not want to leave Paris, it would have meant being far from Philippe. One evening he took me for dinner at Saint-Germain. We stayed out on the terrace for a long time, with Paris laid out at our feet, a black ocean reflecting the twinkling stars in the sky. Couples laughed together in the shadows. Voices sang from arbors. A cricket nearby lulled us with its song. In the car on the way back he told me about his family, and several times he said, "When you come to Gandumas . . . When you get to know my mother . . ." The word *marriage* had never been spoken.

The following morning, he left for Gandumas and spent two weeks there, writing to me a great deal. Before he returned, he sent me the long record of events I have mentioned, the one of his life with Odile. I was interested and surprised by this account. In it I found an anxious, jealous Philippe I would never have imagined, a cynical Philippe too, in some crises. I understood that he wanted to paint himself for me as he truly was, in order to avoid any painful surprises. But this portrait did not frighten me. What did it matter to me if he was jealous? I had no intention of betraying him. And what did it matter if he sometimes diverted himself with the company of young women? I was prepared to accept everything.

Everything about his behavior and the things he said now suggested he had made up his mind to marry me. This made me happy, and yet a slight anxiety spoiled my happiness: it seemed to me that the hint of irritation I sometimes glimpsed when he listened to me talk or watched me do something was growing keener and appearing more frequently. Several times, during the course of evenings that started with our minds in perfect agreement, I felt that something I had said suddenly made him clam up and become wistfully thoughtful. Falling silent myself, I then tried to reconstruct what it was I had said. All my comments struck me as harmless. I tried to understand what had jolted him but found nothing. I found Philippe's reactions mysterious and unpredictable.

"Do you know what you should do, Philippe? Tell me everything you don't like about me. I know there are things . . . Am I wrong?"

"No," he said, "but they're such little things."

"I'd so like to know what they are and try to correct them."

"Well," he said, "next time I go away, I'll write to you about them."

At the end of the month, when he went to spend two days at Gandumas, I received the following letter:

Gandumas, by Chardeuil (Haute-Vienne)

WHAT I LIKE ABOUT YOU:	WHAT I DON'T LIKE ABOUT YOU:
You.	*Nothing.*

Yes, what I've just written is true in a sense, but not entirely. Perhaps it would be more accurate to put the same traits in both columns, because there are some details that I like as fragments of you, when I wouldn't like them in isolation in someone else. Let's try again.

WHAT I LIKE ABOUT YOU:	WHAT I DON'T LIKE ABOUT YOU:
Your dark eyes, your long eyelashes, the line of your neck	*The slightly awkward stiffness in your gestures. The way you*

and shoulders, your
body.

   Mostly a combination
of courage and
weakness, of
propriety and passion.
There is something
heroic about you; it's
very well hidden
under a lack of
willfulness about minor
things, but it's there.

   The girlish side of
you.

   Your sporty dresses.

look like a little girl
caught doing
something naughty.

   Mostly a refusal to
see and accept life as
it is; an idealism
usually found in
Anglo-Saxon
magazines; irritating
sentimentality.
   Your severity about
other people's
weaknesses.

   The old lady side of
you.

   Your yellow smock
dress; the ornamenta-
tion on your hats
(a blue feather);
your dress with
the ocher lace;

everything over-
laden, everything
that alters the
silhouette.

Your conscientious little soul, your simplicity, your orderliness. Your well-kept books and notebooks.	*Your economizing; your caution with household things and emotions.*
Your wisdom.	*Your lack of impulsiveness.*
Your modesty.	*Your lack of pride.*

I could go on for ages with the left-hand column. Everything I've put in the right-hand column is inaccurate. Or I should at least add:

WHAT I LIKE ABOUT YOU:
What I don't like about you.

Because it is all a part of you, and I have no wish to change you, except in the tiniest things that are grafted onto the real you. I know, for example . . . but I really must get on with some work. Hachette are asking me to manufacture a special kind of paper for a new publication, and a foreman has just come in to submit a suggested "composition" for it. Oh, I find it so difficult tearing myself away from a letter to you! One more thing for the list:

WHAT I LIKE ABOUT YOU:
The long voluptuous daydream I fall into the moment I think of you.

Chamfort tells this story: a lady told the Chevalier de B***:
"What I like about you—"
"Ah! Madame," he interrupted. "If you know what it is, I'm lost . . ."
What I like about you, Isabelle . . .

Philippe

That letter made me daydream a great deal too. I went back through my memories and found critical looks from Philippe. I had long since noticed that he attached extraordinary importance not just to the least thing I said but also to my dresses, my hats, every detail of what I was wearing, and this had saddened me, almost humiliated me. I was now surprised to recognize in myself some ways of thinking learned from my mother, as well as her instinctive contempt for luxury. I was amazed to find such concerns in Philippe, in my hero. I realized that he was different from me, but I thought it beneath him to spend any length of time thinking about such minor things. And yet that was his way, and I wanted to please him. And so I made an effort to be as he seemed to wish. I did not altogether succeed, and what worried me most was that I could not see clearly what it was he wanted. My economizing? My lack of impulsiveness? Well yes, that was true. I felt cautious, weighing up everything I did. "How strange," I thought. "All through my childhood I was a fanciful girl, rebelling against sensible, austere surroundings, and now Philippe, looking in from the outside, seems to be finding inherited characteristics I thought hadn't tainted me."

As I read and reread the letter, I couldn't help pleading my case: "A little girl caught doing something naughty. But how could I not look like a scolded child, Philippe? I was raised with a severity you would struggle to imagine. I could not leave the house unless I was escorted by Mademoiselle Chauvière or my mother . . . Oh, Philippe, your Odile spent her childhood with parents who did not mind, who let her go free. You suffered painfully for that . . . My irritating sentimentality? But there was so little sentimentality around me . . . What I want from love is a warm, caressing climate, something my family refused me . . . My modesty? My lack of pride? . . . How could I be sure of myself when all my childhood I was told I was flawed and unremarkable . . . ?" When Philippe came back, I tried to repeat this passionate defense to him, but he smiled and proved so tender that I immediately forgot the letter. The date for our marriage was set and I became perfectly happy.

My parents came back for the ceremony. They did not dislike Philippe. He meanwhile liked my father's aloof irony, and he said that my mother's strict austerity had a particularly "Marcenat" sort of poetry. My family were amazed to discover that we were not to have a "honeymoon." I would have liked to: it would have been such a joy for me to see Italy or Greece with Philippe, but I could tell he did not want to and I did not insist. I understood how he felt, but my parents were very keen that we should observe "the protocol of happiness," and on the day of our wedding my mother predicted a dangerous future for my marriage. "Don't let your husband think you love him too much," she said, "or you'll be lost." I did not hesitate for a moment and replied somewhat tartly, "I'll take care of my own happiness."

. VI .

I still remember the first three months of our life together as the most harmonious of times. The perfect pleasure of living with Philippe. Slow discovery of love. Growing understanding of our bodies. His tactful kindness and consideration. Everything seemed so lovely with you, Philippe, and so easy. I would have liked to drive all the sad memories from your mind and give you every joy, to sit at your feet and kiss your hands. I felt so young. My repressed childhood, my demanding job during the war, my feelings of helplessness as a single woman—I had forgotten them all; life was beautiful.

We spent those first three months at Gandumas, which I liked very much. I had longed to get to know the house and grounds where Philippe grew up. I thought about Philippe as a child, a little boy, with a tenderness that was both voluptuous and maternal. My mother-in-law showed me photographs, school-books, and locks of hair she had kept. I thought her a sensible, intelligent woman. We shared many tastes and the same affectionate but concerned fear for a Philippe who was no longer quite the same one she had raised.

She said that Odile had had a profound and not very good influence on him.

"Before his first marriage, you would never have seen Philippe anxious or highly strung. He was a firm, balanced man; he took great interest in reading and his work, and was very like his father who was first and foremost a slave to duty. Under his first wife's influence, Philippe became much more . . . difficult. Oh, it's only superficial things and his character's stayed the same, but, well, I wouldn't be surprised if you had some trouble in the early days."

I asked her to tell me about Odile. She had not forgiven her for making Philippe so unhappy.

"But, Mother," I said, "he adored her; he *still* loves her. So in spite of everything, she must have given him something . . ."

"I believe he'll be much happier with you," she said, "and I'm grateful to you for that, my dear Isabelle."

We had several conversations that might have seemed strange to anyone listening, because I was the one defending the mythical Odile that Philippe had created and passed on to me.

"You amaze me," my mother-in-law said. "It's true; you appear to have known her better than me, and you never even spoke to her . . . No, I can assure you, I feel only pity for the poor little thing, but we really must speak the truth, and I'm describing her as I saw her."

Time flew by like a magic spell; I felt as if my life had started the day of my wedding. Before leaving for the factory in the morning, Philippe would choose books for me to read. Some of them, particularly the philosophers, remained inaccessible to me, but as soon as there was anything to do with love, I read it quite happily. In a small notebook I copied out the passages that Philippe had marked in pencil in the margin.

At about eleven o'clock I would go for a walk in the grounds. I very much liked accompanying my mother-in-law to the garden village she had had built in memory of her husband on the slopes overlooking the Loue valley. It was a cluster of clean, hygienic houses that Philippe thought ugly, but they were comfortable and practical. In the center of the village, Madame Marcenat had created quite a group of collective institutions that I found interesting. She showed me her school of domestic science, her infirmary, and her child-care center. I helped her, qualified by my wartime experience. I had anyway always had a taste for organization and order.

I even took great pleasure in going to the factory with Philippe. In a few days I learned what it was he did at work. I thought it rather fun; I liked sitting facing him in his office piled high with paper in every color, reading letters from newspaper administrators and editors, and listening to workmen's descriptions of processes. Occasionally, when all the employees had left, I would sit on Philippe's lap and he would kiss me with one eye anxiously on the door. I noticed with delight that he had an almost constant need for my body; the moment I was close to him, he would take me by the shoulders or the waist. I learned that the most perfectly real aspect of him was the lover, and I too discovered a delicious sensuality I had ignored all those years but that now colored my whole life.

I liked being in the slightly wild region of Limousin, a place I felt was suffused with Philippe. The only place I avoided was that observatory in the grounds where I knew he had gone with Denise Aubry and later Odile. I started feeling a peculiar posthumous jealousy. Sometimes I wanted to know. I interrogated Philippe about Odile with almost cruel bitterness. But these flashes of ill temper were fleeting. My only fear was to discover that Philippe was not happy in quite the same way I was. He loved me, I could not doubt that, but he did not have my grateful sense of wonderment about this new life.

"Philippe, I want to scream with happiness!" I said from time to time.

"You're so young, oh my God!" he replied.

. VII .

At the beginning of November we went back to Paris. I had told Philippe that I would like to keep the apartment I had been using in my parents' house.

"I can see nothing but advantages. I don't pay any rent, the apartment's furnished, it's big enough for the two of us, and my parents can't get in the way because they're only in Paris for a few weeks a year. If at some later date they return to France and move back into rue Ampère, then it would be time to look for somewhere else."

Philippe refused.

"You *are* odd sometimes, Isabelle," he said. "I couldn't live in that house. It's ugly and badly decorated, and the walls and ceilings have those monstrous plaster moldings. Your parents would never let you change it. No, I can tell you, it would be a big mistake . . . I wouldn't be happy at home."

"Even with me, Philippe? . . . Don't you think that what's important in life is people, not furnishings?"

"Yes, all right, we can always say things like that and they sound right and true . . . But we'll be lost if you're still going in for superficial sentimentality . . . When you ask, 'Even with me,' I have to reply, 'Of course not, my darling.' Only it's not true: I just know I wouldn't be happy in that house."

I gave in but then wanted to move the furniture, which was mine and had been given to me by my parents, into the new apartment Philippe had found.

"My poor Isabelle," Philippe said. "Which pieces of your furniture are worth keeping? Perhaps a few white bathroom chairs, a kitchen table, if you like, the odd linen press. All the rest is awful."

I was heartbroken. I knew perfectly well that none of the furniture was beautiful, but it had always been there and I did not find it offensive. Quite the opposite, I felt comfortable surrounded by it and, more important, I thought it would be madness to go and buy any more. I knew that when she came back, my mother would criticize me severely, and deep down I would agree with her.

"What do you think we should do with the furniture, then, Philippe?"

"Well, we must sell it, my darling."

"You know we'd get nothing for it. The minute you want to get rid of something, everyone says it isn't worth anything."

"Of course. But it *isn't* worth anything. That mock Henri II dining room furniture . . . Isabelle, I'm surprised you can be attached to horrors like that when you didn't even choose them yourself."

"Yes, perhaps I was wrong, Philippe. Do whatever you like."

This little scene was repeated so frequently, over the most insignificant things, that I actually ended up laughing about it, but in Philippe's red notebook I find this:

> *Good God, I know none of this matters at all. Isabelle is perfect in other ways: her selflessness. . . her wish to make everyone*

around her happy. She transformed my mother's life at Gandumas . . . Perhaps precisely because she herself doesn't have very pronounced tastes, she always seems preoccupied with anticipating mine and satisfying them. I can't mention something I want to her without her coming home that evening with a parcel containing what I wanted. She spoils me the way people spoil children, the way I spoiled Odile. But it saddens me, it frightens me to find that these kindnesses seem rather to distance me from her. I'm angry with myself for this; I fight it but am powerless. What I need . . . what do I need? What has happened? I think what has happened is what always happens with me: I wanted Isabelle to incarnate my Amazon, my Queen, and also in some ways Odile, whom I now confuse with my Amazon in my memories. But Isabelle is not that type of woman. I have given her a role she cannot play. The worst of it is, I know all this and I'm trying to love her as she is, and I know that she's worthy of being loved, and I'm in pain.

But why, Oh God, why? I have that rarest happiness: a great love. I've spent my life yearning for something out of a novel and hoping

*the novel would be a success; now I have it and I
don't want it. I love Isabelle and yet, with her, I
feel an affectionate but invincible boredom. I now
understand how much I must have bored Odile.
A boredom that is absolutely* not *hurtful to
Isabelle, as it was absolutely not hurtful to me,
because it is based not on the mediocrity of the
person who loves us but simply on the fact that,
satisfied with a mere presence, he or she does not
try and has no reason to try to fill life to the brim
and make each minute live . . . Isabelle and I
spent all of yesterday evening in the library. I was
not in the mood for reading, I would have liked
to go out, see new people, do something. Isabelle,
quite happy, looked up over her book from time
to time and smiled.*

Oh, Philippe, dear, silent Philippe, why did you
not say something? I already knew so clearly what
you were writing in secret. No, you would not have
hurt me by telling me such things; quite the opposite, you might have cured me. Perhaps if we had
said everything we might have been able to meet in
the middle again. I knew I was taking a risk when
I said, "Every minute is precious . . . Getting into

a car with you, trying to catch your eye during a meal, hearing your door slam . . ." You are right to say I had only one thing on my mind at the time: being alone with you. Looking at you, listening to you, that was enough for me. *I* had absolutely no desire to see new people. I was afraid of them, but if I had known that you had such a burning need, perhaps I would have behaved differently.

. VIII .

Philippe wanted me to get to know his friends. I was surprised to find there were so many of them. I do not know why I had pictured—hoped for—a more secret, more rarefied life. Every Saturday he spent the end of the afternoon with Madame de Thianges, who seemed to be his great confidante, and whose sister, Madame Antoine Quesnay, he also liked very much. It was a pleasant salon, but it frightened me a little. In spite of myself, I clung to Philippe. I could see he was slightly irritated to find I was always in the same group as him, but I could not help following him.

All the women greeted me very warmly, but I felt no urge to form friendships with them. They had a composure and confidence that I found astonishing and embarrassing. I was particularly surprised to see how intimate they were with Philippe. There was a camaraderie between them and him the likes of which I had never seen in my family. Philippe went out with Françoise Quesnay when she was alone in Paris, or Yvonne Prévost, the naval officer's wife, or a young woman called Thérèse de Saint-Cast who wrote poetry and whom I did not care for. These outings seemed utterly innocent. Philippe and his women friends went to art exhibitions, sometimes a film in the evening or to a concert on Sunday afternoons. In the early days he always invited me to join them, and a few times I did. It was not enjoyable for me.

On these occasions Philippe would behave with an animated gaiety he had once had with me. The spectacle of his pleasure hurt me. It particularly pained me to see him taking an interest in such a variety of women. I feel I would have coped better with a single irresistible passion. It would probably have been appalling and much more dangerous for my marriage, but at least the harm would have had the same stature as my love. What was hurtful was seeing my hero attaching such importance to creatures who may well have been likable but whom I found unremarkable. One day I dared tell him so: "Philippe, darling, I want to understand you. What pleasure do you get from seeing little Yvonne Prévost? She isn't your mistress, you've told me that and I believe you, but what does she mean to you, then? Do you find her intelligent? I can't think of anyone more boring."

"Yvonne? Oh, no! She's not boring. You have to get her to talk about things she knows about. She's the daughter and the wife of naval men; she knows a lot about boats and the sea. Last spring I spent a few days in the south with her and her husband. We swam and sailed; it was great fun . . . and she's so jolly, she has a nice figure, she's pleasant to look at. What more do you want?"

"For you? Well, much more . . . You must understand, darling, I think you're worthy of the most remarkable women, and I see you growing fond of little creatures who are pretty but ordinary."

"You're so harsh and unfair! Take Hélène and Françoise, for example: they're both remarkable women. And anyway they're very old friends of mine. Before the war, when I was very ill, Hélène was commendable. She came and looked after me, she may have saved me . . . You are strange, Isabelle! What is it you want? For me to break off ties with the entire human race and stay alone with you? But I'd be bored after a couple of days . . . and so would you."

"Oh, no, I wouldn't be! *I'd* be quite happy to shut myself away in a prison with you for the rest of my days. Only you wouldn't bear it."

"But nor would you, my poor Isabelle. You want that because you haven't got it. If I made you live that life, you would loathe it."

"Try, darling, you'll see. Listen, it's nearly Christmas. Let's go away together, alone, it would make me so happy. You know I didn't have a honeymoon."

"Willingly, of course. Where would you like to go?"

"Oh, it couldn't matter less to me, anywhere, so long as I'm with you."

It was agreed that we would go and spend a few days in the mountains, and I immediately wrote to a hotel in Saint-Moritz to reserve the rooms.

Just the thought of this trip was enough to make me very happy. But Philippe was still gloomy. He wrote:

Sad feeling of irony as I realize that the relative situations of two human beings are few and far between. In this drama of love, we take turns in playing the role of the more loved and the less loved. All the lines then switch from one performer to the other, but they stay the same. I am now the one who comes home after a long day out of the house and find myself constrained to explain in detail what I have done, hour by hour. Isabelle is trying hard not to be jealous, but I know that evil too well to hesitate diagnosing it. Poor Isabelle! I feel sorry for her and can do nothing to cure her. When I think of the genuine innocence and laborious emptiness of the minutes that seem so mysterious to her, I cannot help thinking of Odile. What would I not have given in times past for Odile to have attributed such value to my every action! But alas! Surely that was what I wanted precisely because she attributed them no value at all!

The more Isabelle and I live together, the more I discover how different our tastes are. Sometimes, in the evening, I suggest we go out to try a new restaurant, go to the cinema or to the music hall. She accepts with such sadness that I feel weary of the evening before it has even started.

"You clearly don't feel like it, so let's not go. Let's stay here."

"If it's all the same to you," she says, relieved, "yes, I'd rather stay here."

When we go out with friends, my wife's lack of enthusiasm chills me to the core; I feel I am responsible for it.

"It's odd," I tell her, "you seem incapable of having fun for just one hour."

"I think it's so pointless," she says. "It feels so much like wasting my time, when I have beautiful books sitting on my table, or work that I'm behind with at home. But if it makes you happy, I'm absolutely prepared to go out."

"No," I say rather irritably, "it doesn't make me happy."

And a few months later, I find this:

Summer evening. I managed, God knows how, to drag Isabelle out to the fair in Neuilly. All around, organs on the rides playing Negro tunes, the banging from shooting galleries, the clatter of the lottery wheel, a warm smell of waffles hanging in the air. We were carried by a slow, dense crowd. I do not know why, but I was happy; I liked the noise, the excitement; I felt there was an obscure but powerful poetry in it. I thought, "These men and women are being borne toward death so swiftly, and they spend the briefest moment throwing a hoop over the neck of a bottle, or making the clown appear by slamming down a mallet. And deep down they are most likely right: standing facing the abyss that awaits us all, Napoleon and Richelieu made no better use of their lives than that little woman and that soldier . . ."

I had forgotten all about Isabelle, who was holding onto my arm. All at once she said, "Let's go home, darling. I find this horribly tiring."

I called a taxi and, as we nosed slowly through the hostile crowd, I thought, "An evening like this would have been so charming and cheerful with Odile! She would have worn that luminous expression she had on her happy days. She would have played every kind of game and been thrilled to win a little boat made of spun glass. Poor Odile, who loved life so much and who saw so little of it, when creatures made to die, like Isabelle and myself, carry on their monotonous existences without particularly wanting to."

Isabelle seemed to guess what I was thinking and took my hand.

"Are you unwell?" I asked. "You're so rarely tired."

"Oh no!" she said. "But I find fairs so boring that they tire me out more quickly than other places."

"Do you find this boring, Isabelle? What a shame, and I like it so much!"

And then out of nowhere—perhaps because the organ on a carousel was playing a tune from before the war—something Odile had said to me a long time ago, as we walked through the same fair, came back to me. Back then she was the one resenting me for being bored. Have I changed so very much? In the same way that a house abandoned by the people who built and decorated it, then bought by new owners, keeps the same smell and even the same spirit of the first owners, I too was impregnated with Odile's spirit and now displayed characteristics that were not entirely my own . . . My true tastes and my cautious Marcenat mind were things I was now far more likely to find in Isabelle, and it was strange to think that, on that evening, I criticized her for the very harshness and dislike of frivolous pleasures that had once been second nature to me and that another woman had erased from my mind.

. IX .

It was nearly time for us to leave for the mountains. The week before, at Hélène de Thianges's salon, Philippe ran into a couple he had known in Morocco, the Villiers. I want to find a word to depict Madame Villier but cannot. Proud, possibly, but also victorious. Yes, that is more what it is: victorious. Beneath a mass of blond hair, her profile is pure, precise. She was reminiscent of a beautiful thoroughbred animal. She came over to us as soon as we arrived.

"Monsieur Marcenat and I went on a wonderful excursion in the Atlas Mountains," she told me. "Do you remember Saïd, Marcenat? Saïd," she added for my benefit, "was our guide, a little Arab with shining eyes."

"He was a poet," said Philippe. "When we took him in the car with us he sang about the speed of Europeans and of Madame Villier's beauty."

"Are you not taking your wife to Morocco this year?" she asked.

"No," said Philippe, "we're only going on a very short trip, to the mountains. Aren't you tempted?"

"Is that a serious invitation? Because, believe it or not, my husband and I want to spend Christmas and New Year's in the snow. Whereabouts are you going?"

"To Saint-Moritz," said Philippe.

I was furious; I tried to catch his attention, but he did not notice. In the end I stood up and said, "We have to go, Philippe."

"We do?" he asked. "Why?"

"I've arranged to see the managing agent at home."

"On a Saturday?"

"Yes, I thought it would be more convenient for you."

He looked at me with some surprise but said nothing and stood up.

"If you like the idea of the trip," he said to Madame Villier, "telephone me; we'll make some plans. It would be great fun to do this with another couple."

When we were outside he said rather abruptly, "Why on earth arrange a meeting at six o'clock on a Saturday? What a peculiar idea! You know perfectly well it's Hélène's day and I like to stay late."

"But I haven't arranged to meet anyone, Philippe. I wanted to leave."

"What a fabrication!" he said, astonished. "Are you unwell?"

"Of course not. I just don't want those Villiers with us on our trip. I don't understand you, Philippe. You know that, for me, the whole pleasure of vacations is spending them alone with you, and you go and invite people you hardly know, whom you met once in Morocco."

"Such vehemence! Such a different Isabelle! But the Villiers aren't people I hardly know. I spent two weeks with them. I spent exquisite evenings in their garden in Marrakesh. You can't imagine how perfect that house is: the ponds, the fountains, the four cypress trees, the smell of flowers. Solange Villier has exquisite taste. She had arranged it so well: all

Moroccan-style divans and thick carpets. No, truly, I feel closer to the Villiers than friends in Paris whom we meet at dinners three times through the winter."

"Oh, well! That's as may be, Philippe. I could have been wrong, but leave me my trip. I was promised it, it's mine."

Philippe laughed and put his hand on mine. "Well, Madame, you shall have your trip."

The following day when we were having coffee together after lunch, Madame Villier telephoned Philippe. I gathered from what he said that she had spoken to her husband, he approved of the plan, and they would both come to Switzerland with us. I noticed that Philippe did not make much of it and even discouraged the Villiers, but his last words were, "Well, then, we'd be delighted to meet up with you there."

He hung up the receiver and looked at me, rather embarrassed.

"You heard yourself," he said. "I did what I could."

"Yes. But what's happening? Are they coming? Oh, Philippe, that's too much!"

"But what do you want me to do, darling? I really can't be rude."

"No, but you could think of an excuse, say we're going somewhere else."

"They would have gone there. Besides, don't make so much of all this. You'll see, they're very kind and you'll be glad to have them as companions."

"Listen then, Philippe. Do this: you go alone with them. *I* don't like the idea anymore."

"You're mad! They won't understand at all. And I don't think it's very kind of you. I didn't have any intention of going anywhere, of leaving Paris; you're the one who asked me to. I agreed to it to make you happy, and now you're trying to make me go on my own!"

"Not on your own . . . with your dearest friends."

"Isabelle, I'm tired of this ridiculous scene," Philippe said with a violence I had never seen in him. "I've done you no wrong. I didn't invite the Villiers. They invited themselves. Anyway, they mean absolutely nothing to me. I've never made overtures to Solange . . . I've had enough," he went on, hammering out the words and pacing up and down the dining room. "I can feel how jealous and anxious you are, and I daren't do or say anything anymore . . . Nothing reduces life more drastically than that, you can take it from me . . ."

"What reduces life," I told him, "is sharing it with everyone."

I listened to what I was saying in amazement. I sounded sarcastic, hostile. I was busy irritating the only person in the world I was interested in, and I could not help myself doing it.

"Poor Isabelle!" Philippe said.

And—because, thanks to him, I knew his past life so well and probably lived in his memories more than he did himself—I could see he was thinking, "Poor Isabelle! It's happening to you too, it's your turn . . ."

I slept very badly that night, blaming myself entirely. What grievances did I actually have? There was certainly no intimacy between my husband and Solange Villier because they had not seen each other for a long time. So I had no legitimate grounds to be jealous. Meeting them might even have been fortuitous. Would Philippe have had fun alone with me in Saint-Moritz? He would have come home to Paris grumpy, feeling as if I had forced him to make a pointless and rather lackluster trip. With the Villiers he would be in a good mood, and some of his happiness would reflect on his wife. But I felt sad.

. X .

We were meant to leave a day before the Villiers but our departure was delayed, and all four of us ended up taking the same train.

In the morning, Philippe woke early, and when I came out of the compartment I found him standing in the corridor deep in conversation with Solange, who was also up and ready. I watched them for a moment and was struck by how happy they looked. I went over to them and said, "Good morning!" Solange Villier turned around and, in spite of myself, I wondered, "Does she look like Odile?" No, she did not look like Odile; she was much more vigorous, and her features were less childlike, less angelic. Solange looked like a woman who had measured herself up against life, who had dominated it. When she smiled at me, I was momentarily won over. Then her husband came to join us. The train was traveling between two tall mountains, and a torrent ran alongside the tracks. I found the scenery otherworldly and sad. Jacques Villier talked to me about boring topics; I knew (because everyone said so) that he was an intelligent man: not only had he been very well received in Morocco, but he had also become a major businessman. "He does a bit of everything," Philippe had told me, "phosphates, ports, mines." But the truth is I was trying to listen to the conversation between Philippe and Solange, and the clatter of the train was robbing me of half of it. I heard (*Solange's voice*): "Well, what would you say charm is?" (*Philippe's voice*): ". . . very complex . . . the face plays a part, and the body . . . but particularly the natural . . ." (a word I missed, then *Solange's voice*): "And taste too, impulsiveness, a spirit of adventure . . . wouldn't you say?"

"That's it," said Philippe. "A combination. A woman has to be capable of gravity and childishness . . . What's intolerable . . ."

Again the noise of the train snatched the end of the sentence away. The mountains rose up before us. Cut wood, gleaming with resin, was piled up next to a chalet with a wide shallow-sloping roof. Was I going to suffer like this for a whole week? Jacques Villier ended a long description with, ". . . Anyway, you can see the operation is quite superb."

He laughed. He had most probably explained some ingenious device to me; all I remembered of it was a name: the Godet Group.

"Superb," I replied, and I could see he thought me stupid. It did not matter to me. I was starting to hate him.

In my memory, the end of that journey was like a state of delirium. The overheated little train climbed through a backdrop of dazzling white, shrouding itself in clouds of steam that hovered briefly over the snow. It followed mysterious wide curves, which made the white crests topped with fir trees revolve around us. Then a precipice appeared to one side of the tracks and, far down below, we could see the black curve we had just left behind. Solange watched this display with childish glee and kept drawing Philippe's attention to details in the scenery.

"Look, Marcenat, it's so beautiful the way the trees keep the snow on their branches . . . You can just feel the strength of the wood holding all that weight without bowing . . . And there . . . Oh, there! . . . Look at that hotel glittering up there on the peak, like a diamond nestled in white velvet . . . And the colors on the snow . . . Do you notice how it's never white, but bluish white, pinkish white . . . Oh, Marcenat, Marcenat! I do so love it!"

None of this was spiteful, and even when I think about it in all honesty, there was something gracious about the way she said it, but she irritated me. I was amazed that Philippe, who claimed to prize naturalness above everything else, tolerated this lyrical monologue. "Maybe she's happy," I thought, "but still, at thirty-three (perhaps thirty-five . . . her neck looks drawn), she can't be happy the way a child is . . . And, anyway, we can all see that the snow's blue and pink . . . Why say so?" I felt Jacques Villier was thinking along the same lines as me because, from time to time, he punctuated his wife's sentences with a cynical and slightly weary "y-es." When he said that "y-es," I liked him for a moment.

I did not understand the Villiers' relationship. They displayed great courtesy toward each other and she treated him with a familiar sort of tenderness, calling him sometimes Jacquot and sometimes Jacquou, and even kissing him for no apparent reason, just skimming him with her lips. And yet, after spending a few hours with them, it was very clear they were not lovers, that Villier was not jealous and accepted his wife's excesses in advance with haughty resignation. What did he live for? For another woman? For his mines, his boats, and his Moroccan fields? I could not tell and besides was not interested enough in him to try to tell. I looked down on him for being so indulgent. "He doesn't want to be here any more than I do," I thought, "and if he had a bit of drive, neither of us *would* be here." Philippe, who had bought a Swiss newspaper, was trying to convert prices on the stock exchange into French francs and, thinking this would please Villier, talking about share values. Villier nonchalantly swept aside the strange names of Greek and Mexican factories like a famous writer raising a weary hand when a flatterer quotes from his works. He turned to me and asked whether I had read *Koenigsmark*. The little train was still snaking around between the fluid white shapes.

Why when I remember Saint-Moritz does it appear as the set for a play by Musset, simultaneously cheerful, unreal, and melancholy? I can still see the way out of the station by night, the lights on the snow, the piercing hearty cold, the sleds, and the mules whose harnesses were laden with small bells and red, yellow, and blue pompoms. Then the wonderful embracing heat of our hotel, the English in evening dress in the hall, and, in our vast, warm room, the happiness of being alone with my husband for a few minutes, at last.

"Philippe, kiss me, we must consecrate this room . . . Oh, I would so love to have dinner here alone with you! And we're going to have to dress up, meet up with those people and talk and talk . . ."

"But they're very nice."

"Very nice . . . on condition that we don't have to see them."

"You're so harsh! Didn't you think Solange was pleasant on the journey?"

"Come on, Philippe, you're in love with her."

"Never in my life. Why?"

"Because if you weren't in love with her you wouldn't put up with her for two minutes . . . I mean, what did she talk to you about? Can you think of a single idea in everything she's told you since this morning?"

"Well, yes . . . She has a strong feeling for nature. She spoke very prettily about the snow, the fir trees . . . wouldn't you say?"

"Yes, she occasionally comes out with an image, but I do too. All women would if they let their tongues run away with them . . . it's our natural way of thinking . . . The big difference between Solange and me is that I have far too much respect for you to tell you everything that comes into my head."

"My dear friend," Philippe said with tender irony, "I've never doubted your aptitude to think pretty things, nor your modesty that keeps you from telling them to me."

"Don't make fun of me, darling . . . I'm being serious . . . If you weren't slightly tempted by that young woman, you'd see that she's incoherent, she jumps about from one subject to another . . . Isn't that true? Be honest."

"It's not true at all," said Philippe.

. XI .

In my memory that trip to the mountains is like an appalling form of torture. Before we left I knew I was naturally inept at all physical activities but had thought Philippe and I would tackle the difficulties together, as a couple of novices, and that it would be fun. On the very first morning I discovered that Solange Villier had a divine ability for these games. Philippe was less experienced than her but was supple and relaxed. From the first day I had to watch them skating together jubilantly while I dragged myself along awkwardly, supported by an instructor.

After dinner, Philippe and Solange pulled their chairs closer together in the hotel foyer and chatted all evening, while I had to listen to Jacques Villier's financial theories. It was the days of the sixty-franc pound, and I remember him saying, "You know, that's a very long way from the true value of the pound: you should tell your husband to put at least some of his fortune in foreign currency because, you see . . ."

Sometimes he also talked to me about his mistresses, even naming them. "You must have heard that I'm with Jenny Sorbier, the actress? That's no longer the case . . . No . . . I loved her very much, but it's over . . . I'm now with Madame Lhauterie . . . Do you know her? She's a pretty woman, and very gentle . . . A man like me, who's constantly battling in his business life, needs to find tenderness in women, a tenderness that's very calm, almost an animal quality . . ."

Meanwhile I would be maneuvering to get closer to Philippe to try and instigate a general conversation. When I succeeded, there was immediately evidence, between Solange and myself, of the irremediable opposition derived from two different philosophies of life. Solange's great theme was "adventure." That is what she called a search for unexpected and dangerous incidents. She claimed to abhor "comfort," moral or physical.

"I'm glad I'm a woman," she told me one evening, "because a woman has many more 'possibilities' before her than a man."

"What do you mean?" I asked. "A man has his career. He can *do* something."

"A man has *one* career," Solange said, "while a woman can live the lives of all the men she loves. An officer brings her war, a sailor the ocean, a diplomat intrigue, a writer the pleasures of creation . . . She can have all the emotion of ten lives without the day-to-day disadvantages of living them."

"What an awful thought!" I cried. "That presupposes she loves ten different men."

"And that all ten of them are intelligent, which is highly unrealistic," Villier interjected, putting a great deal of emphasis on the word *highly*.

"Mind you," said Philippe, "you could say the same of men. They too are brought different lives by the successive women they love."

"Yes, perhaps," said Solange, "but women are so much less individual; they have nothing to bring."

Something she said one day particularly struck me because of the tone in which she delivered it. She had been talking about the pleasure to be gained from escaping civilized life, and I had said, "But why escape, if you're happy?"

"Because happiness never stands still," Solange said. "Happiness is the respite between periods of worry."

"Quite right," said Villier, and this sentiment from him surprised me.

So, in order to please Solange, Philippe picked up on the theme of escape. "Oh yes!" he said. ". . . To escape . . . that would be wonderful."

"You?" Solange asked. "You're the last person who wants to escape."

Her words hurt me on his behalf.

Solange rather liked stirring people's self-esteem with a crack of the whip like that. As soon as Philippe behaved as if he loved me or said a kind word to me, she would treat him sarcastically. But most of the time she and Philippe seemed like a courting couple. Every morning Solange came down in a new brightly colored sweater, and every time Philippe would murmur, "Goodness, you have such taste!" Toward the end of our stay, he had become very intimate with her. What really hurt me was the familiar, tender way they talked together, and the way he helped her into her coat, it looked like a caress.

Besides, she knew he liked her, and she played on her power. She was terribly catlike. I can think of no other way to describe it. When she came down in evening dress, I thought I could see electric currents running the length of her naked back.

As we arrived back in our room, I could not help asking, though without bitterness, "So, Philippe, do you love her?"

"Who, my darling?"

"Solange, of course."

"Oh! God no!"

"And yet you really look as if you do."

"Me?" Philippe asked, secretly delighted. "But in what way?"

I explained at length what I felt I had seen, and he listened accommodatingly. I had noticed that as soon as it was to do with Solange, Philippe took an interest in what I had to say.

"They do have a peculiar relationship, though," I said the day before we left. "He told me he spends six months of the year in Morocco, and his wife goes there only once every two years, and just for three months. So she stays in Paris alone for whole seasons. If you had to live in Indochina . . . or the

Kamchatka Peninsula, I know *I'd* follow you anywhere . . . like a little dog . . . mind you, you'd
find me terribly annoying, wouldn't you, Philippe?
When it comes down to it, she's the one who's right."

"In other words she's found the best way to ensure he doesn't tire of her."

"A lesson for Isabelle?"

"You're so sensitive! No, not a lesson for anyone;
a statement of fact: Villier adores his wife . . ."

"She's the one telling you that, Philippe."

"Well, he certainly admires her."

"And doesn't keep an eye on her."

"Why would you want him to keep an eye on
her?" Philippe asked rather irritably. "I've never
heard anyone say she behaved badly."

"Oh, Philippe! I haven't known her three weeks
and I've already heard three of her former lovers
mentioned."

"People say that about all women," Philippe
muttered with a shrug.

I felt I had stooped to pettiness, baseness almost,
something entirely new for me. Then, because I was
not unkind in my heart of hearts, I pulled myself
together, made a great effort to be friendly toward

Solange, and made a point of going for a walk with Villier to leave her alone with Philippe at the skating rink. I passionately longed for that trip to be over and was scrupulous not to say a word that would bring it to an end.

. XII .

When we returned to Paris, Philippe found that his director was unwell, and he had to work more than usual. He often could not come home for lunch. I wondered whether he was seeing Solange Villier but did not dare put the question to him. When we went to the Thianges' on Saturdays, if Solange was there, Philippe made straight for her, took her off into a corner, and did not leave her side all evening. It could have been a favorable sign. If he were seeing her freely during the week, perhaps he would have feigned avoiding her on Saturday. I could not help myself talking to the other women about her; I never said anything detrimental, but I listened. She was said to be a dreadful coquette. One evening when I was sitting next to Maurice de Thianges, he saw Jacques Villier arrive and said under his breath, "Goodness! Hasn't he left yet? I'd have thought his wife would have sent him back to his Atlas mountains by now!" Almost everyone who mentioned Villier added the words, "Poor fellow!"

Hélène de Thianges was a friend of Solange's and we spoke about her at length. She painted a portrait of her that was at once rather lovely and rather worrying.

"First and foremost," she told me, "Solange is a beautiful creature with very strong instincts. She loved Villier passionately at a time when he was very poor, and it was because he was handsome. It was brave. She was the daughter of a certain Comte de Vaulges, a Picardy family, very highborn; she was ravishing; she could have made an excellent marriage. She decided instead to go off to Morocco with Villier, and in the early days they led a colonial life there, a tough life. When Villier was ill for a time, Solange had to keep the books and pay the workmen herself. It's worth pointing out that she has the tremendous pride of the Vaulges: that sort of life must have grated on her, and yet she played the game. In that sense, she really does have the qualities of an honest man. Only she has two great failings or, if you like, two great weaknesses: she's terribly sensual and has a need to triumph wherever she goes. For example, she tells people (not men, she says this to women) that whenever she's wanted a man, she's always had him, and it's true, and with quite different types of men."

"Has she had a great many lovers, then?" I asked.

"You know how difficult it is to be sure with these things. People know when a man and woman see a great deal of each other. But are they lovers? Who knows? . . . When I say 'she had them,' what I really mean is she took hold over their minds and they became dependent on her, she felt she could get them to do what she wanted, do you understand?"

"Do you think her intelligent?"

"Very intelligent for a woman . . . Yes . . . Well, there's nothing she doesn't know about. Of course, she depends on the man she loves for her topics of interest. In the days when she adored her husband, she was brilliant on colonial and economic issues; when it was Raymond Berger, she was interested in things to do with art. She has a great deal of taste. Her house in Morocco is a marvel, and the one in Fontainebleau is very unusual . . . She's driven more by love than intellect. But, all the same, she has tremendous judgment when she has a clear head."

"What would you say it is that's so attractive about her, Hélène?"

"It's mostly that she's so feminine."

"What do you call 'feminine'?"

"Well, a combination of qualities and faults: tenderness, prodigious devotion to the man she loves . . . for a time, but also a lack of scruples . . . When Solange wants a new conquest, she'll overlook everyone else, even her best friend. It's not nastiness, it's instinctive."

"Well, *I* would call it nastiness. You could just as easily say a tiger isn't nasty when it eats a man, because it's instinctive."

"Exactly," said Hélène. "A tiger isn't nasty, or at least not consciously so . . . What you've just said is actually very accurate: Solange is a tigress."

"But she seems so gentle."

"Do you think? Oh, no! There are flashes of steel; that's one element of her beauty."

Other women were less indulgent. Old Madame de Thianges, Hélène's mother-in-law, said, "No, I don't like your little friend Madame Villier . . . She made a nephew of mine very unhappy, he was a charming boy and he literally went off and had himself killed in the war, not *for* her, if you will, but *because* of her . . . he'd been so terribly hurt. He had a position in Paris and it was absolutely right for him . . . She won his heart, drove him mad, then abandoned him for someone else . . . Poor Armand didn't want to stay and he died, so pointlessly, in a flying accident . . . I won't have her in my house anymore."

I did not want to relate this malicious gossip to Philippe, and yet I always ended up reporting it back to him.

He remained calm, "Yes, that could be true," he said. "She may have had lovers. She has a right to, it's none of our business."

Then, after a while, he became agitated: "In any event, I'd be most surprised if she were cheating on him at the moment because her life is so transparent. You can call her at almost any time of day. She is at home a great deal and, if you want to see her, she's always free. A woman who had a lover would be much more secretive."

"But how do you know that, Philippe? Do you telephone her? And go to see her?"

"Yes, sometimes."

. XIII .

A little later I had proof both that they had long conversations together and that these conversations were innocent. One morning after Philippe had left, I received a letter to which I could not reply without his opinion. I asked to be put through to his office, and it so happened that I ended up on the same line as Solange Villier. I recognized her voice and Philippe's. I should have hung up but did not have the strength to, and I listened to their cheerful exchange for some time. Philippe came across as amusing and witty, a side of him I never saw anymore and had almost forgotten. I myself preferred the serious, melancholy Philippe as Renée had once described him to me and whom I met immediately after the war, but I also knew the very different Philippe who was currently saying pleasant, light-hearted things to Solange. What I heard was reassuring. They were telling each other what they had been doing and what they had read in the last couple of days; Philippe summarized a play we had been to see together the day before, and Solange asked, "Did Isabelle like it?"

"Yes," said Philippe, "I think she quite liked it . . . How are you? You didn't look very well on Saturday at the Thianges'; I don't like seeing you that sallow color."

So they had not seen each other since Saturday, and it was now Wednesday. All at once I felt ashamed and hung up. "How could I have done that?" I asked myself. "That's as despicable as opening a letter." I could not understand the Isabelle who had wanted to listen.

A quarter of an hour later I called Philippe back. "I want to apologize," I said. "I asked to speak to you earlier and you were talking to someone. I recognized Solange's voice and I hung up."

"Yes," he said without a hint of embarrassment, "she telephoned me."

The whole episode seemed very clear and straightforward to me, and it calmed me down for a while. Then I started finding new signs of Solange's influence in Philippe's life. First, he was now going out two or three evenings a week. I did not ask him where he went, but I knew people saw him with her. She had a good many enemies among the women I knew, and they—seeing me as a natural ally— tried to befriend me. Those who were good-natured (I mean as good-natured as women can be toward one another) treated me with unvoiced pity and referred to my misfortune only with aphorisms and generalizations; those who were unkind pretended to believe I was resigned to facts that I actually did not know, so that they could have the pleasure of disclosing them to me.

"I understand why you wouldn't want to go and watch acrobats with your husband," one of them said. "It's so boring."

"Philippe went to watch acrobats?" I asked in spite of myself, curiosity gaining the upper hand over my pride.

"What? But he was at the Alhambra yesterday evening. Did he not tell you? He was with Solange Villier. I thought you knew."

The men, on the other hand, affected concern so they could offer to console me.

If we received an invitation to dinner or if I suggested we do something, Philippe would often reply, "Yes, why not? But let's wait twenty-four hours before making a decision; I'll let you know tomorrow."

I could find no explanation for this delay unless Philippe wanted to telephone Solange in the morning to ask whether she had been invited to the same dinner or whether she wanted to go out with him that evening.

I also felt that Philippe's tastes and even his character now bore this woman's imprint, very subtly so, but it was nonetheless visible. Solange loved the countryside and gardens; she knew how to tend plants and animals. She had had a bungalow built on the edge of the forest at Fontainebleau and often spent the second half of the week there. Philippe told me several times that he was tired of Paris and would like to have a small plot of land somewhere nearby.

"But you have Gandumas, Philippe, and you go there as little as possible."

"That's not at all the same. Gandumas is seven hours from Paris. No, I'd like a house I could nip to for a couple of days, or even go in the morning and be back in the evening. In Chantilly for example, or Compiègne or Saint-Germain."

"Or Fontainebleau, Philippe."

"Or Fontainebleau, if you like," he said, smiling involuntarily.

That smile almost pleased me: it took me into his confidence. "Oh, yes," Philippe seemed to be saying, "I know that you know. I trust you."

And yet I could tell I must not press the point and he would not give me any precise information, but I was sure there was a connection between this sudden love of nature and my anxieties, and that a large proportion of Philippe's life now depended on Solange's decisions.

Interestingly, Philippe's influence on Solange's tastes was no less striking. I think it was invisible to anyone but me, but even though I am not usually very observant, I noticed the tiniest detail wherever those two were concerned. At Hélène's Saturday salons I often heard Solange talking about what she was reading. It turned out she was reading the books Philippe loved, the ones he had given me to read, some of them books that François had once recommended to Odile and she had suggested to

Philippe. I recognized the "François heritage" of strong cynical material; Cardinal de Retz was there, and Machiavelli. Then there were Philippe's true tastes: Stendhal's *Lucien Leuwen*, Turgenev's *Smoke*, and the first volumes of Proust. The day I heard Solange talking about Machiavelli, I could not help smiling sadly. I as a woman knew only too well that Machiavelli meant as little to her as ultraviolet rays or Limousin enamelwork but that she was capable of taking an interest in any one of them and talking about it sufficiently intelligently to create an illusion for a man if she believed that would please him.

When I first met Solange, I noticed her love of strong colors, which suited her very well. For several months now, almost every time I saw her in the evening, she was in a white dress. White was one of Philippe's preferences, inherited from Odile. To think how often he told me of Odile's dazzling whiteness! It was strange and sad to think that, through Philippe, poor little Odile lived on in other women, in Solange, in me, each of us striving (perhaps, in Solange's case, without realizing it) to reconstitute her long-lost grace.

Yes, it was strange and sad, but for me mostly sad and not only because I was painfully jealous but also because I suffered to find Philippe being, as I saw it, unfaithful to Odile. When I met him, I liked his faithfulness and saw it as one of his fine character traits. Later, when he gave me the record of his life with Odile and I knew the truth about her flight, I had even more admiration for Philippe's steadfast respect for the memory of his only love. I admired it and understood it all the better because I had formed an image of Odile that was itself admirable. Her beauty . . . her fragility . . . her naturalness too . . . her lively, poetic intelligence . . . Yes, having once been jealous of her, I too now loved Odile. As described by him, she alone seemed worthy of Philippe as I perceived him and perhaps as I alone saw him. I accepted being sacrificed to such a noble religion; I knew I was beaten, I wanted to be beaten, I bowed before Odile with accommodating humility and in that very humility I found a secret satisfaction and, no doubt, a hidden source of pride.

Because, despite appearances, my feelings were not entirely pure. If I accepted that Philippe's love for Odile endured, if I even wanted it to and if I willfully forgot Odile's faults and her all too obvious extravagances, then it was because I believed this dead woman could protect me from the living. I am now painting myself as darker and more calculating than I was. No, I was not thinking of myself but of my love for Philippe. I loved my husband so much that I wished he were bigger and better than anyone else. His attachment to this quasi-divine creature (because death had shielded her from human imperfections) gave him that stature in my eyes. But how could it not pain me to see him enslaved to a Solange Villier, whom I could see and judge and criticize every day, who was of the same flesh and blood as myself, whom other women denigrated in front of me, whom I deemed beautiful and fairly intelligent but certainly not divine or superhuman?

. XIV .

Philippe had on several occasions said, "Solange has really tried to get close to you, but you're evasive. She feels you're hostile, odd . . ." It is true that, since our trip to Switzerland, Madame Villier had often telephoned me, and I had refused to go out with her. I felt it more dignified to see little of her. But to please Philippe and demonstrate my goodwill, I promised to go to her house once.

She received me in a small boudoir that struck me as quite "Philippe style," very pared down, almost bare. I felt awkward. Solange, relaxed and cheerful, lay herself down on a divan and immediately started talking to me in confidential tones. I noticed she called me "Isabelle" while I was hesitating between "Madame" and "my dear friend."

"How strange," I thought as I listened to her. "Philippe loathes familiarity and impropriety, and for me the most striking thing about this woman is precisely the fact that she has no reserve whatsoever; she says everything. Why does he like her? . . . There's something gentle in her eyes . . . She seems happy . . . But is she?"

An image of Villier with his balding head and tired voice flitted across my mind. I asked for news of him. He was away, as usual.

"I don't see Jacques very much, you know," said Solange. "But he's my best friend. He's such a frank, straightforward fellow . . . It's just, after thirteen years together, sustaining the myth of a great love would be hypocritical . . . and I'm not like that."

"But you married for love, didn't you?"

"Yes, I adored Jacques. We had some wonderful times. But passion never lasts long . . . And the war kept us apart. After four years, we were so used to living separately . . ."

"That's so sad! And you didn't try to rebuild what you'd had?"

"You know, when you no longer love each other . . . or, to be more precise, when there's no longer any physical desire (because I have a great deal of affection for Jacques), it's difficult to remain, to outward appearances, a unified couple . . . Jacques has a mistress; I know that. I approve of her . . . You won't understand that yet, but there comes a time when we all need our independence . . ."

"Why? I would have thought marriage and independence were contradictory terms."

"That's what people say in the early days. But marriage, as you perceive it, has an element of discipline to it. Are you shocked by this?"

"A little . . . It's just . . ."

"I'm very forthright, Isabelle. I can't bear posturing . . . By pretending to love Jacques . . . or to hate him . . . I would earn your support. But I wouldn't be me . . . Do you understand?"

She was talking to me but not looking at me, drawing little stars in pencil on the cover of a book. When her eyes were lowered like this, her face looked quite hard and seemed to bear the mark of some obscure suffering. "Deep down, she's not all that happy," I thought.

"No," I said, "I don't really understand . . . A chaotic, disjointed life must be so disappointing . . . And anyway, you have a son."

"Yes. But you'll see for yourself when you have children: there's hardly any grounds for communication between a woman and a twelve-year-old schoolboy. When I go to see him, I feel I'm boring him."

"So would you say maternal love is posturing too?"

"Of course not . . . It all depends on the circumstances . . . You are aggressive, Isabelle!"

"What I don't understand about you is that while you say, 'I'm forthright, I won't tolerate hypocrisy,' you've never dared take that to its logical conclusion . . . Your husband has reclaimed his independence and gives you complete freedom . . . Why aren't you divorced? It would be more loyal, more clear-cut."

"What a peculiar idea! I don't want to remarry. Neither does Jacques. So why should we divorce? Besides, we have common interests. Our land in Marrakesh was bought with my dowry, but it's Jacques who's farmed it, made something of it . . . And I'm always very happy to see Jacques again . . . It's all more complicated than you think, my dear Isabelle."

Then she talked of her Arabian horses, her pearls, and her hothouses in Fontainebleau. "It's interesting," I thought. "She claims to feel contempt for these luxuries, that her life is elsewhere, but she can't help talking about them . . . And perhaps that's something else Philippe likes, the childish pleasure she derives from things . . . Still, it's quite funny seeing the difference between her lyrical monologues in front of a man and this inventory of her assets in front of a woman."

When I left, she laughed as she said, "You're probably scandalized by what I've told you, because you've not been married very long and you're in love . . . That's all very nice. But don't overdramatize things . . . Philippe does love you, you know, he talks about you very kindly."

Having Solange reassuring me about the state of my marriage and Philippe's feelings for me felt unbearable. She said, "See you soon; come back and see me." I never went back.

. XV .

A few weeks after that visit I felt unwell; I was coughing and shivering. Philippe came and spent the evening beside my bed. The half-light, and perhaps my fever too, gave me courage, and I talked to my husband about the changes I had noticed in him.

"Philippe, you can't see yourself, but it's almost unbelievable for me . . . Even the things you say . . . It really struck me when you were talking with Maurice de Thianges the other evening—there was something so hard about your opinions."

"Good God! You pay such attention to everything I say, my poor Isabelle, far more than I do, I assure you. What did I say the other evening that was so bad?"

"I've always liked your ideas about loyalty, about oaths and respecting contracts, but this time, if you remember, it was Maurice who was putting that argument forward and you were saying life's so short that men are miserable creatures with few opportunities for happiness, and they should grab those they are offered. So you see, Philippe . . ." (and to say this I turned away and did not look at him) "so it seemed to me you were talking for Solange, who was listening."

Philippe laughed and took my hand.

"You're so feverish," he said, "and you've such an imagination! Of course I wasn't talking for Solange. What I said was true. We almost always tie ourselves down without knowing what we're doing. Then we want to be honest; we don't want to hurt the people we love, and, for muddled reasons, we refuse ourselves certain pleasures that we later regret. I was saying that there's a cowardly sort of goodness in this, that we almost always resent those who've made us abandon our own longings in this way, and, when all is said and done, it would be better for them as well as ourselves if we had the courage to know what we want, and to meet life head on."

"But what about you, Philippe, is there something you regret at the moment?"

"You always bring general ideas back to the two of us. No, I don't regret anything. I love you very much and I'm perfectly happy with you, but I would be even happier if you weren't jealous."

"I'll try."

The following morning the doctor came and found I had a nasty case of tonsillitis. Philippe stayed with me a lot of the time and oversaw the care I was given with great devotion. Solange sent me flowers and books, and came to see me as soon as I was well enough to receive guests. I felt I had been unfair and hateful, but when I was better and ready to start living like everyone else, I was struck once more by the intimacy between them and started worrying as I had before. In fact I was not alone in worrying. Monsieur Shreiber, the director of the paper business, shyly intervened one day when I had gone to see Philippe at his office and did not find him there. Shreiber was a Protestant from Alsace, he had often come to lunch with us at home, and I had taken to him as a friend because I thought him very upright and steadfast.

"Madame Marcenat," he said, "I apologize for asking you this, but do you know what's wrong with Monsieur Philippe? He's not the same man anymore."

"In what way?"

"He doesn't care about anything, Madame. He very rarely comes back to the office in the afternoons now, he misses meetings with his best customers, and it's three months since he's been to Gandumas . . . I'm doing my best, but it's not my company . . . I can't replace him."

So when Philippe told me he was taking care of business, he was sometimes lying—this man I had known to be so scrupulous and loyal. But surely he was lying in order to reassure me? And, besides, had I made it easy for him to be honest? Sometimes I just wished he could be happy, and I promised myself I would not disturb his peace of mind, but, more often than not, I tormented him with questions and resentment. I was sour, insistent, loathsome. He responded with tremendous patience. I felt he had been better with Odile than I was with him in fairly similar circumstances, but immediately forgave myself, thinking the situation far worse for me. A man does not gamble his whole life on one love; he has his work, his friends, his ideas. A woman like me lives only for her love. What was there to replace it with? I hated women and was indifferent to men. I had finally, after a long wait, won the only hand I had ever wanted to play: having a unique and absolute emotion. I had lost it. I could see no end or remedy to this terrible sorrow.

That was how the second year of my marriage was spent.

. XVI .

There were, however, two things that reassured me. For some time Philippe had needed to go to America to study various work processes in the paper industry and the American workman's way of life. I really longed to make this trip with him. Every now and then he started making plans for it and sent me to the transatlantic company to inquire about departure dates for steamers and the cost of the passage. Then, after hesitating for a long time, he would decide we would not be going. I ended up thinking we would never make the trip and actually made up my mind to be resigned to everything before it even happened. "I'm the one who has adopted

Philippe's ideas about chivalrous love," I thought. "I love him and I will continue to love him whatever happens, but I will never be totally happy."

One evening in January 1922 Philippe said, "This time I've made up my mind. We shall go the United States in the spring."

"Me too, Philippe?"

"Of course you too. It's largely because I promised you this trip that I want to go. We'll spend six weeks there. I'll finish all my work within a week so we can travel and see the country."

"You're so kind, Philippe! I'm thrilled."

I thought this really was very good of him. Self-doubt fosters tremendous naïve humility. I honestly could not believe that Philippe would derive any great pleasure from traveling with me. I was particularly grateful to him for relinquishing any opportunity to see Solange Villier for two months. If he loved her as much as I had sometimes feared, he could not have left her like that, particularly as I knew how anxious he was by nature where people he cared for were concerned. So everything must have been less serious than I thought. I remember being gay and clearheaded all through January, and I did not pester Philippe with my questions and complaints at all.

In February I discovered that I was pregnant. This delighted me. I passionately wanted a child, particularly a son; I felt he would be another Philippe but, this time, a Philippe who would be entirely mine, at least for fifteen years. Philippe himself welcomed the news happily, and that too was a pleasure for me. But the early weeks of my pregnancy were terrible and it soon became clear I would not be able to cope with the sea voyage. Philippe offered not to go. I knew he had already written many letters and arranged factory visits and meetings, and I insisted he change none of his plans. When I try now to understand why I subjected myself to a separation I found so painful, I can think of several motives. First, I felt ugly at the time, my face was tired and I was afraid Philippe would not find me appealing. Also, the thought of distancing Philippe from Solange was still precious to me, perhaps more precious than having my husband beside me. Last, I had often heard Philippe propounding the idea that a woman's great strength was absence, that when we are far away from people we forget their faults and obsessions, we realize they contribute something valuable and indispensible to our lives, something we had not even noticed because it was too intimately tied up with ourselves. "It's like salt," he used to say. "We don't even know we're eating it, but if you took it out of all our meals we would most likely die."

If only, while he was far from me, Philippe could discover that I was the salt of his life . . .

He left in early April, having told me I should keep myself entertained and see people. A few days after he left, I felt better and tried to get out a bit. I had no letters from him; I knew I would have none for a couple of weeks, but I needed to shake off the melancholy that hung over me. I telephoned a few friends and felt it would be both right and shrewd to call Solange. I had a lot of trouble getting hold of anyone; eventually a manservant told me she had gone away for two months. This had a dramatic effect on me. I thought—ridiculously, in fact, because it was so unlikely—that she had gone with Philippe. I asked if anyone had an address for her and was told she was at her house in Marrakesh. But of course, she was on her regular trip to Morocco. Even so, once I had hung up, I had to lie down on my bed, feeling very uncomfortable, and I thought sadly about the facts for some time. So that was why Philippe had so willingly accepted the idea of this trip. I especially resented him for not telling me and for allowing me to accept the offer as a generous sacrifice. Now, looking back, I am far more indulgent. Powerless to tear himself away from her but still affectionate toward me, Philippe had done his best and tried to give me whatever he could spare from a passion that was becoming all too obvious.

Besides, the first letters I received from America erased my fears. They were tender and colorful; he seemed sorry I was not there and wished he could share with me experiences he was enjoying. *This country would suit you, Isabelle, it is a country of comfort and perfection, a country of order and jobs well done. New York could be one gigantic household run by a precise, all-powerful Isabelle.* And in another letter: *I miss you so much, my darling! I would so love to come back to you in the evenings in this hotel room peopled only by an overactive telephone. We could have one of those long conversations I love; we could talk over the people and events of the day, and your clear little mind would give me valuable ideas. And you would ask, probably hesitantly and with apparent indifference, "Do you really think she's pretty, that Mrs. Cooper Lawrence you spent the whole evening with?" And on that note I would kiss you and we would catch each other's eyes and laugh. Wouldn't we, darling?* As I read those words, I did indeed smile, and I was grateful to him for knowing me so well and accepting me.

. XVII .

Everything in life is unexpected and perhaps it remains so right to the end. This separation that I had so dreaded has stayed with me as a time of relative happiness. I was fairly solitary but I read and worked. Besides, I was very tired and slept for part of the day. Illness offers a sort of moral respite because it imposes firm limits on our wishes and concerns. Philippe was a long way away, but I knew he was happy and well. He wrote me charming letters. There was never a quarrel between us, never a shadow over us. Solange was in deepest Morocco, with seven or eight days' sea voyage between her and my husband. The world felt like a better place;

life seemed easier and kinder to me than I had known it for a long time. I now understood something Philippe had once said and I had deemed monstrous at the time: "Love tolerates absence and death better than doubt and betrayal."

Philippe had made me promise to see friends. I dined with the Thianges once, and with Aunt Cora two or three times. She was aging rapidly. Her collection of old generals, old admirals, and old ambassadors was no longer a full set because death had intervened. Several splendid specimens were missing altogether, having not been replaced. She herself occasionally fell asleep in her chair, surrounded by friendly ironic conversation. People said she would drop dead halfway through a dinner. I myself was grateful to her; it was at her house that I had met Philippe, and I continued to visit her faithfully. Two or three times I even lunched alone with her, which was counter to all tradition on the avenue Marceau, but one evening I started confiding in her and she encouraged me to continue. I ended up telling her my whole story, first my childhood, then my marriage, then Solange's role and my jealousy. She listened and smiled.

"Well, my poor little friend," she said, "if you never have problems more serious than that, you'll be a happy woman . . . What are you complaining about? That your husband's unfaithful? But men are never faithful . . ."

"Forgive me, Aunt Cora. But my father-in-law . . ."

"Your father-in-law was a hermit, that's a known fact, and I knew him better than you did . . . But where's the merit in that! Edouard spent his entire youth in the provinces, in the most unbelievable surroundings . . . he never had any temptations . . . but take my poor Adrien, for example. Do you think he was never unfaithful to me? My dear Isabelle, for twenty years of my life I knew my best friend, Jeanne de Casa Ricci, was his mistress . . . Of course, I won't say I didn't find it tricky in the beginning, but everything sorted itself out . . . I remember for our golden wedding . . . I invited all of Paris . . . Poor Adrien, whose mind was starting to go, he made a little speech and talked indiscriminately about me, Jeanne Casa, and the admiral . . . People around the table laughed, of course, but at the end of the day it was all very kindly meant, we were very old and we'd done the best we could with our lives, we hadn't ruined anything irremediably . . . Everything was all right and, besides, the dinner was so good that people hardly thought about anything else."

"Yes, Aunt Cora, but it all depends on character. To me, my love life is all-important, social life doesn't mean a thing. So . . ."

"But my poor dear, who's told you not to have a love life? Of course I love my nephew very much and I'm not the one to recommend you take a lover . . . No, clearly . . . But all the same, if it so pleases Monsieur Philippe to play away when he has such a pretty young wife, I'm also not the one to hold it against you if you too try to fill out your life . . . I know full well that even here on the avenue Marceau there are plenty of men who find you attractive . . ."

"Alas! My dear aunt, I believe in marriage."

"Well, that's as it should be . . . I believe in marriage too, I've proved I do. But marriage is one thing and love is another . . . You have to have a solid canvas; there's nothing to stop you embroidering a few arabesques . . . It's just down to how you do it . . . What I don't like with young women these days is they have no manners."

Philippe's elderly aunt talked at length in these terms. I found her entertaining; we even loved each other, but we were not really designed to understand each other.

I was also invited out by the Sommervieus, associates of Philippe's in a number of businesses. I thought it my duty to accept because it could be useful to Philippe. When I arrived at their house I regretted coming because I saw immediately there was no one I knew. It was a beautiful house, furnished in a way that was rather too modern for my liking but with real taste. Philippe would have been interested in the paintings: there were some Marquets, a Sisley, and a Lebourg. Madame Sommervieu introduced me to men and women I did not know. The women, who were mostly polite, were covered in magnificent jewels. The men were almost all the industrial engineer type with robust bodies and energetic faces. I listened to the names without really concentrating, well aware I would forget them. "Madame Godet," my hostess said. I looked at Madame Godet, who was a pretty, slightly faded blonde. Monsieur Godet was also there, an officer of the Légion d'honneur who seemed rather authoritarian. I knew nothing about them and yet I kept thinking, "Godet? Godet? I think I know that name."

"Who is Monsieur Godet?" I asked my hostess.

"Godet," said Madame Sommervieu, "is the biggest name in metallurgy. He's associate director of Steelworks for the West. He's also very powerful in coal mining."

I thought Philippe must have mentioned him to me, or was it Villier?

Godet was next to me at dinner. He peered at my name card with interest because he had not caught my name and then said immediately, "You wouldn't be Philippe Marcenat's wife by any chance?"

"Indeed I am."

"Oh! I used to know your husband very well. It was with him, or rather with his father, that I first started out in Limousin. A very lowly start. I had to take care of a paper factory; I didn't find it very interesting. I had a subordinate role. Your father-in-law was a strict man, difficult to work with. Oh, yes! Gandumas is full of bad memories for me!" He laughed and added, "I do apologize for saying that."

While he was talking, I suddenly understood. Misa . . . he was Misa's husband . . . All of Philippe's account came back to me as clearly as if I had every sentence before my eyes. So that pretty woman with

the soft, doleful eyes, the one over there at the far
end of the table, smiling brightly to the man next to
her, she was the one Philippe took in his arms one
evening while they sat on cushions before a dying
fire. I could not believe it. In my mind's eye, the
cruel, the voluptuous Misa had acquired the voice
and manners of a Lucretia Borgia or a Hermione.
Had Philippe described her so badly? But I had to
talk to the husband.

"Yes, that's right, Philippe has often mentioned
you." Then I added with some difficulty, "Am I
right in thinking Madame Godet was a great friend
of my husband's first wife?"

He stopped looking at me and he too seemed embarrassed. ("What does he know?" I wondered.)

"Yes," he said. "They were childhood friends.
Then there was some trouble. Odile didn't behave
very well toward Misa, I mean Marie-Thérèse, but I
call my wife Misa."

"Yes, of course."

Then, realizing this was a little strange, I changed
the subject. He explained the relationship between
France and Germany in the world of steel, coke, and
coal. He showed how major industrial issues influenced foreign policy. He had far-reaching ideas and

ANDRÉ MAUROIS

I found them interesting. I asked him whether he
knew Jacques Villier.

"The one from Morocco?" he asked. "Yes, he's
on one of my committees."

"Do you think him an intelligent man?"

"I hardly know him; he's successful . . ."

After dinner I maneuvered to ensure I was alone
with his wife. I knew Philippe would not have allowed me to do this, and I had made an effort to
forbid myself, but passionate curiosity drove me on
and urged me toward her. She seemed surprised.

"During dinner," I said, "your husband reminded me that you once knew mine very well."

"Yes," she said coldly. "Julien and I lived at Gandumas for several months."

She threw me a strange look, both questioning
and sad. She seemed to be thinking, "Do you know
the truth? And is this apparent friendliness false?"
The strange thing is I did not dislike her. Quite the
opposite. I warmed to her. I was touched by her
grace, her serious, melancholy expression. "She
looks like a woman who has suffered a great deal,"
I thought to myself. "Who knows? Perhaps she
wanted Philippe to be happy? Perhaps, because she
loved him, she wanted to warn him against a woman

who could only possibly make him unhappy? Is that such a great crime?"

I sat near her and tried to bring her out of her shell. After an hour I managed to get her to talk about Odile. She could not do so without a degree of discomfort, which showed how raw the feelings these memories stirred still were.

"I find it very difficult to talk of Odile," she said. "I really loved her and really admired her. Later she hurt me and then she died. I don't want to sully her memory, particularly for you."

She glanced at me again with that strange look in her eyes, loaded with questions.

"Oh!" I said. "Please don't think I'm hostile to her memory. In fact, I've heard so much about her I've ended up thinking of her as a part of who I am. She must have been so beautiful."

"Yes," she said sadly, "she was remarkably beautiful. And yet there was something in her eyes that I didn't like. A bit of . . . no . . . I don't want to say falsity . . . that would be too . . . it was—I don't know how to explain it—it was something like triumphant cunning. Odile needed to dominate. She wanted to impose *her* will, *her* version of the truth. Her beauty had given her a lot of self-confidence and she believed, almost in good faith, that if she said something then it became true. This worked with your husband, who adored her, but not with me, and she resented me for that."

I listened to her and suffered. I was seeing Renée's Odile, my mother-in-law's Odile, almost Hélène de Thianges's Solange, and not Philippe's Odile, whom I liked.

"It's so strange," I said. "The person you're describing is strong and willful. When Philippe talks about her, I get the impression she was frail, always having to lie down, rather childlike and good at heart."

"Yes," said Misa, "that was true too, but I think that was on the surface. The real Odile deep down had a sort of audacity like . . . well, I wouldn't know how to put it . . . the audacity of a soldier, a partisan. For example, when she wanted to hide . . . But no, I don't want to tell you about that, not you."

"What you call audacity, Philippe called courage; he says that was one of her great qualities."

"Yes, if you like. That's true in a way, but she didn't have the courage to set limits on herself. She had the courage to do the things she wanted. Which is still a fine thing but not so difficult."

"Do you have children?" I asked her.

"Yes," she replied, looking down. "Three: two boys and a girl."

We talked for the whole evening and parted having sketched the beginnings of a friendship. For the first time, I completely disagreed with a verdict of Philippe's. No, this woman was not spiteful. She had been in love and jealous. Who was I to blame her? At the last moment I did something impulsive that I later regretted. I said, "Goodbye. I'm glad we talked. I'm on my own at the moment, we could go out together."

As soon as I left the salon, I realized this had been a mistake and Philippe would not approve. When he learned that I had become friendly with Misa, he would be fiercely critical and would probably be right.

She too must have derived some pleasure from our conversation. Perhaps she was curious about me and my marriage, because she did indeed telephone two days later and we agreed to meet for a walk in the Bois de Boulogne. What I wanted was to get her to talk about Odile, to find out about Odile's tastes and habits and foibles from her, and I hoped that, with this knowledge, I might find more ways of pleasing

Philippe, whom I dared not ask about the past. I asked Misa countless questions: "How did she dress? Who was her milliner? People said she arranged flowers very well . . . but how can something like flower arranging be so personal? Please explain . . . Oh, it's so strange, you tell me and everyone tells me she had so much charm, but some details you're giving me are actually quite hard, almost unpleasant . . . So what exactly constituted her charm?"

But Misa proved quite incapable of giving me even an idea of this, and I could tell she herself had often pondered this question without ever finding an answer. All I found in what she told me about Odile was the love of nature that Solange had too, and a spontaneous vivacity that I lacked. "I'm too methodical," I thought. "I'm too wary of my own enthusiasm. I think Odile's childish side and her gaiety charmed Philippe as much as, if not more than, her moral qualities." Then we started to talk more intimately about Philippe, and I told her how much I loved him.

"Yes," she said, "but are you happy with him?"

"Very happy. Why?"

"No reason . . . I was just asking. Besides, I completely understand your loving him; he's endearing.

But, at the same time, he has such a weakness for women like Odile that it must make him very difficult to have as a husband."

"Why do you say 'women'? Have you known others besides Odile in his life?"

"Oh no! But I can tell. You see he's a man who's more likely to be driven away by devotion and passionate love . . . Well, here I am saying that when I know nothing about it. I don't know him very well, but that's what I imagine. Back when I knew him, I found he had moments of futility and frivolity that let him down slightly. But, you know, once again, nothing I say means very much. I've seen so little of him in my life."

I felt very uncomfortable; she seemed to be enjoying this. Was Philippe right? Was she spiteful? When I arrived back home I had a terrible evening. I found a tender letter from Philippe on the mantelpiece and hoped he would forgive me for doubting him. Yes, he was weak, but I liked that weakness too, and all I chose to see in Misa's ambiguous pronouncements about him was her own disappointment in love. She asked me to go out with her several times and even invited me to dinner. I declined.

. XVIII .

Philippe's absence was coming to an end, which made me tremendously happy. My health was now restored, and I was even feeling better than before the pregnancy. The waiting, the sense of a life forming inside me, lent me a mood of calm and serenity. I worked hard to ensure Philippe was pleasantly surprised when he came home. He must have seen very beautiful women and perfect houses in America. In spite of my condition, because of my condition, I took great care with my dresses. I changed a few details in the furnishings because Misa had given me some ideas about what Odile might have liked. The day he was due back I filled the house with a ridiculous profusion of white flowers. That day I succeeded in overcoming what Philippe jokingly called my "sordid economizing."

When Philippe stepped off the transatlantic train at Saint-Lazare station, I thought he looked younger and in high spirits, his face tanned from his days at sea. He was full of memories and stories. The first few days were very pleasant. Solange was still in Morocco; I had made a point of checking. Before going back to work, Philippe allowed himself a week's vacation, which he gave entirely to me.

It was during this week that an incident clearly demonstrated my husband's true nature. One morning I went out just before ten o'clock because I had a fitting. Philippe stayed in bed. He told me later that after I left, the telephone rang. He went to answer, and a man's voice he did not recognize said, "Madame Marcenat?"

"No," he said. "This is Monsieur Marcenat. Who's calling?"

A sharp click informed him that the man had hung up.

He was surprised and called the switchboard operator to find out who had been on the line. This required lengthy negotiations and he was eventually told, "a booth at the stock exchange," which must have been a mistake and explained nothing.

"Who could have telephoned you from the stock exchange?" he asked when I came home.

"From the stock exchange?" I asked, surprised.

"Yes, the stock exchange. They asked for you, I said it was me, and they hung up."

"How odd! Are you sure?"

"That question's beneath you, Isabelle. Yes, I'm sure. Anyway, the voice was perfectly clear."

"A man's voice or a woman's?"

"A man's of course."

"Why 'of course'?"

We had never talked quite like that; in spite of myself I looked embarrassed. Even though he had said "a man's voice," I was convinced it was Misa who had telephoned (she often called me), but I dared not name her. I was angry with Philippe, he almost seemed to be accusing a wife who adored him, and yet I was slightly flattered. So could he be jealous of me, then? I felt a woman I did not know blossoming in me with astonishing speed, an Isabelle who could be a little sarcastic, a little coquettish, a little sympathetic. Dear Philippe! If he only knew how utterly my life revolved around him and for him, he could have rested easy, too easy. After lunch he asked with a nonchalance that reminded me of some of my own questions, "What are you doing this afternoon?"

"Me, nothing, a bit of shopping. Then I'm going to tea with Madame Brémont at five o'clock."

"Would it bother you if I went with you, given I'm on vacation?"

"Oh, no, I'd love it. I'm not used to you being so kind to me. I'll meet you there at six o'clock."

"What? You said five o'clock."

"Well, it's like all these teas. The invitation says five o'clock but no one gets there before six."

"Couldn't I come with you to do your shopping?"

"Of course . . . I thought you wanted to go to the office to look at your mail?"

"There's no rush. I'll go tomorrow."

"You're a wonderful husband when you come home from abroad, Philippe."

So he went out with me and we spent the afternoon in a completely new mood of constraint. There is a note about this in Philippe's book; it reveals feelings that, at the time, I had not realized were so intense.

I feel as if, while I was away, she developed a sort of strength, a self-assurance she did not have before. Yes, that is it, self-assurance. Why? It's strange. She stepped out of the car to buy some books and, as she got out, she looked at me tenderly, but I felt there was something odd about that look. At Madame Brémont's house she had a long conversation with Doctor Gaulin. I was surprised to find myself trying to work out in what terms they were talking. Gaulin was describing experiments on mice.

"You take virgin mice," he said, "and put them with newborn mice. They don't look after them; they'd leave them to die of hunger if you didn't intervene. If you inject them with ovarian extract, they become exemplary mothers in a couple of days."

"How fascinating!" said Isabelle. "I'd very much like to see that."

"Come to my laboratory. I'll show you."

Then, for a moment, I thought it was Gaulin's voice I had heard on the telephone.

I have never had a better measure of how absurd jealousy is than reading that note, because no suspicion was ever more foolish. Doctor Gaulin was a likable, intelligent man who was very fashionable in society circles that year and I enjoyed listening to him, but the thought that I could take an interest in him as a man had never occurred to me. Since my marriage to Philippe, I had become incapable of even "seeing" another man; I viewed them all as large objects that might be to Philippe's advantage or disadvantage. I could never have conceived of myself loving them. And yet I find this on a scrap of paper pinned to the page I have just cited:

Accustomed as I am to confusing love with the agonies of doubt, I find myself thinking I might be feeling its effects once more. The same Isabelle who, three months ago, I deemed too assiduous, too ever-present, I now find hard to keep beside me as much as I would like. Did I really have that sense of invincible boredom when I was with her? Now I'm not so outwardly happy but I'm not bored for one moment. Isabelle is completely astonished by my new attitude; she's so modest that the true meaning of this change in me remains a mystery to her. This morning she said, "If you don't mind, I'd like to go to the

Pasteur Institute this afternoon to see Gaulin's experiments."

"Absolutely not," I said. "You won't go."

She looked up, dumbstruck by my vehemence. "But why not, Philippe? You heard what he was talking about the other day. I think it's very interesting."

"Gaulin has a way of behaving around women that I don't like."

"Gaulin? What a peculiar idea! I saw a lot of him last winter and never noticed anything. But you hardly know him; you saw him for ten minutes at the Brémonts' . . ."

"That's just it. It was in those ten minutes . . ."

And then, for the first time since I have known her, Isabelle smiled a smile that could have been Odile's.

"Are you jealous?" she asked. "Oh, that's too funny! That really does make me laugh."

I remember that incident. I did actually find it quite amusing and, as I said earlier, it made me rather happy. Philippe's mind had been closed to me such a long time, it was an elusive thing that I tried in vain to pin down and open up, but all of a sudden I felt I had a hold on it. It was very tempting and, if I have a right to any indulgence in my life, I feel it should be for that period, because it seemed to me that—had I wanted to play a particular game, a mysterious, coquettish game—I could have secured my husband's affections with a quite new assurance. There was no question about it. I allowed myself two or three harmless experiments. Yes, that was how Philippe was made. He was tortured and captivated by doubt. But I also knew that doubt meant constant suffering for him, it was an obsession. I knew because I had read the story of his earlier life, and I saw proof of it every day. Anxious about what I said and did, he fell to wistful meditation, slept badly, and stopped taking an interest in his work. How could he succumb to such wild imaginings? I was expecting a child in four months' time and all I could think of was this child and him. He could not see that.

I did not want to play that hand even though I could have won it. That is the only small credit I would ask, it is the only important sacrifice I made, but I did make it. And I would like to think that, because of it, you forgave me, Philippe, for my sad, grim jealousy and the pettiness that sometimes—quite rightly—irritated you. I too could have tied you to me, stripped you of your strength, freedom, and happiness; I too could have filled you with the painful anxiety that you feared, that you sought. I did not want to. I wanted to love you without trickery, to fight with an open heart. I handed myself over to you with no defenses, while you yourself were handing me the weapons. I think I did the right thing. I think love should be a greater thing than the cruel war between lovers. It should be possible to admit loving someone and yet also succeed in being loved. That was your weakness, my darling, this need to be spared boredom by the indiscretions of the women you loved. That was not how I saw love. I felt capable of total devotion, slavery, even. There was nothing in the world for me but you. Some catastrophe could have annihilated every single man we knew, but if you were spared it would not have felt calamitous to me. You were my world. Perhaps it was unwise to let you see and know that. With you, my love, I did not want to observe sensible policies. I was incapable of pretence or caution. I loved you.

In just a few days my clear-cut behavior and placid way of life restored Philippe's peace of mind. I stopped seeing Gaulin (which, incidentally, I regretted because he was a nice man) and I almost completely shut myself up at home.

The last months of my pregnancy were quite difficult. I felt so altered and did not want to go out with Philippe because I was afraid he would not like the way I looked. In the last weeks he kept me company very devotedly, spending time with me every day and reading to me. Our relationship was never closer to what I had always dreamed. We had both returned to some of the great novels. In my youth I had read Balzac and Tolstoy but had not fully understood them. Now everything seeemed loaded with meaning. The character of Dolly at the beginning of *Anna Karenina* was me; Anna herself was partly Odile, partly Solange. When Philippe read, I could tell he was making the same comparisons. Sometimes a sentence so closely resembled our relationship or me that Philippe looked up at me from his book with a smile he could not contain. I smiled too.

I would have been very happy if Philippe had not still seemed sad. He did not complain of any trouble and was in good health, but he often sighed, sat in his chair beside my bed, wearily stretched his long arms and ran a hand over his eyes.

"Are you tired, darling?" I asked.

"Yes, a little. I think I need a change of air. Being in that office all day . . ."

"Of course, particularly as you then stay with me all evening. Go out, darling . . . Have some fun . . . Why have you stopped going to the theater and concerts?"

"You know I hate going out on my own."

"Won't Solange be back soon? She was only meant to be away two months. Have you heard from her?"

"Yes, she's written to me," said Philippe. "She's stayed on in Morocco. She didn't want to leave her husband on his own."

"What? But she leaves him on his own every year . . . Why this sudden concern? How odd."

"How would I know?" Philippe asked irritably. "That's what she wrote, that's all I can tell you."

. XIX .

Solange *eventually came back* a few weeks before my baby was due. The abrupt transformation in Philippe made my heart bleed. One evening he suddenly seemed young and cheerful. He brought me flowers and some of the plump pink prawns I liked. He walked briskly around my bed with his hands in his pockets and told me amusing stories about his office and the editors he had seen during the course of the day.

"What's got into him?" I wondered. "What's given him that glow?"

He ate his dinner beside my bed and,

nonchalantly, without looking at him, I asked, "Still no news of Solange?"

"I beg your pardon?" Philippe asked with rather exaggerated casualness. "Didn't I tell you she telephoned this morning? She's been back in Paris since yesterday."

"I'm happy for you, Philippe. You'll have a companion to go out with just when I won't be able to keep you company."

"You must be mad, Isabelle. I'm not going to leave you for a moment."

"I insist that you leave. Besides, I won't be on my own because my mother will be in Paris soon."

"That's true," said Philippe, clearly delighted. "She can't be too far away now, your good lady mother. Where was her last telegram from?"

"It was radioed from the boat, but judging by what the shipping company told me, she should be in Suez tomorrow."

"I'm very happy for you," said Philippe. "It's very kind of her to have made this huge journey to attend a birth."

"My family's like yours, Philippe, births and deaths are high points. I seem to remember my father's happiest memories were of his provincial cousins' funerals."

"When my Marcenat grandfather was very old," said Philippe, "his doctor forbade him from going to any funerals, and he complained bitterly. 'They won't let me follow poor Ludovic's cortege,' he said. 'It's not as if I have many other forms of entertainment.'"

"You seem very cheerful this evening, Philippe."

"Me? Oh, no . . . But the weather's so lovely. You're feeling well. This nine-month nightmare is about to end. I'm happy. It's only normal."

I was humiliated to see him so alive and to know the cause of this resurrection. That evening he ate with an appetite I had previously seen in Saint-Moritz and which, to my considerable anxiety, he had lost for many months. After dinner he became agitated. He kept yawning.

"Would you like us to read a little?" I asked. "The Stendhal you started yesterday evening was very good . . ."

"Ah, yes!" said Philippe. "*Lamiel* . . . Yes, it was quite splendid . . . If you like." He gave a bored pout.

"Listen, Philippe. Do you know what you ought to do? Go and say hello to Solange. You haven't seen her for five months, it would be nice."

"Do you think? But I don't want to leave you. And I have no idea whether she's at home or whether she's free. Her first evening back she must be with her family, and her husband's."

"Telephone her."

I had hoped he would defend his position better, but he immediately succumbed to the temptation.

"Oh well! I'll give it a try," he said and left the room.

Five minutes later he came back, his face beaming, and said, "If it's all the same to you, I'm going to nip over to see Solange. I'll be there a quarter of an hour."

"Stay as long as you like. I'm delighted, it'll do you so much good. But come and say good night when you come in, even if it's very late."

"It won't be very late. It's nine o'clock now. I'll be back at a quarter to ten."

I saw him again at midnight. While I waited, I had read a little and cried a lot.

. XX .

My mother arrived from China a few days before my child's birth. When I saw her again I was amazed to find I was closer and yet more estranged from her than I would have thought. She found fault with our way of life, our servants, our furniture, and our friends, and her criticisms struck invisible, long-buried chords in me that reverberated feebly to the same tune. Even the family base inside me had already been covered with a thick "Philippe layer," and things that amazed and shocked her seemed quite normal to me. It was not long before she commented on the fact that, in the last weeks of my pregnancy, Philippe was not entirely as attentive as he could have been. It pained me when she said, "I'll come and keep you company this evening, because I don't imagine your husband will have the heart to stay at home," and I regretted that it hurt more because of my pride than my love. I was sorry she had not arrived before Solange returned, when, outside his working hours, Philippe had not left my side. I would have liked to show her that I too could be loved. She often stood by my bed, looking at me with a critical eye that reignited all my childhood anxieties. She was attentive, almost hostile as she brought a finger down onto the parting in my hair. "You're graying," she said. It was true.

If Philippe came home after midnight when there were fewer and fewer pedestrians on the street, I would listen to their footsteps, trying to recognize his. I can still remember that disappointing sound growing louder, awakening the hope that it might stop, then carrying on, growing quieter and fading away. A man who is really going to stop by a door starts slowing down several paces in advance; I eventually recognized Philippe from this dying rhythm. The soft sound of a bell in the house, a faraway door closing; he was back. I promised myself

I would be bright and indulgent yet almost always greeted him with complaints. I myself was hurt by the monotony and vehemence of the things I said to him then.

"Oh, Isabelle!" Philippe would say wearily. "I can't take this anymore, I tell you . . . Can't you see you're contradicting yourself? You're the one begging me to go out; I do as I'm told and then you bombard me with criticism . . . What do you want me to do? Shut myself away in this house? Well, then, say so . . . I'll do it . . . Yes, I promise, I'll do it . . . Anything rather than this constant quarreling . . . But please don't try to be generous at nine o'clock in the evening and then so mean at midnight . . ."

"Yes, Philippe, you're right . . . I'm awful. I swear I won't do it again."

But the following day an inner demon dictated the same pointless words to me. In fact it was mainly Solange who irritated me. I felt that at this particular point in my life she should have had the tact to leave me my husband.

She came to see me, and conversation was fairly awkward. She had a beautiful sable coat and recommended her furrier at some length. Then Philippe arrived; she must have told him she would be visiting because he was home much earlier than usual. The coat became a useless, almost invisible prop, and the garden in Marrakesh took center stage.

"You can't imagine what it's like, Isabelle . . . In the morning, I walk barefoot over the warm tiles between the orange trees . . . there are roses and jasmines intertwined around all the columns. You can see the pale blue Zellige tiles through the flowers and foliage . . . and over the rooftops, the snow on the Atlas mountains gleaming like a magnificent diamond ("We already had the diamond back in Saint-Mortitz," I thought) . . . And the nights! The cypress trees seem to be pointing at the moon like black fingers . . . Oh! Marcenat, Marcenat, I do so love it . . ."

She tilted her head back slightly and seemed to smell her jasmines and roses.

When she left, Philippe saw her to the door and came back looking slightly sheepish, and leaned against the chimney breast in my bedroom.

"You should come to Morocco with me one day," he said after a long silence. "It really is very beautiful. Oh, by the way, I've brought you a book by Robert Etienne about the Berbers, about their way of life . . . It's a sort of novel . . . but also a poem . . . It's remarkable."

"My poor Philippe," I said. "I do feel sorry for you having to deal with women. Such actresses!"

"What makes you say that, Isabelle?"

"I say it because it's true, darling. I know plenty about them, women, I mean, and they're not at all interesting."

At last I felt the first pains. The labor was long and difficult, but I was happy to see Philippe's reaction: he was white, more frightened than I was. I could see he cared for my life. His emotion gave me strength: I completely mastered my nerves in order to reassure him, and I talked about our little boy, because I was sure I would have a boy.

"We'll call him Alain. His eyebrows will be slightly too high like yours; he'll walk up and down with his hands in his pockets when something's tormenting him . . . Because he'll be terribly tormented, won't he Philippe? With parents like us . . . What an inheritance!"

Philippe tried to smile, but I could see he was moved. When I was not in pain I told him to hold my hand.

"Do you remember my hand on yours, Philippe, when we went to see *Siegfried* . . . That was the beginning of everything."

From the bedroom I was in, I heard Doctor Crès talking to Philippe a little later.

"Your wife's incredibly brave," he said. "I've rarely seen anything like it."

"Yes," said Philippe, "my wife is a very good woman. I hope nothing will happen to her."

"What do you think's going to happen to her?" asked the doctor. "Everything's normal."

They decided I should have chloroform for the end, although I did not want it. When I opened my eyes, I saw Philippe beside me with a happy tender expression on his face. He kissed my hand. "We have a son, darling." I wanted to see him and was disappointed.

My mother and Philippe's had made themselves comfortable in the little sitting room next to my bedroom. The door was open and, as I lay half asleep with my eyes closed, I could hear their pessimistic prognostications about the child's upbringing.

Although they were very different and doubtless disagreed on almost any subject, they had a generational loyalty in rebuking a younger couple.

"Oh, it's going to be a pretty sight!" said Madame Marcenat. "With Philippe taking care of everything except his son's upbringing, and Isabelle only taking care of Philippe, you'll see, the child will do whatever he pleases . . ."

"Well, of course," said my mother, "the young can think of only one thing: happiness. Children must be happy, the husband must be happy, the mistress must be happy, the servants must be happy and, in order to achieve that, they abolish the rules, ignore barriers, they do away with punishments and sanctions, and they forgive everything before forgiveness has even been—I won't said deserved—but asked for. It's unimaginable. And with what results? If at least they were much 'happier' than we were, you and I, I mean, Madame, then I might understand. But the funny thing is they're not as happy as us, much less so. I can see my daughter . . . Is she asleep? Are you asleep, Isabelle?"

I did not reply.

"It's odd for her to be so sleepy on the third day," said my mother.

"Why was she chloroformed?" asked Madame Marcenat. "I told Philippe that, in his shoes, I wouldn't have allowed it. Women should have their children themselves. I had three children myself; sadly, I lost two, but I had them all naturally. These artificial births are bad for the child and for the mother. I was very angry when I heard Isabelle had been so soft. I think you could search through our whole family (there are Marcenats in ten different provinces), and you wouldn't find one woman who'd agreed to that."

"Really?" My mother asked politely, having herself recommended that I have chloroform but, as a diplomat's wife, not wanting a conflict that might be unfavorable to the combined offensive she was currently enjoying with Madame Marcenat against the younger generation . . . "As I was saying," my mother went on very quietly, "I can see my daughter. She says she's unhappy? Well, it's not Philippe's fault, he's a very kind husband and no more of a womanizer than the next man. No, it's because she analyzes herself the whole time, she frets and constantly checks the barometer of her relationship, of 'their love,' as she calls it . . . Did you ever give much thought to the state of your marriage,

Madame? I gave it very little thought. I tried to help my husband in his career; I had a demanding household to run; we were very busy and everything was fine . . . It's the same with bringing up children. Isabelle says what she wants most is for Alain to have a nicer childhood than she did. But I can assure you she didn't have an unpleasant childhood. I brought her up quite strictly; I don't regret that. You can see the results."

"If you hadn't brought her up the way you did," Madame Marcenat said, and she too was talking very quietly, "Isabelle wouldn't have grown into the delightful young woman she is. She owes you a great debt of gratitude, and so does my son."

I did not move a muscle because their conversation amused me. "Who knows? They could be right," I thought.

They stopped agreeing when the subject of how Alain was fed was discussed. My mother-in-law thought I should nurse him myself and abhorred English nannies. My mother had told me, "Don't try. With your nerves, you'll give up after three weeks, by which time you'll have made the child ill." Philippe did not want me to either. But I attached symbolic importance to the decision and dug my heels in. The results were as my mother had predicted. Everything since that longed-for birth disappointed me. I had had such high hopes that reality was powerless to satisfy them. I had thought this child would be a new and much stronger connection between Philippe and myself. He was not. In fact, Philippe took little interest in his son. He went to see him once a day, amused himself speaking English with the nanny for a few minutes, then was back to the Philippe I had always known, gentle and distant, with a haze of boredom encroaching on his tender and melancholy courtesy. I even thought that it was now much more than boredom. Philippe was sad. He did not go out so often. I thought at first this was out of kindness, because he did not feel it right to leave me on my own when I was still so weak. But more than once, when my mother or a friend had said she would visit me, I said, "Philippe, I know you find these family conversations boring. Telephone Solange and take her to the cinema this evening."

"Why on earth are you always forcing me to go out with Solange?" he replied. "I *can* last two days without seeing her."

Poor Philippe! No, he could *not* last two days without seeing her. Although I did not know precisely why, or know anything about Solange's private life, I sensed that something had changed between them since she had returned from Morocco, and that Philippe was suffering because of her.

I did not dare ask him about this, but just from the look on his face I could track the progress of his ailing morale. In a few weeks he had lost an almost unbelievable amount of weight; his complexion was yellow, his eyes had dark rings around them. He complained that he was not sleeping well and he had the blank stare usually associated with sleeplessness. At mealtimes he was silent, then had to make an effort to speak to me; this visible effort pained me even more than his silence.

Renée came to visit me and brought a little gown for Alain. I noticed at once how much she had changed. She had organized her life as a working woman and talked about Doctor Gaulin in terms that made me think she had become his mistress. This liaison had been a topic of conversation at Gandumas for several months, but only for its existence to be denied. The family was keen to remain on cordial terms with Renée and would have felt obliged, by its own codes, to stop receiving her if her virtue could not be taken for granted. But when I saw her I knew that, consciously or not, the Marcenats were wrong. Renée was full of joy, she looked like a woman who loved and was loved.

Since my marriage I had grown apart from her a great deal and, in several situations, had found her hard and nearly hostile, but on that day we almost immediately achieved the same mood of our long wartime conversations. We eventually talked about Philippe and talked about him intimately. Renée told me for the first time, very frankly, that she had loved him and it had hurt her terribly when I married him.

"In those days, Isabelle, I almost hated you, and then I rearranged my life and it all seems so far removed from me now . . . Even our strongest emotions die, don't you think? And we can look back to the woman we were three years ago with the same curiosity and detachment as if it were someone else."

"Yes," I said, "perhaps. I haven't got to that stage yet. I love Philippe as much as when we were first in love, much more, even. I feel I could make sacrifices for him now that I wouldn't have been able to make six months ago."

Renée looked at me for a moment in silence, appraising me as a doctor would.

"Yes, I believe that," she said eventually. "Do you know, Isabelle, I said earlier I didn't regret anything, but it's actually stronger than that. Do you mind if I'm completely frank? I congratulate myself every day for not marrying Philippe."

"And me for marrying him."

"Yes, that's right, because you love him and you've adopted his appalling habit of trying to find happiness in suffering. But Philippe is a terrible creature, not at all unkind—quite the opposite—but terrible because he's obsessed. I knew Philippe when he was a little boy. He was already the same man, except that then there might have been other possible Philippes in him. Then along came Odile and she set his personality as a lover, and probably set it forever. For him, love is associated with a particular sort of face, a particular form of extravagant behavior, a particular gracefulness that is slightly disturbing, not altogether candid . . . And because he's also absurdly sensitive, this type of woman, the only type he can love, makes him very unhappy . . . Wouldn't you say?"

"It's true and it's not, Renée. I do realize that it's absurd ever to say, 'I'm loved,' but Philippe does love me, I can't be in any doubt about that . . . It's just, at the same time, you're quite right, he needs completely different women, women like Odile, like Solange . . . Do you know Solange Villier?"

"Very well . . . I didn't dare mention her to you, but I was thinking of her."

"Oh, but you can talk about her; I'm not at all jealous anymore. I was . . . Are people saying Solange is Philippe's mistress?"

"Oh no! . . . Absolutely not. In fact they're saying that, during her last trip to Morocco, she fell for Robert Etienne, you know, the man who wrote that fascinating book about the Berbers . . . In her last few weeks in Marrakesh she spent all her time with him. He's just come back to Paris . . . He's a major writer and a wonderful person. Gaulin knows him and thinks very highly of him."

I was lost in thought for a moment. Yes, it was just as I had suspected, and this name, Etienne, gave me an explanation for several conversations my husband had instigated. He had brought all Etienne's books home, one after the other. He had read brief passages from them to me, asking me what I thought of them. I had liked them, particularly the long meditation called *Prayer to the Oudaïas Gardens*. "It's beautiful," Philippe had said. "Yes, it really is beautiful, it's wild." My poor Philippe, he must have been in such pain! He was now probably analyzing Solange's every utterance and every move, as he had once analyzed Odile's, to look for traces of this man he did not know. It was likely to be this pointless, tortuous task that filled his sleepless nights. Oh, I suddenly felt so angry with that woman!

"You were right, Renée, what you said earlier about the appalling habit of deriving pleasure from suffering . . . It's just that when circumstances have dictated that you begin your love life in that way, which is what happened in Philippe's case and in mine, is it still possible to change?"

"I think we can always change, if we really want to."

"But how do you want to, Renée? Don't you already need to have changed for that?"

"Gaulin would say, 'By understanding the mechanism and overcoming it.' In other words, by being more intelligent."

"But Philippe is intelligent."

"Very, but Philippe makes too much use of his sensitivity and not enough of his intelligence."

We chatted happily until it was time for Philippe to come home. Renée had a scientific way of talking about things, which soothed me because it made me simply one individual like so many others in a clearly labeled group of women in love.

Philippe seemed happy to see Renée, asked her to stay for dinner with us, and for the first time in several weeks talked animatedly throughout the meal. He liked science, and Renée told him about new experiments he had not yet heard of. When she mentioned Gaulin's name for the second time, Philippe asked abruptly, "Gaulin? do you know him well?"

"I would think so," said Renée. "I work for him."

"Isn't he a friend of Robert Etienne, the one from Morocco, I mean the one who wrote the *Prayer to the Oudaïas*?"

"Yes," said Renée.

"What about you?" asked Philippe. "Do you know Etienne?"

"Very well."

"What sort of man is he?"

"Remarkable," said Renée.

"Ah!" said Philippe. Then he added with some difficulty, "Yes, I too think he's talented . . . But sometimes the man is inferior to the work . . ."

"That is not the case here," said Renée, merciless.

I looked at her beseechingly. Philippe was silent for the whole rest of the evening.

. XXI .

I watched as Philippe's love for Solange Villier died beside me. He never talked to me about her. On the contrary, he obviously wanted me to think nothing had changed in their relationship. Besides, he still saw her often, but much less than before, and it did not give him such unmitigated pleasure. When they went for walks, he no longer came home young and happy, but serious and sometimes almost despairing. Occasionally I thought he might confide in me. He would take my hand and say, "Isabelle, you're the one who chose the better course."

"Why, darling?"

"Because . . ."

Then he would stop, but I understood perfectly. He continued to send Solange flowers, and to treat her as someone he loved dearly. Don Quixote and Lancelot remained faithful. But the notes I find in his papers from 1923 are quite sad:

April 17—Walk with S., Montmartre. We went all the way up to the place du Tertre and sat at a café terrace. Croissants and lemonade. Solange asked for a bar of chocolate and had her snack there in the open, like a little girl. Rekindled exactly various feelings I had forgotten since the Odile-François days. Solange wants to be natural and affectionate; she's very tender with me and very good to me. But I can see she is thinking of someone else. She has the same languor I noticed in Odile after her first escapade and, like her, avoids any explanations. The moment I try to talk about her, about us, she avoids it and comes up with a game. Today she looked at passersby and had fun guessing what their lives were like from the way they moved and how they looked. With a taxi driver who stopped by our café and sat at a table with two women he had been driving around in his car, she invented a whole novel. I try to stop loving her, but do not manage very well. I find her as attractive as ever—she looks so strong, her face so sun kissed.

"My dear," she says, "you're sad. What's the matter? Don't you think life's fun? Just think, in every one of those funny little houses there are men and women whose lives would be fascinating to watch. And think that, all over Paris, there are hundreds of squares like this, and dozens of Parises in the world. It is amazing!"

"I don't agree, Solange. I think life's quite an interesting performance when you're very young. When you get to forty like me, when you've seen the prompt, you know the actors' ways, and have worked out the threads of the plot, you feel like walking out."

"I don't like you talking like that. You haven't seen anything yet."

"But I have, my poor Solange, I've seen the third act. I didn't think it was very good or very cheerful. It's always the same situation, I can see it's going to be like that right to the end, and that's enough for me. I don't feel like watching the outcome."

"You're a bad audience," said Solange. "You have a delightful wife, charming girlfriends . . ."

"Girlfriends?"

"Yes, sir, girlfriends. I know about your life."

This is all terribly Odile. What I can barely forgive myself is that I take pleasure in this misery. There's a mysterious satisfaction in viewing life as a mournful performance like that, a satisfaction no doubt based on pride—a Marcenat vice. What I ought to do is stop seeing Solange. Then perhaps everything would settle down, but it is impossible to see her and not love her.

April 18—Yesterday evening I had a long conversation about love with one of my friends, a man of over fifty who is said to have been one of the Don Juans of his day. What struck me as I listened to him was how little happiness he derived from all the adventures that other men envied him.

"When all is said and done," he said, "I loved only one woman: Claire P., and even with her, my goodness, I was tired of her in the end!"

"And yet she's so charming," I said.

"Oh, you can't judge her now," he said. "She's all mannerisms and simpering. She's taken behavior that used to be quite natural to her and now wears it like a mask. No, I really can't even see her anymore."

"What about the others?"

"The others were nothing."

I mentioned the woman who is still regarded as the one who fills his life.

"I don't love her at all," he said. "I just see her out of habit. She's hurt me terribly; she was unfaithful to me many times. Now I can judge her. No, really, it's nothing."

Listening to him makes me wonder whether romantic love actually exists, whether I should give up on it. As in Tristan und Isolde, *death alone saves love from failure, but of course death condemns it.*

April 19—Trip to Gandumas. The first for three months. A few workmen came to tell me their woes: poverty, sickness. Confronted with these real problems, I blushed to think of my own imaginary ones. And yet, among the workmen too there are troubles in love.

Spent a completely sleepless night thinking about my life. I think it's been one long mistake.

To be honest, my only occupation has been pursuing an absolute happiness that I thought I would find through women, and there is no more fruitless pursuit. Absolute love does not exist any more than a perfect government, and the heart's opportunism is the only wisdom in human affections. It is most important not to take pleasure in a particular behavior. Our feelings are all too often only the images of our feelings. I could free myself from this obsession with Solange in a flash if I agreed to look at the real Solange, the one I have had in me ever since I met her, which has always been in me, drawn by a cruel, exacting master, and that I refuse to see.

April 20—Even though Solange hardly cares for me now, the minute I try to break away, she pulls a little on the string and draws it tighter. Coquettishness or charity?

April 23—Where does the blame lie? Solange has changed like Odile. Is that because I made the same mistakes? Or because I made the same choice? Should we always hide what we feel in order to keep what we love? Do we have to be cunning, must we devise and disguise just when we want to let ourselves go? I don't know anymore.

April 27—Every ten years we should eradicate a few ideas that experience has proved to be misguided or dangerous.

Ideas to eradicate:

A) Women can be tied down by a promise or an oath. *False. "Women have no morals, the way they behave depends on what they love."*

B) There is such a thing as the perfect woman, with whom love would be a succession of undiluted pleasures for the senses, the mind, and the heart. *False. "Two human beings moored next to each other are like two boats rocked by the waves; their hulls collide and creak."*

May 28—Dinner on the avenue Marceau. Aunt Cora dying among her fattened chickens and her orchids.

*Hélène came over to talk to me about Solange.
"Poor Marcenat!" she said. "You've looked so miserable the last few weeks . . . I understand, of course, you're hurting."*

"I don't know what you're talking about," I replied.

"Yes you do," she said. "You're still in love with her."

I protested.

. XXII .

The red notebook reveals a Philippe who was far more lucid and in control of himself than I recognized at the time. I think his intelligence was already freer, but in his secret depths there was still an enslaved Philippe. He seemed so unhappy that, more than once, I wondered whether I should go and see Solange and beg her to show him some consideration. But it felt such a ridiculous step to take that I did not dare to. Besides, I now loathed Solange. I felt that alone with her I would not be able to restrain myself. We carried on seeing her at the Thianges', and then Philippe refused to go to Hélène's Saturday salons (something he had never done).

"You go, so she sees we're not angry with her. That wouldn't be fair, Hélène's kind. But I can't do it anymore, I tell you. The older I get the more I despise the social scene . . . a corner by the fire, a book, you . . . that's happiness for me now."

I knew he meant it sincerely. I also knew that if, at that moment, he had met a pretty, frivolous young woman and she, by some invisible communication, had given him the signal he was waiting for, he would instantly and unwittingly have altered his philosophy and explained that, after a day's work, what he really needed was to see new people and have some fun. Early in our marriage, I remember being saddened by the eternally impenetrable skulls of those we love, hiding their thoughts from us. Philippe had become transparent to me. Through a fine membrane pulsating with a network of delicate vessels, I could now make out his every thought, his every weakness, and I loved him better than ever. I remember one evening in his study looking at him for a long time without a word.

"What are you thinking about?" he asked, smiling.

"I'm trying to see you as I would if I didn't love you, and still to love you like that."

"God, that's complicated! And can you?"

"Love you like that? Yes, effortlessly."

That evening he suggested we go to Gandumas earlier in the year than usual.

"There's nothing to keep us in Paris. I can take care of my work just as well there. And the country air will be very good for Alain, and my mother won't be so alone. I can see nothing but advantages to going."

This trip was all I could have wished for. At Gandumas, Philippe would be entirely mine. My only fear was that he would be bored there, but in fact I noticed he immediately seemed more balanced. In Paris, even though he had lost Solange, he still had tenacious—but most likely unfounded—hopes. He still reacted instinctually when the telephone rang, a response I knew so well and of which he was not yet cured.

When we went out, because I was painfully aware of Philippe's every quiver, I could tell he was afraid we might meet her at any moment, but he also longed for this. He knew he still cared for her terribly and that, if she wanted to, she would have him back in a flash. He knew this, but he also knew that both his dignity and fears for his happiness demanded that he should not allow himself to be taken again. At Gandumas, in a setting that had never been associated with Solange, he gradually started to forget her. After a week, he already looked better; his cheeks were fuller, his eyes brighter, he was sleeping better.

The weather was magnificent. We went for long walks together. Philippe told me he now wanted to follow his father's example and take an interest in smallholdings. We went to la Guichardie, les Bruyères, and Resonzac every day.

Philippe spent only the mornings at the factory; every afternoon he went out with me.

"Do you know what we ought to do?" he asked. "We should take a book and read to each other in the woods."

There were lovely shady retreats around Gandumas. Sometimes it was a mossy bank beside a wide walkway where the branches met overhead, forming the side aisle of a soft green cathedral, sometimes a fallen tree trunk, sometimes on a bench put there years before by Grandfather Marcenat. He very much liked Balzac's *Study of a Woman* and his

Secrets of the Princesse Cadignan, and various novellas by Mérimée such as *The Double Misunderstanding* or *The Etruscan Vase*, as well as some Kipling stories and some of the poets.

Sometimes he would look up and ask, "I'm not boring you, am I?"

"What a thought! I've never been more perfectly happy!"

He would look at me for a moment and then carry on. When the reading was over, we discussed the characters and their personalities, and often ended up talking about real people. One day I was the one who brought along a small book and refused to show Philippe its title.

"What is this mysterious book?" he asked once we were sitting down.

"It's something I took from your mother's bookshelves, and it's played a part in your life, Philippe; at least you once wrote that it did."

"I know what it is, it's my *Little Russian Soldiers*. Oh, I'm really pleased you found it, Isabelle. Let me see."

He leafed through it and seemed slightly amused and slightly disappointed. "'They proposed to elect a queen, a young schoolgirl we all knew very well:

Ania Sokoloff. She was a remarkably beautiful, slender, elegant, and able girl . . . Bowing our heads before the queen, we swore to obey the laws.'"

"Oh, but it's charming, Philippe, and it's so you . . . 'Bowing our heads before the queen, we swore to obey the laws.' It also has such a nice story: something the queen wants and the hero goes to great trouble to find . . . '"My God, my God!" said the queen. "What trouble you've gone to! Thank you." She was very pleased. Shaking my hand once more as I bid her adieu, she added, "If I am still your queen, I shall tell the general to reward you handsomely." I bowed to her and withdrew, and I too was very happy . . .' You've so completely stayed that little boy your whole life, Philippe . . . Only the queen has kept changing."

Philippe, sitting beside a bush, plucked off small branches, snapped them in his fingers, and threw them into the grass.

"Yes," he said, "the queen has kept changing. The truth is I've never met the queen . . . well, never exactly her, do you understand?"

"Who's been the queen, Philippe?"

"Several women, my darling. Denise Aubry a bit . . . but a very imperfect queen. Did I tell you poor Denise Aubry died?"

"No, Philippe . . . She must have been very young . . . What did she die of?"

"I don't know. My mother told me the other day. Hearing about it felt very strange, as if it was a trifling piece of news, the death of a woman who, for several years, was the center of the universe to me."

"Who was the queen after Denise Aubry?"

"Odile."

"And was she the closest to the queen of your dreams?" I asked.

"Yes, because she was so beautiful."

"After Odile? . . . Hélène de Thianges for a while?"

"Perhaps for a while," he said after a moment's thought. Then he added, "But definitely you, Isabelle."

"Me too, really? For a long time?"

"A very long time."

"Then Solange," I said.

"Well, yes, then Solange . . ."

"Is Solange still the queen, Philippe?"

"No," he said quietly. "But in spite of everything, I don't have unpleasant memories of Solange. There was something so alive, so strong about her. I felt younger with her; it was nice."

"You should see her again, Philippe."

"Yes, I'll see her again when I've recovered more, but she won't be the queen any longer; that's over."

"And what about now, Philippe, who's the queen?"

He hesitated for a moment, then looked at me and said, "You are."

"Me? But I was deposed long ago."

"Yes, you may have been deposed because you were jealous and petty and unfair. But in the last three months you've been so brave, so straightforward, that I've given you your crown back. Anyway, you can't imagine how much you've changed, Isabelle. You're not the same woman anymore."

"I know that, my darling," I said. "Deep down, a woman in love never has a personality; she says she has one, she tries to make herself believe she has, but it's not true. No, she tries to understand the woman that the man she loves wants to see in her and to become that woman . . . It's very difficult with you, Philippe, because it's not very clear what you want. You need faithfulness and tenderness, but you also need coquettishness and uncertainty. What's a woman to do? I chose faithfulness, which was closest to my own character . . . But I think you're going to carry on needing someone else for a long time, someone who's unreliable and elusive to you. The great victory I've won over myself is accepting this other woman, I even accept her with resignation, happily. The really important thing I've realized in the last year is that if we truly love we mustn't attach too much importance to the things that the people we love do. We need them; they alone mean we can live in a particular 'atmosphere' (your friend Hélène calls it a 'climate' and that's exactly right) that we can't get by without. So long as we can keep them, hold on to them, good God, what does the rest matter? Life's so short, so difficult . . . Philippe, do I have the strength to haggle with you over the few hours' happiness these women might give you? No. I've come a long way, I'm no longer jealous, it doesn't hurt anymore."

Philippe lay down on the grass and put his head on my knees.

"I haven't quite reached the same stage as you," he said. "I think it could go on hurting me, hurting a lot. The fact that life's short isn't a consolation for me. It's short, yes, but compared to what? For us, it's everything . . . Even so, I feel I'm gradually coming to a calmer period. Do you remember I used to talk about my life as a symphony that combined different themes: the theme of the Knight, the Cynic, and the Rival. I can still hear them all loud and clear. But I can also hear one isolated instrument in the orchestra. I don't know what it is, but it keeps firmly yet gently repeating a quiet, soothing theme made up of just a few notes. It's the theme of serenity; it's rather like the theme for old age."

"But you're young, Philippe."

"Oh, I know that! And that's why it sounds so quiet. Later it will drown out the whole orchestra and I'll miss the days when I heard all the others."

"What makes me sad sometimes," I told him, "is thinking how long the apprenticeship is. You tell me I'm a better person than I used to be, and I think that's true. When I'm forty perhaps I'll start understanding life a bit, but it will be too late . . . Still . . . Darling, do you think it's possible for two people to be in perfect agreement, without a single cloud?"

"It's just been possible for the last hour," said Philippe, getting to his feet.

. XXIII .

My time of true marital happiness was that summer at Gandumas. I think Philippe loved me twice: for a few weeks before we were married, and during those three months, from June to September. He was tender, with absolutely no ulterior motive. His mother had as good as forced us to share a bedroom; she thought this very important, could not understand how a husband and wife could be separate. This brought us even closer. I liked waking in Philippe's arms, and then Alain would come and play on our bed. His teeth were hurting, but he was very brave. When he cried, Philippe would say, "You must smile, Alain. Your mother's so stoic, little boy." I think the child ended up understanding the two words "smile, Alain," because he always tried to stop his crying and open his mouth to try to look happy. It was very touching and Philippe was starting to love his son.

The weather was gorgeous. When my husband came home from the factory, he liked to "toast himself" in the blazing sun. We had two chairs carried out onto the lawn in front of the house, and we sat there in silence, lost in drifting daydreams. I liked to think we might both have the same images in mind: the heather, the ruined château at Chardeuil quivering in the scorching air, farther away the hazy curve of the hills, and perhaps even farther away, Solange's face and the slightly hard expression in her eyes; on the horizon perhaps the Florentine landscape, the wide, shallow-sloping roofs, the domes, the cypress trees instead of firs on the hills, and Odile's angelic face . . . Yes, they were in me too, Odile and Solange, and I thought this quite natural and necessary. From time to time Philippe would look at me and smile. I knew we were wonderfully at one; I was happy. The bell for dinner drew us from our voluptuous languor.

"Oh, Philippe!" I sighed. "I'd like to spend my whole life beside you like this, listless, with nothing more than your hand, the warmth in the air, the heather . . . It's blissful and at the same time so melancholy, don't you think? Why is that?"

"Beautiful moments are always melancholy. We can tell they're only fleeting, we wish we could pin them down, but we cannot. When I was little, I always felt like that at the circus, and later at concerts, when I was too happy. I used to think, 'In two hours it'll all be over.'"

"But now, Philippe, we've got at least thirty years ahead of us."

"That's nothing, thirty years."

"Oh! I couldn't ask for more."

My mother-in-law also seemed to hear the soft, pure note of our happiness.

"I'm finally seeing Philippe living as I've always hoped he would live," she told me one evening. "My dear Isabelle, do you know what you should try to do if you were wise? Persuade Philippe to come back to Gandumas for good. Paris does nothing for him. Philippe's like his father: deep down, he was shy and sensitive despite his inscrutable outward appearance. All that hustle and bustle in Paris, all those complicated feelings—it makes him ill."

"Sadly, Mother, I think he would be bored."

"I don't think so," she retorted. "His father and I lived here for sixteen years, the best years of our lives."

"Perhaps, but he's adopted other habits. I know *I* would be happier because I like living alone, but he . . ."

"He would have you."

"That won't always be enough."

"You're too modest, my dear Isabelle," she said. "And you have no confidence. You mustn't give up the fight like that."

"I'm not giving up the fight, Mother . . . Quite the opposite. I'm sure now that I can win . . . that I'll stay the course while the others will be brief phases and will hardly feature in his life . . ."

"The others!" my mother-in-law said, surprised. "You really are extraordinarily weak."

She often came back to her plan; she was gently insistent. But I was careful not to mention it to Philippe. I knew that a constraint like that would immediately wreck the perfect harmony I was so enjoying. In fact, I was so worried Philippe would be bored that several times I suggested spending Sundays with neighbors, or going to visit some spot in the Périgord or Limousin that he had told me about and I did not know well. I liked him taking me around his region; I loved the slightly wild countryside and, on its sheer cliffs, the châteaux with huge walls that looked down over pretty views of rivers. Philippe told me old legends and anecdotes. I had always loved the history of France and was quite moved to hear familiar names once more: Hautefort, Biron, Brantôme. Sometimes, shyly, I would make a connection between what Philippe was telling me and something I had read, and was delighted to see him listen to me attentively.

"You know so much, Isabelle," he said. "You're very intelligent, perhaps more than any other woman."

"Don't make fun of me, Philippe," I begged.

I felt I had finally been discovered by a lover whom I had loved for a long time without a shred of hope.

. XXIV .

Philippe wanted to show me the caves in the Vézère valley. I really liked the black river twisting between rocks carved and polished by the water, but I was disappointed by the caves. In oppressive heat, we had to climb steep paths, then ease through narrow corridors of stone to look at bisons sketched vaguely on the walls in red.

"Can you see anything?" I asked Philippe. "It's a bison if you try hard enough, but even then . . . the wrong way up."

"I can't see a thing," said Philippe. "I want to get out, I'm freezing."

After the heat of the climb, I too felt an icy chill. Philippe was quiet on the way back. That evening he complained of catching a cold.

The following morning he woke me early. "I don't feel well," he said.

I got up quickly, opened the curtains, and was terrified by the sight of him: he was pale and looked anxious, his eyes had dark rings under them, and his nostrils, which looked pinched, palpitated oddly.

"Yes, you look ill, Philippe, you caught cold yesterday . . ."

"I'm having trouble breathing, and I've got a raging fever. I'm sure it's nothing, darling. Give me some aspirin."

He did not want to see the doctor and I did not dare insist, but when my mother-in-law, on my request, came to our room at about nine o'clock, she made him take his temperature. She treated him like a sick little boy, with an authority I found surprising. Despite Philippe's protests, she called Doctor Toury up from Chardeuil. He was quite a shy, very gentle man who always peered at you for a long time through his tortoiseshell glasses before speaking. He listened to Philippe's chest very methodically.

"Full-blown bronchitis," he said. "Monsieur Marcenat, this will take a week at least."

He gestured for me to leave the room with him. He looked at me from behind his glasses, his expression well-meaning but uncomfortable.

"Well, Madame Marcenat," he said, "this is quite tricky. Your husband has bronchopneumonia. The stethoscope picked up rattling throughout his chest, almost like pulmonary edema. And his temperature's at 104, his pulse at 140 . . . It's a bad case of pneumonia."

I felt half paralyzed. I did not fully understand.

"But he's not in danger, is he, Doctor?" I asked, almost jokingly because it seemed so unrealistic for my vigorous Philippe to be so ill overnight.

He seemed surprised. "Pneumonia's always dangerous. I'll have to wait before giving a prognosis."

Then he told me what I needed to do.

I remember hardly anything of the next few days; I had been hurled into the mystical, cloistered life of illness. I looked after Philippe, doing as much as I could because I felt that being useful would keep away the terrible, mysterious threat. When there was nothing I could do, I stayed beside him, wearing a white tunic, watching him and trying—just by looking at him—to transmit some of my strength to him.

He went on recognizing me for a long time. He was so prostrate he could not speak; he thanked me with his eyes. Then he became delirious. There was a terrible moment for me, on the third day, when he thought I was Solange. All of a sudden, in the middle of the night, he started talking with great difficulty.

"Oh!" he said. "You came, my dear Solange, I knew you'd come. How kind."

He was really struggling to get the words out but looked at me desperately tenderly.

"My dear Solange, kiss me," he whispered. "You know you can. Go on, I'm so ill."

Not really knowing what I was doing, I leaned over and, on my lips, he kissed Solange.

Oh! I would have given you Solange with all my heart, Philippe, if I had thought her love could save you. I think that if I ever loved you perfectly it was at that moment, because I had abdicated; I existed only for you. During that period of delirium, my mother-in-law was in the room several times when Philippe mentioned Solange. Not once did I experience a rebellious surge of wounded pride. All I could think was, "Let him live, my God, let him live!"

On the fifth day I had a little hope. When I took his temperature in the morning it had dropped, but when the doctor came and I said, "It's better at last, it's only 100.4," I noticed that he still looked gloomy. He examined Philippe, who was almost insensible.

"So?" I asked shyly when he stood back up. "Are things better?"

He sighed and looked at me sadly. "No," he said, "quite the contrary. I don't like these sudden drops. It's false defervescence . . . A bad sign."

"But not a sign of the end?"

He did not answer.

That same evening, Philippe's temperature went back up and his features collapsed alarmingly. I now knew he was going to die. I sat beside him and took his burning hand; he did not seem to feel me. I thought, "So you're going to leave me on my own, my darling." And I tried to imagine that inconceivable thing: life without Philippe. "My God!" I thought. "How could I be jealous! . . . He had only a few months to live, and . . ." I then swore to myself that, if by some miracle Philippe was saved, I would never want for any happiness but his.

At midnight, my mother-in-law wanted to take over from me; I shook my head forcefully. I could not speak. I was still holding Philippe's hand in mine, it was now covered in cloying sweat. His difficult breathing physically hurt me. All of a sudden he opened his eyes and said, "Isabelle, I can't breathe. I think I'm going to die."

These few words were spoken in a very clear voice, and then he fell back into his torpor. His mother took me by the shoulders and hugged me. The pulse I held beneath my fingers became imperceptible. At six o'clock in the morning, the doctor came and gave him an injection that revived him a little. At seven o'clock Philippe breathed his last without regaining consciousness. His mother closed his eyes. I thought of the words he had written when his father died: *Will I be alone, then, when I face death? I hope it will be as soon as possible.*

It came very soon, Philippe, just as you hoped, and it was such a shame, my dear darling. I do believe that, if I had been able to keep you, I would have made you happy. But our fates and our wishes almost always play to a different rhythm.